# The
# Kaibab Resolution

*Ron Culley*

Kennedy & Boyd
an imprint of
Zeticula
57 St Vincent Crescent
Glasgow
G3 8NQ
Scotland

http://www.kennedyandboyd.co.uk
admin@kennedyandboyd.co.uk

ISBN-13 978-1-904999-28-7

Guns is bad!

lots a love,

The
Kaibab Resolution

# Acknowledgements

I am much obliged to those who encouraged me to re-visit this novel, first drafted in 1996, for a new public. Now it also heralds a sequel, scheduled for release in 2011.

It represents a piece of work which engaged my spare attention almost completely at a time when my wife Jean was equally pre-occupied with the *travails* of pregnancy.

Our son Conor was born just shortly after I wrote the words "*The End*" and our son Ciaran was born as I finished the redrafts a year later.

I'm most grateful to my eldest son, Ron, who proof-read the manuscript and did so with almost unerring accuracy; I am also grateful to his younger brother, Campbell, for not annoying Ron while he undertook this task.

Others, too numerous to mention, are also to be thanked for reading the manuscript and proposing changes. Not only was their feedback extremely helpful but it was invariably delivered with courtesy and warmth. It was almost all acted upon.

If you've made your way through these acknowledgements, you might be giving thought to reading the novel. I hope that you do and that in doing so, you find as much enjoyment as I did in writing it.

*Ron Culley.*
*December 2010.*

# Preface

Doctor Liam Brannigan, a Dublin born economist working in the white hot political atmosphere of Capitol Hill in Washington, USA follows his boss, a newly retired Senator to Las Vegas to assist in a straightforward business project.

Unknown to him, his quiet life of cool research and calm persuasion, is to be turned upside down when he inadvertently becomes involved in witnessing the slaughter of a group of priests waiting innocently at a taxi rank.

As his relationship with the beautiful Susan Lattanzi deepens, he is drawn into a murky world of violence and confusion - not knowing whether to trust the Vegas police, the FBI or the Mafia.

Brannigan's life is put in danger as he tries to survive the attempts of *Posse Commitatus* - an undercover right wing group dedicated to the protection of their version of the American way – and who are committed to the assassination of his boss.

The Middle American, liberal values of his employer begin to erode as those who preach right wing evangelism, non payment of Federal taxes and violence towards minority groups, pursue Liam and threaten his life and that of those he holds dear.

# Prologue

Nine year old Joseph Lattanzi parted the heavy velvet curtain just sufficiently to permit one eye to observe the body of his late uncle Giovanni which was lying in an open coffin in the back room of his father's funeral parlour. Dressed as if he were about to visit chapel, the body had the pallid but restful look which denoted the high standards of cosmetic care for which Joseph's father had become renowned.

Joseph had seen dead bodies before but never one whom he had known in life. It was strange looking at a real person who only days before had tousled his hair and given him ten cents for bringing him a newspaper. But now he was stilled.

His uncle Giovanni was one of the many uncles who seemed to surround him as he grew up in his home in lower Manhattan in New York City. In fact, Joseph had only two uncles and two aunts - all still living in Naples, Italy - but was generously endowed with a collection of adults of varying ages who, almost without exception were warm, friendly and generous in their attentions.

Outside, the December snows covered New York's cobbled streets. Young Joseph shivered behind the curtain he'd now closed, his attention taken by the voices of two men, one of them recognisably his father, as they entered the room occupied by Giovanni.

"God help us all now!" said Paulo Rossini, speaking in English but with a thick Italian accent.

"I brought my family here to America to escape the European wars and now I find that they have followed us here."

"The Japanese could invade at any time now that they have sunk the American fleet," said Rossini, his pessimism deepening. "Although it will mean more work for you and your funeral parlours."

Franco Lattanzi sighed. "I would rather my family and my friends lived in peace than my businesses flourished through war. Fathers burying their sons and daughters should never happen. Even yet I cannot bring myself to find words of comfort for a mother or a father who has lost their child. It is the worst of all tragedies."

"But you'll still take their money."

"Yes," sighed the undertaker. "I'll take their money. I look after my family and we all have to eat. But I wanted more. I wanted my two children, young Sophia and Joseph to live a better life. Joseph to get an education and Sophia to marry well. This world offered so much and now the Japanese have dropped their bombs on American ships. It is a black day for all of us. Including the Japanese."

Joseph had been receiving his education for the past four years, his younger sister for the past three, in fulfilment of their father's ambitions for them.

**

Franco Lattanzi had left Italy for America with his young bride Maria shortly after they were married in 1928, four years before Joseph was born. Naples offered Franco little other than the warmth of his extended family where, at night round an open fire, he was told exaggerated tales of the successes of friends and relations who had gone to America.

Exaggerated tales or not, few now returned. The climate was similar to Naples, there was a Little Italy springing up in all of the great cities and there was work. Opportunities abounded. So having discussed it with Maria, Franco announced at the dinner table one Sunday afternoon that he and his bride intended leaving for the New World within the year once they had saved enough money for the sea fare.

The farewell proved more difficult than Franco had imagined. Always a close family, the emigrant Lattanzis found themselves promising to return within the year despite all on the quay-side knowing in their hearts that this was improbable in the foreseeable future.

Arriving in New York, they didn't travel far, heading straight from the stunningly ornate Ellis Island, where they both underwent a medical to ensure they weren't suffering from any 'loathsome or contagious disease' to an Italian community on the lower east side. There, Franco and Maria took any work that was available until they could afford to rent a small apartment of their own. After a year, Franco took a job in an undertaker's parlour preparing bodies for burial. He showed himself to be a diligent worker who came not only to handle the back-room practicalities of death but who excelled in his empathic understanding of those bereaved. Two years later, with the help of a loan from a wealthy countryman, Franco bought out the Dutchman who ran the establishment and also opened a second establishment in the lower west side.

Franco often worked long hours but young Joseph was happy in the bosom of his family. Neighbours were kind and he and Sophia had many friends, all of whom spent as much time in each other's parents' apartments as they did their own. Both children were popular - Joseph because he was bright, polite and helpful, and Sophia because she was an angel. Everyone commented on her beauty and her temperament. She radiated a happiness which was infectious and which rendered her as popular with adults as with her friends. Untypically perhaps, she and her brother Joseph were closer than any brother and sister had any right to expect. They played together, studied together and helped around the home with good grace.

When Joseph was twelve and Sophia was nine, one of their 'uncles' asked if they would run an errand taking a parcel containing some business papers to another of their uncles who lived only two blocks away. The recipient of the parcel was their uncle Dino who was distinguishable from certain of their other uncles in that he had never attempted to master the English language and communicated only in Italian. In addition, Dino was always better dressed as a consequence of money he earned from his activities as a foot soldier of the Mafia. Joseph had never felt himself comfortable in the presence of Dino who, alone among his many uncles, could be irascible as well as extremely generous.

On the evening when Joseph and Sophia were requested to deliver the parcel to their uncle Dino, a gunfight broke out on the corner of his apartment involving Dino as one of the participants. Joseph had seen gunfights before and pulled his sister by the elbow and protected her by wrapping her arms around her as they cowered next to a stairway.

Dino was shot dead by one of the assailants, a bullet through his heart. Tyres screeching, the car carrying the other gunmen moved off at pace before the police arrived. As it became evident that the danger was over, people began to emerge from their cover, drawn irresistibly towards the blood stained sidewalk on which Dino lay, his gun still in his hand.

Satisfied that the shooting had stopped, a frightened Joseph peered over the steps of the stoop in order to confirm his perception and loosened his grip on Sophia who slumped to the ground, the back of her head having been smashed by a ricochet from one of Dino's bullets.

She died in his arms.

Franco and Maria were inconsolable with grief at the loss of their daughter. In their desolation, they drew Joseph closer to them but were further anguished at his apparent inability to share their tears. Joseph was quiet and uncommunicative. He spent hours on his own, walking from his home to the East River where he would sit, staring into its blackness, immobilised apart from an occasional effort to throw a sad and unhappy pebble into the river.

A police officer had spoken with him about the shooting of his sister but Joseph would not answer any questions, despite the promptings of his mother.

One night, three days after Sophia's death, Joseph slipped from his bedroom and took the spare keys to the parlour from his father's 'secret cupboard'. Pausing to ensure that he hadn't wakened anyone, Joseph slipped quietly from the apartment and made his way to the funeral parlour from which Sophia's body would be taken the following day to its final resting-place. On arrival, he opened the door and, locking it behind him, entered, lighting a kerosene lamp to find his way.

The back room was traditionally where the body was kept overnight before a funeral and was where those who wished to pay their last respects would attend before the burial ceremony. The dim light from Joseph's lamp found two coffins. Both were closed and were set on a raised dais in the middle of the floor. It was evident that one was the coffin of a child. The other was a sturdy box which would have been of a size consistent with that required to contain an adult. Joseph approached and held the lamp above his head. With his other hand he raised the coffin lid, keeping it open just sufficiently to establish that it contained the body of Dino Ciardi.

Closing the lid, he stepped over to the small white coffin and opened the lid fully, revealing the body of his little sister Sophia who lay, her arms crossed across her chest, her eyes closed, looking as angelic in death as she was in life.

What began as a single tear rolling unbidden from the corner of an eye became a flood as the emotions Joseph had kept from everyone, including himself, overcame him. His body racked and heaved with sobs for long minutes before he stood on his toes and laid his head on her chest for a farewell hug. He stepped back, repelled as the cold body reminded him again of the actuality of her death. Moments passed as Joseph struggled with his emotions. Still sobbing, he wiped the tears from his eyes with his sleeve and returned to Dino's coffin, opening the heavy oak lid with difficulty.

It swung open, falling on its hinged side with such force that the lid almost wrenched itself from the main structure. Joseph's chin was level with the top edge of the coffin. Inside, Dino Ciardi was dressed in his finery although his heavily jowelled chin overflowed the collar of his white shirt making him look uncomfortable as he prepared to meet the Almighty.

From behind his back, Joseph wrestled with a revolver he'd taken earlier from his father's 'private cupboard' to which no one but Franco was meant to gain entrance but to which Joseph and Sophia had had almost unrestricted entry due to the flimsiness of the lock. His waistband yielded eventually and Joseph peered again over the coffin. He raised the handgun and rested its weight on the top of the coffin where he directed it at Dino's dead body. Squeezing his eyes tight shut, Joseph pulled the trigger and fired the revolver sending the first bullet into the side of Dino's nose. Despite the thunderous and frightening crash of the bullet exploding in the gun's chamber, a further five shots followed, reducing Dino's face to unrecognisable pulp. Slowly, Joseph lowered the gun and inspected his handiwork. Satisfied that not even his father could repair the damage before Dino would have to explain his injuries at the heavenly gate, Joseph returned to the side of his sister who still looked as though she might wake at any moment and propose some joint activity for the upcoming day as so often she used to do.

He left the kerosene lamp on a table in a position where his sister would be illuminated by its warm glow and retreated to his favourite hiding place of some years before, behind the heavy velvet curtains where he could climb up into a shelved alcove and look down on the scene below.

*En route* to the funeral parlour, Joseph had been unconcerned about the prospect of his actions being brought to the attentions of the authorities. However, as he sat in his eyrie looking down at his beautiful sister, thoughts of self-preservation began to course through his mind. He took the revolver and prised open a loose board in the wall he'd used as a youngster and secreted the weapon behind it. Once the board had been replaced, no indication could be found of any hide hole.

Only occasionally wondering whether the gunshots would have been reported to the police, young Joseph Lattanzi sat above the parlour through the night, holding back the red velvet curtains, looking at his sister, fighting his fatigue and thinking of what might have been and what would be in the future.

# Chapter One

Las Vegas had suggested itself as a gradual golden glow in the night sky when the plane was still some ten minutes flying time from McCarran Airport. Liam Brannigan shifted uncomfortably in his seat and folded the in-flight magazine he'd already read disinterestedly on the outward leg of what had proved to be a relatively productive visit to Washington. His lazy gaze fell on a shapely stewardess making final landing arrangements before being drawn back to the diamond bright cluster of light emanating upwards from the city in which he had lived for the past two years.

Doctor Liam Brannigan was an economist. Educated at Trinity College, Dublin then Glasgow University, Scotland where he completed his Ph.D, he found early employment in Washington as a very junior research assistant on Capitol Hill. There, his popularity with a couple of the harder working Senators resulted in a Green Card, promotion and introductions to a raft of individuals who made many of the decisions of consequence in the States. He also obtained some very quiet financial information that brought him assets such as apartments in Washington and Las Vegas and a bank account of four million dollars. And all this before he'd really got started.

Getting started involved moving to Las Vegas where he continued his friendship with the now ex-Democratic Senator Joseph Lattanzi as an Aide in order to advise on the development of the building of Lattanzi's new hotel - then unnamed. Brannigan knew as much about hotel developments as Lattanzi knew about economics but was aware of his mentor's perception of him as a can-do, streetwise guy whom he liked and trusted.

The DC 10 banked over Lake Mead, its nose lining up with the runway lights. Within the compartment, Brannigan could still see the beginnings of passenger activity as people began tidying up around them as a prelude to disembarking.

"Home at last," said his neighbouring co passenger who'd attempted some earlier social exchanges but who'd given up and turned his fire on an aisle seat occupant who hadn't mastered Brannigan's ability to grimace a concluding response to unwelcome transactions "Yeah," said Brannigan as the wheels hit the tarmac with a screech and the roaring engine noise ended any further prospect of conversation.

McCarran International Airport was as busy as ever. Only ever an occasional gambler and then pretty much only on horses or sports games, Brannigan was inured to the main attraction of Vegas but understood precisely why so many flocked to its tables and basked in its sunshine. After all, that was stuff he was meant to know about, even if Joe seldom involved him in these matters any more.

Having departed for Washington earlier that morning for a discrete meeting with a White House Aide, Brannigan had only hand luggage and moved as swiftly as the throngs would permit along the walkway to the rest rooms in the main terminal building. Entering, Brannigan headed for an unoccupied washhand basin and laid his briefcase between his feet. A doused cigarette butt floated in a pool of nicotine stained water into which the previous user appeared to have coughed up his phlegm-ridden lungs. Brannigan cursed under his breath and reached for his hand luggage.

Stepping over to an area more recently attended to by the washroom assistant, Brannigan rubbed the weariness from his eyes as a precursor to splashing some tepid water on his ace. Behind him he could see the reflection of two priests standing at adjacent urinals attempting both micturation and conversation. They dried their hands in the warm air blower before continuing their apparently affable discussion on their way to the door of the mensroom. Brannigan finished his ablutions and turned towards the exit just in time to see the Hispanic attendant's eyes light upon a briefcase obviously left by one of the two departed clerics.

"Is priest's," said the elderly attendant, stooping and proffering it to Brannigan. "Yeah," said Brannigan, none too pleased at his enforced involvement. "Hand it to Lost Property." The cleaner shrugged his shoulders and continued to offer up the briefcase. "Is priest's," he repeated. "Brannigan groaned. "Okay, give it here," and stuffed a couple of dollar bills into the breast pocket of the uniformed attendant with a look that shouted *thanks for nothing*.

He stepped outside and glimpsed a back view of the priests heading towards the front entrance. Attempting a half hearted wave at the back of their heads and realising his folly as he did so, Brannigan stepped briskly after them, apologising as his haste caused others to step aside, and arrived outside where the humid blast of hot desert air reminded him he'd returned to Vegas.

The priests had by this time joined a party of other dogcollared colleagues who stood around their suitcases, apparently awaiting transport. Figuring they had reached a destination which would detain them for a period, Brannigan slowed his pace and smiled despite himself at the notion of Vegas becoming a shrine for the holy. As a child growing up in Dublin he'd been thoroughly indoctrinated into the ways of the Catholic Church and was aware of the significance of places like Lourdes in France. *But Vegas? God alone knows why a group of a dozen or so priests find it necessary to visit this city, he thought.*

The queue for cabs was long enough but was diminishing rapidly as three skycaps choreographed the speedy arrival and departure of city residents, businessmen and tourists. The priests had found themselves a corner where customised arrangements had obviously been made to collect them and were chatting amiably when a cab pulled up some yards from the group. Acknowledging its arrival disinterestedly, Brannigan's mouth began silently to shape the words *what the ....* as a man sitting in the rear of the vehicle pointed an automatic weapon from the window of the cab and unleashed its contents in a thunderous crash of noise and smoke, sending a hail of bullets into the waiting priests. After the initial burst, which left no man standing, the machine pistol erupted once more, pouring more rounds into the bloody, twisted mess of people who lay in an orgy of death on the sidewalk.

**

"In the name of the Father, the Son and the Holy Ghost, Amen." Brother Patrick Sheridan smiled his affection for his young congregation as the slightly discordant strains of the ailing church organ signified an end to another Sunday Mass. It was a beautiful, spring Dublin evening and the friendliness of those exiting from the tiny chapel on Exchange St on the banks of the Liffey combined to persuade Patrick that all was well with the world. His responsibility that evening had been to celebrate Mass for around thirty teenagers, many of whom had taken up studies at Trinity and most of whom he'd got to know quite well due, in no small measure, to the proximity of his church to the Temple Bar area of the city where inner area development had bestowed a grand collection of bars and drinking houses.

Not much older than most of his charges, Patrick was tasked with working with the younger elements of the parish and saw it almost as a duty to spend time socialising with  them over a few glasses of Guinness. Patrick sometimes thought to himself that maybe he wasn't much up to the priesthood. He'd discussed this with those responsible for his development before for sure, but had always been persuaded that self-doubt went with the territory and that his love of God would see him through.

Patrick had admonished himself in the past for enjoying a good drink but Father Michael had once counselled him that in the priesthood generally and that in the Dublin priesthood in particular, concern should only set in when he began to enjoy a "fierce drink." No one had ever managed to define the increments by which "good" became "fierce" became "terrible" and had not old Father McLaughlin, one of the most beloved and respected of men, been referred to only last week as a " terrible man for the drink?" Patrick was confused, but in the meantime he'd see his young parishioners off the premises then join them again later down at the Liffey Bar for a jar and a blether. He'd also heard of a well-known priest in Cork who'd developed a taste for a "terrible fierce drink." Patrick obviously had nothing to worry about yet. He stepped back into the shadow of the arched doorway and re entered the chapel where he noticed a celebrant, head bowed, still seated in a rear pew. Pausing only to pick up a hymn book which had fallen to the floor, Patrick didn't even hear the muffled thwack of the silenced bullet which tore a hole in his throat and sent him reeling backwards through the doorway he'd just entered.

**

Las Vegas Police Lieutenant John Regan enunciated his words with a staccato growl.

"Your problem is your attitude stinks, son. Now why don't you pick your things up off my desk and get out of my face?"

Regan glared at the back of the already departing, embarrassed traffic cop.

"I hear you been dealin' with the public like that again, I'll have you directing the goddam traffic, you sonofabitch".

"He *already* directs the traffic, boss" corrected Sergeant Bilk, known ubiquitously and for obvious reasons as "Bilko."

Regan shouted after the disappearing cop. "I'll have you directing traffic with this night-stick shoved up your ass, you sonofabitch."

"Some of the guys figure he's gay as well, but I guess he'll get the point," said Bilko.

Regan and Bilko had worked the streets of Las Vegas for the best part of twenty-five years each. Both married, both divorced, the only relationships either had found enduring were the ones they had with the force and with each other.

The phone rang and the Desk Sergeant spoke to Bilko. "We've a whole bunch of people shot down at McCarran."

"Who's attending?" asked Bilko.

"Some airport people. And we've got some scene of crime boys on the way."

"Everything under control?"

"Yeah, 'cept all of the stiffs is priests."

Bilko covered the lower half of the handset with his palm. "Major fatalities at McCarran. All of em's priests."

Regan rubbed his bleary eyes, shook his head wearily and spoke slowly. "Jeeeesus Christ. Get people down there. We'll follow once I've phoned the Mayor. He'll have the press crawlin' all over him plus he'll go friggin' nuts, he thinks his tourist trade's gonna take a punch. Get me all the information you can, as quickly as you can."

Bilko spoke to the phone. "Okay, we're on our way. Swamp the place. Call Traffic and have some wheels brought round front."

**

Susan Lattanzi was in the kitchen drinking a glass of water before heading upstairs to bed. Still only twenty-three, she had the poise and elegant beauty of her mother and, according to her father, the intelligence of her father. She had arrived rather later in the life of her parents due to them only marrying when her father was in his early forties and her mother was thirty – the first marriage for both of them. Joe had been too busy earning money and making his way in politics to have room in his life for wedlock. Nonetheless, when he met Susan's mother Liz Kemp at a Washington function, it was love at first sight and their marriage had been the stuff of '50s textbooks. Liz had happily stepped back from her role as a freelance journalist to become a housewife and only a year later, a mother.

The phone rang in the hallway and startled Susan. It was late. She padded along the deep piled hall carpet towards the phone, her woollen bed socks rather at odds with her sleek, silk kimono.

"Hello?" she asked tentatively.

"Susan, it's Liam. Is your father there? It's pretty urgent."

"He's sleeping but I can wake him. Is something wrong?"

"I'm phoning from the police station. The forces of law and order are asking me a few questions about some murders!"

Susan had become used to Liam's light-hearted banter over the years and often had fallen for his good natured story telling which usually ended in her laughter and an affectionate mid-air swipe in his direction.

"Liam, it's a bit late for any nonsense. If I waken Dad and it's one of your jokes, he'll come after you with a shotgun."

"This is serious, Susan. I was caught up in a shooting at the airport. God only knows how many are dead. And to be honest, I should have been one of them. I've never been as scared in my life. Listen, would you ever wake your father up and tell him what's happened? He'll want to get Jimmy St James down here to look after things."

"My God! Liam, are you hurt?" asked Susan, suddenly possessed of his earnestness.

"No, I'm okay. But I'd feel better if St James was talking to the cops instead of me. And so would your father. Tell him I'm fine and the cops haven't fingered me for the murders just yet."

"Liam, do they think it was you?" Susan asked disbelievingly.

Brannigan laughed.

"They don't know what to think just yet but I look like being a major witness so one way or another I'm going to be entertaining them for a while so how about you go and tell Joe?"

Bilko waited just out of earshot until Brannigan had finished his call. He stepped forward. "That you finished?"

Brannigan nodded his head.

"The family lawyer's coming over. I told him not to bother but he insists. He figures that me being a stranger to your country would leave me like putty in your hands. He's been watching too many of those TV programs. I told him I just wanted to tell you what happened so we could all go home."

"Then just tell us now."

"And disobey my counsellor? Christ, he's twice my size. He won't be long and then we'll get this all sorted out."

"Mister, we got seven stiffs and five shot up bad and we ain't got no accused. No one saw the gunmen up close 'cept you, no one can tell us anything specific 'cept you an' you wanna wait for a friggin mouthpiece?"

Brannigan levered himself off the desk edge on which he'd propped himself to make his phone call and held Bilko's gaze.

"Sounds like you understand my position perfectly, officer."

"Lieutenant Regan, it's so nice to meet you again even at this ungodly hour of the morning".

Jimmy St James entered the office offering his hand to Regan who shook it perfunctorily and while still seated.

"And Sergeant Bilk. How delightful".

He turned to Regan. "I wonder if I might have a few moments alone with my client?"

"Your client, counsellor, has been sitting here for the last hour wasting our friggin' time. Somethin' stinks here," interrupted Bilko. "Either he's been involved in this carnage or I'll eat my own ass."

St James smiled reassuringly. "No sergeant, it's called the individual's right to silence. My specific instructions to him."

He turned to Regan. "Now may I speak with Mr Brannigan briefly while Sergeant Bilk eats his own ass?"

Regan nodded assent "A couple of minutes. We'll be right outside."

The door closed and St James looked at Brannigan. "Well Liam, I suppose you better tell me why Joe had me come down here."

Brannigan told the story.

After the gunfire had subsided, Brannigan peered over the trunk of the cab behind which he'd thrown himself only to see the assailant sped away by his driver while he himself, raked the queue of taxi cabs with gunfire ensuring that any which might be tempted to attempt a pursuit would be unable to do so.

"Next thing all hell breaks loose and I'm on my way here."

"Have you provided a statement?" asked St James.

"No."

"Then I suggest you do. We'll be out of here soon. Just tell them what you've told me."

**

Regan and St James spent the next while observing Brannigan and Bilko's dialogue move from initial skirmishing to outright enmity.

Brannigan's eyes looked heavenwards in exasperation. "Look, obviously it wasn't Frank Sinatra who shot the priests. I'm just saying he *looked* like Frank Sinatra. Around the time when he was in that movie 'Von Ryan's Express' in the mid-sixties. If you put out a photofit of Ole Blue Eyes, you're sure to nail him."

"Son, this is a serious business," said Regan raising his voice. " I appreciate you and Mr. St James takin' the time to sit with us here but I gotta go see the Mayor in ten minutes an' you're sayin' to me I gotta tell him that we got a bunch of dead priests and that they got shot up by Quentin Tarrantino and Frank Sinatra?"

Equally frustrated, St James raised his hand inviting Regan to pause. "Lieutenant, I feel that my client has been as accommodating as possible and I'm sure your technical people can make some use of his descriptions of these two men. Now, given your imminent appointment with his honor the Mayor and to permit Mr Brannigan and myself some sleep, perhaps we could continue our conversation later and at a more respectable hour of the day."

Bilko stepped forward towards a still seated Brannigan, stooping until he was almost nose to nose.

"I guess you figure you got that Irish blarney, son. What is it you call it, 'the gift of the gab'? Well to me it's all just a pain in the tits crock a' shit. We got stuff to do here and you been more smartass than helpful. So you go right on home now. Just don't park on a double yellow on *my* shift."

"Sound advice, Sergeant Bilk. I'll see to it that my client pays heed to your caution." Jimmy St James rose to his feet and, gesturing Liam towards the door, smiled affably. "It's been a stressful night for Mr Brannigan. We'll both be available should you need us again."

Outside, St James turned to Brannigan. "You've had quite an evening, Liam but I don't think you've made a lifelong friend of Sergeant Bilk. Joe says you're to sleep at his ranch tonight, or what's left of it. He'll be up and I suppose he'll want to go over everything again with you. Still, sleep isn't everything it's cracked up to be."

Brannigan grimaced ruefully and they walked to St James' car. Turning a corner into the car park, both men were immediately besieged by a mob of cameramen, photographers and journalists shouting questions and flashing light bulbs. Jimmy St James took charge.

"Ladies and gentlemen", he said, speaking in his normal tones to quiet the bustling pack. "My client will not make a statement nor will he answer questions. He has been a witness to a most dastardly slaying and has passed on his information to the police. He now intends to get some rest in order to continue his efforts to assist the forces of law and order bringing to justice the people who committed this heinous crime."

As they attempted to move towards St James' car they were caught up in a maelstrom of shouted questions, none of which either man attempted to answer. St James smiled angelically at the cameras and moved Brannigan unsteadily towards and into the passenger seat of his car. They moved off slowly followed by an ever-reducing number of cameramen and photographers until, with no further impediments slowing the car, it growled into life and sped towards Boulder Ranch.

**

Franco and Maria Lattanzi never recovered from the death of their daughter Sophia. They lavished attention upon Joseph who responded by working diligently at his studies during the day and by supporting his father in running the family's funeral business at weekends. Joe's early teenage years was a solitary period but his natural ebullience gradually re emerged and he found that his dark good looks, his genuine charm and his reputation as a hard working, intelligent young man found favour with women of his own age. He was also held up as the archetypal 'good son' by mothers in the neighbourhood and was spoken of as a man to watch by businessmen who were impressed by the role he played in supporting his father's business when Franco's health began to fail him.

Joe Lattanzi had been put through Law School by his father Franco and was on the fringes of Camelot when John Fitzgerald Kennedy was wooing the American electorate in the late fifties. Younger than both JFK and his brother Bobby, he had nevertheless been close to Edward and had enjoyed friendships with many of the young ladies who had formed part of that magic circle. The nineteen sixty election had been the closest call imaginable with a majority of less than one percent giving Kennedy the nod over Nixon. Joe had worked tirelessly for a Democrat victory not just because he had found Jack Kennedy's easy charm irresistible and believed absolutely in the dreams he was chasing but also, by extension, because he loathed Nixon.

The Kennedys were famed for their attitude of *"Don't get mad, get even"* and they understood the importance of looking after your own people.

Joe was second generation American and his folks had lived the Dream, arriving penniless in the States but going on to make a fortune in the funeral business in New York. Educated, charming and wealthy with an Italian Catholic background Joe, although not Irish, was quintessentially "own people" and was eventually rewarded with a seat in the Senate representing Rhode Island following a stint in the Attorney General's office, working in support of Bobby's vendetta against organised crime.

His early reputation had been that of a hell raiser - both socially and politically - but marriage to Liz brought a new gravitas and seriousness to his politics although he remained the most affable and popular of men in private life.

Over the years he served with distinction on the Hill, never holding office but always reliable for a measured sound bite. With his patrician good looks and articulacy, he was a natural for television and grew in status over the years until his retirement with the first Clinton election in 1992.

Now in his mid-sixties, Joe had retained his looks and charm. Retirement to the year round warmth of Nevada had relaxed him and he appeared happy and re invigorated, spending time with his young wife and a daughter he loved more than life itself.

His "retirement project" as he termed it, was building a fifteen hundred bed hotel with the almost obligatory gaming rooms, on a large gap site on the Strip. That, coupled with occasional forays into journalism and looking after his ranch, was enough to keep him occupied. Joe Lattanzi was the archetypal good citizen.

Only six other men were aware of the fact that he was also one of the most senior members of the Mafia west of Denver.

**

The ambulance stood impatiently at a blocked intersection on Pearce St, flashing and wailing impotently at the stalled vehicles ahead, which, with every passing second, reduced the likelihood of its human contents becoming mere cargo. Inside, Father Patrick Sheridan was being attended by a paramedic working desperately to stem the flow of blood before its further escape extinguished a life now ebbing finally from the young priest.

"Get the van moving Sean, or this fellah's not going to make it."

Eventually a gap opened and the ambulance pushed its way into an inside traffic lane which appeared to have been coned off for no apparent reason other than perhaps because the good Lord had seen fit to provide a clear route to the hospital for one of His own.

Radioing ahead, the driver had ensured that medical staff were on their toes and squealing to a halt outside Accidents and Emergencies, the ambulance disgorged its contents to the care of the medics before pulling round the corner to clean up.

A porter waited until the stretcher had taken Patrick into the hospital before stepping into the bay just vacated by the ambulance. Pausing and peering as if to confirm his identification of the object on the ground, he bent forward and, using the tips of his thumb and forefinger, picked up a blood red dogcollar.

Patrick's jugular vein normally constrained itself to its function of returning deoxygenated blood from his

*24*

head to his heart. The bullet had provided options when it ruptured his jugular vein and oesophagus permitting spurts of blood to spill internally and externally, bringing him to the very edge of extinction. It destroyed his right laryngeal nerve, condemning him immediately to a speechless future, and clipped his trachea before exiting.

Dr. Sam Scott had spent six weary years as a surgeon in Belfast and as a result had amassed invaluable practical experience of dealing with gunshot wounds. He had not expected to put these to use so soon after his arrival in Dublin only two months previously. However, just as a higher deity had provided Patrick with a traffic free lane to the hospital, so too did He now arrange for Sam Scott to be bending over him in the Operating Room. Patrick would later reflect ruefully that despite almost being killed and having the power of speech snatched from him, this was his lucky day.

## Chapter Two

Vatican Secretary of State, Cardinal Pierre Martine sat at a desk in his apartments in the City State fingering a faxed communication and pursing his lips. He directed his voice at an intercom. "Please ask Bishop Vittorio to come in."

Since the scandals which had undermined the integrity of the Vatican Bank in the early seventies, great strides had been taken to restore public confidence and much of this had been due in no small measure to the prodigious efforts of 'God's Banker' Cardinal Martine's guest, Bishop Vittorio Grassini.

The Cardinal rose and walked towards the door in order to greet his caller.

"My dear Vittorio, I am so pleased to see you again. Thank you for coming over to meet with me."

They embraced warmly as would befit a friendship that had lasted more than thirty years. Grassini smiled.

"Your Eminence, I was about to witness the humiliation of my Torino heroes playing against Juventus on television. Whatever you have to tell me is unlikely to improve my mood unless you have been informed of some goals being scored by blue shirts."

"This year has not been a good year for your football team," the Cardinal agreed. "But come and sit down so we might discuss some information which I have just received. If it is true, it is both tragic and worrying. I fear I may have need of your services."

The organisation which leads almost one fifth of the world's population in faith has an inevitable responsibility to protect itself. When Stalin asked rhetorically, "*How many divisions does the Pope of Rome have?*" he was merely acknowledging the reality that the Pope did not lead an army. Since the fifteenth century, the church had had to rely on the protection of others to protect its considerable interests. But times change and occasionally, the pressure for change comes from the most unexpected of sources. Even from within.

In the seventies, the Vatican Bank was accused of major financial frauds involving the Italian Government, the Banca Cattolica del Veneto, a secret society - P2, the Mafia and the Banco Ambrosiano. Pressure to restore its credibility had been increased by President Lyndon Johnston's visit to Rome to meet Pope Paul V1 and subsequently by his successor visitor Nixon, both of whom were concerned by the high level of speculation by the Vatican Bank in American institutions and by allegations of money laundering on a massive scale. Additionally, both also shared the view that "President meets Pope" headlines read well whatever the circumstances.

It wasn't until May 1984 that Pope John Paul ll finally reorganised the *Curia* - the church's elaborate bureaucracy - and set up a unit within the bank to ensure the highest standards of fiscal probity. Secretly, he also took steps to ensure that the unit was given a preventative role, that its portfolio of responsibilities was all embracing and that certain of its activities would be deniable.

Cardinal Martine was currently the man charged with looking after Vatican interests which might not be amenable to prayer and his old friend Bishop Grassini was his link with those outwith the Vatican who could assist. They all had work to do.

**

Joe Lattanzi had spoken to Brannigan by car phone upon his departure from police headquarters and having quizzed Jimmy St James, judged that it was better to encourage everyone to catch a few hours sleep before taking stock.

Only Susan was awake when St James' Merc pulled into the driveway.

Dressed now in a warmer gown, she stood, arms folded, silhouetted against the interior lights of the hallway.

"Liam, it's on every channel. God, it's awful. Are you okay?" asked Susan, as Brannigan attempted both to greet her and signal acknowledgement of St James' departure.

"I'm okay, but there's some folks on their way to the morgue tonight and some others only just hanging in there. Jesus it was a slaughter. Over in seconds. I was only a couple of paces away from the group of priests when these guys drew up and one of them lets loose with a semi automatic. It's a bloody miracle I wasn't shot." He shivered involuntarily as they entered the hallway. "Sweet Jesus, Susan, I could be doing with one of Joe's whiskies."

She obliged.

Emptying a large measure in one gulp, he returned the empty glass to Susan who poured another equally generous shot and listened as Liam told and retold the story before his tired yawns prompted Susan to recognise his fatigue and to arrange for his sleeping arrangements in one of the guest rooms.

**

The sunshine had deserted Dublin.

Eamon O'Farrell rested his forearms on the steering wheel and nodded in the direction of the entrance to Accidents and Emergencies.

"Well now, for all your much vaunted professionalism, Mr Tyler, it appears that your victim is still alive, given the haste with which they took him inside there."

The passenger in O'Farrell's battered Fiat removed his now quite unnecessary sunglasses and glowered through a drizzle of girning rain at the hospital attendant picking up the blood stained dog collar of Father Patrick Sheridan.

"Trust me, they're carrying in a dead man."

"Mister Tyler, as you would imagine, I've seen my share of killing and we have our own fellows who are fairly bloodthirsty all right but that man did you no harm at all."

Tyler replaced his sunglasses and turned to O'Farrell.

"He insulted me and he insulted my country. People who do that get very dead."

A match flared, igniting O'Farrell's cigarette.

"Well, it must have been some insult Mister Tyler. It certainly escaped me. I mean the man's a Priest, a man of God. I thought you people were into God and country, or is it just country now?"

"Listen, O'Farrell, we just finished our business here so why don't you do what your bosses told you to do and get me to the airport. I'm feelin' homesick for some American sunshine."

"My bosses made no mention of you shooting a Priest, Mister Tyler, but fortunately for you they have agreed it would be wise to get you out of the country no matter the lunacy of your actions."

He rapped his fingers on a bag on Tyler's lap. "If you leave that gun of yours under your seat, I'll get rid of it."

"How can I begin to thank you, Mister O'Farrell," said Tyler sarcastically. "You'll get it at the airport and not one second before. I do not enjoy being separated from my weapon."

"Mister Tyler, we had a business deal. You bring us the guns we want and our folk stateside give you lots of your American dollars. You've kept your part of the bargain and I understand that our bank draught has been cleared. Our relationship is now terminated. Shooting that Priest was not the cleverest thing you've ever done and will cause us trouble here in Dublin, be in no doubt. If things were different, I daresay that my elders and betters would not be so forgiving but they tell me I've just to get you back to America. If it was up to me, you would certainly find yourself called to account for your misdeeds but we're disciplined over here so I'll leave you to get on with your business. Now let's be getting to that airport before you decide that I've insulted you and your country."

Tyler smiled. "You never said a truer word, sonny boy. Let's drive."

**

Before sunup, Joe Lattanzi rose and left to drive the twenty-five miles from his ranch to Las Vegas. The cool morning air refreshed him, in counterpoint to the searing heat of the desert which, as night follows day, would soon begin to blister the inhabitants of the settlements around Boulder City just off the Nevada Highway along which he cruised.

Previously more at home on the east coast, Joe had spent his years representing the good citizens of Rhode Island from a secluded mansion in Newport and from his townhouse in Georgetown, Washington D. C. In 1970, he bought a ranch a few miles outside Boulder City close to Las Vegas and had come to love the place. He had grown his family and his fortune there and, over the years, had come to know its powerbrokers better than anyone. For many years he had the perfect lifestyle, spending his week in Washington and Rhode Island and, whenever time allowed, Friday through Sunday on Boulder Ranch. He was on first name terms with every President other than Nixon and was especially close to Jimmy Carter who, even yet would stay overnight - occasionally longer - if he was in Nevada.

Joe had fallen in love with the Kennedy dream back in the late fifties and the early sixties and although no lawyer, had jumped at the opportunity to work with Bobby Kennedy in the Justice Department.

He'd never really given much thought to organised crime although he'd been exposed to its street manifestations while running his funeral business in New York. In those days he paid protection money. His father had paid and he paid. Italians understood the Mafia. Sure, the Brotherhood was involved in all of the seamier sides of life and everyone had heard of its violent excesses but there was always the protective side, the benevolent side. "They may be gangsters," his father would tell him, "but they're *our* gangsters." Over the years, Joe had come to accept the Mob as part of life in the big city. Even the Kennedys acknowledged the significance of the Mafia and had leaned heavily on the influence which could be and was exerted by such as Momo Salvatore "Sam" Giancana, head of the Chicago syndicate, in order to ensure a win for Jack Kennedy in his runoff against Richard Nixon.

Joe's life changed immeasurably after Bobby was appointed Chief Counsel to the Senate Permanent Investigations Sub Committee. The destruction of organised crime had become an obsession for the Kennedy brothers - especially Bobby - but faced with the prospect of working with Bobby Kennedy, Joe would have pursued the very devil himself if he'd been asked to.

In 1957, now working in the background supporting Bobby on the McClellan Committee, the devil he was asked to pursue was Jimmy Hoffa, at that time the Vice President of the Teamsters Union. Hoffa was reputed to have entered into a pact with the Mafia which would see him rise to power within the union in exchange for him giving them huge sums from their pension funds and as a consequence, was called publicly to account by Kennedy's committee for his alleged misdeeds.

His arm wrestling with Bobby Kennedy throughout the enquiries of the McCllelan Committee Hearings became ever more irascible as each sought not only to present and have vindicated their version of the truth but to insult and taunt the other in an increasingly personal way.

In February of '57, only a month after the Hearings had begun, Kennedy was informed by a Washington lawyer that Hoffa had approached him and had offered him $2000 a month if he'd attempt to secure someone a place on Kennedy's team and act as an informant. Kennedy was delighted at this turn of events and immediately had an arrangement cleared with the all-powerful head of the FBI, John Edgar Hoover, that the lawyer could facilitate this. Keenly excited by his first venture into the world of bluff and double bluff, Kennedy arranged - with some difficulty - that one of his junior researchers whom he knew could be trusted completely was engaged covertly by the Teamsters Union and given the task of passing on any useful information.

And so it was that the young Joseph Lattanzi found himself working for - and being paid by - two of the most powerful men in America at the same time; younger brother of the President of the United States, Majority Counsel Robert Kennedy heading the State's drive to quash organised crime and Jimmy Hoffa, one of the most senior underworld character of his day.

**

Only forty five minutes after leaving Boulder Ranch, Lattanzi's powerful German engineered car pulled into the driveway of the Mayor's Mansion. He was admitted by a guard who recognised the driver's features as identifying one of very few visitors who were to be admitted without hesitation at any hour of the day or night.

Mayor Nick Guthrie was in one of the large downstairs rooms using a hunched left shoulder to hold a phone to his ear in order to free his hands to take notes. Raising a hand in silent welcome, he acknowledged Lattanzi's entrance with a barely perceptible raise of his jaw.

"I can assure everyone that these assailants will be caught and punished. We've seen acts of madness like this all over the world and it's difficult to guard against attacks on innocent people who are just going about their lawful business. This is not a Vegas problem. This is society's problem." He fell silent as the journalist posed another question.

"No, there is no evidence to suggest that these people were targeted but obviously we'll be looking into every possibility. I'll make a more formal statement at a press conference at ten o'clock once we have more information."

He paused momentarily to allow his caller to thank him for the telephone interview.

"Thank you too, Jim. For God's sake put a decent spin on this one. I owe you a beer." He put the phone in its cradle and offered his hand in friendship to Lattanzi.

"Joe, it's good to see you."

"This is a hell of a business, Nick. One of my men witnessed the whole thing. He said it was a massacre."

"That's for sure. I've had every news station you can think of calling me and there's plane loads of media people heading for Vegas right now. And there's not a goddam thing I can tell them."

Lattanzi nodded his understanding. "Reports from Forensic?"

"Nothing yet. We've got cops all over the State looking for a yellow cab. Cab drivers are keeping a look out for any of their cars which look suspicious but we've had no reports of a cab being stolen." He shook his head and reached for a question, any question, which might shed some light on matters. "What's your boy saying?"

"I only spoke to him by phone after he'd left police headquarters. He's at my ranch just now getting some sleep. I was going to wait up for him but I figured I'd catch him later once he's a bit more alert. He won't have told me anything he didn't tell your people."

Guthrie mulled over the weight of Lattanzi's comments and dismissed them, his mind still racing. "Anyway, I'm glad you came over, Joe. I'm going to have to try to keep the hotel owners in line. We're going to have every one of them in the firing line once the media hit town and we're going to need them all singing from the same hymn sheet to keep confidence up or the tables'll take a hit. They won't be a problem, they just need to be organised. You make a few calls for me?"

Ever since Lattanzi had moved to Boulder Ranch he had cultivated a relationship with all of the key people on the Strip. He was better placed than anyone to organise this task.

"Okay, Nick. Let me use an office."

**

Vittorio Grassini left the apartments of Cardinal Martine and headed towards the Curial offices. The Cardinal had told him of the events in Las Vegas and had asked his advice although Vittorio was quite certain that his old friend had decided some time earlier to invoke his powers of commission.

When Pope John Paul had reorganised the *Curia* in 1984, three special units had been set up, bolstering those already in place; one dealing with financial probity, one strengthening Papal security and one looking after diplomatic and political affairs. A small independent section, under the direction of Bishop Grassini, was established covertly within Unit 3 to protect the interests of the Church. Perhaps because of his experiences in Poland before becoming the head of the Church of Rome, Pope John Paul recognised that excellent intelligence was a necessary prerequisite in protecting the interests of any national or global entity.

During this period of reorganisation, urgent voices encouraged the Holy Father to establish a fully fledged secret service including the formation of active operating units to protect the church but the Pope could not be persuaded. Across the world, Grassini reasoned, the Church must nevertheless have access to an unparalleled network of contacts - legal, governmental, media, business, even underworld if necessary. Grassini's job was to sit astride that network and ensure that the Church could reach out and arrange for events to be shaped in a way which suited its purposes. Grassini created covert operation and it would be to this network which he would now turn.

As he entered his office, a surprised Father Paulo stood up excitedly.

"Bishop Grassini, we have been trying to contact you. We have grave news."

He followed Grassini into his personal office.

"A report has come to us that six priests have been shot dead in Las Vegas in America. Six others are very seriously wounded and we have been told that some of them are expected to die before very much longer."

Grassini placed his hand on his colleague's shoulder. "I know, Father. I was informed by Cardinal Martine."

"About the shooting of a young priest in Dublin, also?" he enquired.

Grassini's eyes narrowed. "There was a Priest shot in Dublin?"

"Yes, I'm afraid so, Bishop. A young Priest called Patrick Sheridan. He was shot in church as he finished Mass, and he too is very seriously wounded."

"Dear Lord, it has been a terrible night. May God forgive those who have brought this to pass. May He care for the souls of those who have died." He grimaced. "Do we have any other information?"

"I regret not although I've asked that information is passed to us immediately it comes to hand. You can imagine the press interest in all of this."

"It's hardly surprising, Paulo," said Grassini wearily. "It just lies beyond my comprehension that people should behave in this way."

He sat down. "I would appreciate a few minutes on my own, Father. I would like to think and I would like to pray."

# Chapter Three

Joe Lattanzi placed the phone on the receiver and sighed wearily to an empty room. "God Almighty, we live in an insane world." He rose and walked the few paces back through to the room he'd earlier vacated where Nick Guthrie was again on the phone.

"Yeah, yeah, yeah." Guthrie said into the mouthpiece.

Lattanzi smiled despite himself at the thought of Guthrie innocently echoing the Beatles at a time that called for earnestness and solemnity.

"Look, I'll say more at the press conference. Gimme a break Hank, I've gone off the record as much as I can. I honest to God don't know any more information or I'd tell you." He listened briefly to further imprecations. "Jeeesus, you're persistent Hank. I hope that editor of yours pays your goddam phone bill. You must cost him twice as much as any other journalist." He listened again and laughed. "I promise Hank, I promise. Trust me. What d'ya think I am for chrissake, a politician? Of course I'll keep my word!"

His smiling demeanour became a frown before the handset hit the cradle.

"I swear this job would be a zillion times easier if it wasn't for those press guys."

"I guess so," said Lattanzi." But you've got to figure they'll be all over you for a while."

"The hotel people goin' along with our script?" asked Guthrie.

"Yes, although Shultz is a bit shaky. He appears to have financial targets he's in danger of missing. My guess is that a crisis like this would provide some much needed camouflage for his next meeting with his board of directors but I was able to lean on him. I don't imagine he'll stray far from the position he and I agreed."

"You haven't lost any of your powers of persuasion, Joe. I promise I won't forget your help in this."

"I'm sure my hotel plans will continue to find favour with your colleagues, Nick."

"You can be assured I've taken steps to ensure that there will be no problems Joe."

"As you would imagine, Nick, I've already taken all of those steps some time back. I need you to make sure that all of the various ordinances which might cause me problems in the future don't cause me problems."

"Like I said, Joe. Like I said." Guthrie stood and looked out of the window. "You know Joe, you sitting next to me at that press conference would sure give me a shade more credibility in this affair."

"This has got nothing to do with me, Nick. I'm only concerned to ensure there's no impact on the tables."

"Exactly Joe. But you got to look long term. We don't handle this just right, we got a long-term problem on our hands. People just are not going to feel safe here. They're going to go to Atlantic City or Reno in case they get shot up. By the time your hotel expects to be making dollar bills we may not have recovered. And another thing, I thought you had one of your boys almost shot dead in this craziness?"

Lattanzi sighed and relented. "Okay, Nick. But you'd better understand, you owe me big for this. I came to Vegas to bow out of the limelight, not to make the headlines for CNN."

"Just as you say, Mister Lattanzi. Just as you say."

**

Joe Lattanzi took time to freshen up but resisted the temptation to have a suit brought out to him calculating that his casual attire would remind viewers that he'd retired and was only back in front of the lenses because of the calamity that had occurred.

Lattanzi returned to Guthrie's still vacated office and phoned the ranch to inform his wife Liz that he'd be detained in Vegas rather longer than he'd anticipated due to his promise to the Mayor. Among the calls she listed as having been received in his absence was one from a long time friend of the family, Father Frank Carlucci.

He dialled the number Liz had given him. "Father Frank, its Joe. Sorry we've not been in touch recently. Life's been hectic. Are you well?"

"I'm fine, Joe and all the better for speaking with you. I spoke briefly with Liz this morning. God's blessed you with a fine wife and daughter."

"That's for sure but listen, I imagine you're calling about the shooting of the priests."

"And not just those who were shot at the airport. Did you hear that a young priest was shot in Dublin earlier?"

"What in God's name is happening?" said Lattanzi reflecting upon man's capacity for inhumanity to man.

"That's pretty much what I hoped you could find out for me," said Carlucci. "We've been friends since we walked the same streets as kids in lower Manhattan. And you've told me a number of times that you are in a position to help me out any time I found myself in a deep hole. Well, I'm not in trouble but I've been contacted by some of our people in Rome - and believe me Joe, that's very unusual - and it was suggested that I might know someone who could get to the bottom of what was going on. Why they made contact with me, I don't know and how they might have known about our friendship escapes me but I sure would like to help them get a handle on this. Essentially, they want to know if it's sectarian and whether more shootings might follow."

"I've just promised the Mayor I'd help out with the media on this and I suppose I could ask a few questions but right now I'm as puzzled as you are. The Dublin side is probably beyond me but one of my staff - in fact the one who witnessed the shootings - is from Dublin and may be able to throw some light on this."

"I dare say that Rome is making its own enquiries in Ireland but anything you come up with would be welcome. And of course, it goes without saying that everything would be treated in the most absolute confidence."

"I'm happy to help out Frank. It certainly makes a difference from your usual freeloading requests for widows and orphans."

"Ah well, you've always allowed me to play on our friendship in the past in regard to financial support for good causes. You're a good man Joe, and generous, but now it's information I need, not money"

"I'll do everything in my power, Frank. You know I will."

**

Some while later he found himself in front of a battery of cameras and microphones the like of which he'd been used to only on special occasions in Washington. Seated on the left of Mayor Guthrie was Lieutenant Regan. Lattanzi sat on his right.

Guthrie started by telling the world how shocked everyone was, went on to talk up Vegas's good record in offences committed per head of the population -all the details expected from a politician -and acquitted himself well. Next up was Regan who told the story but who didn't have much to tell. Regan had been given the task of responding to the media's questions. Guthrie didn't have much to learn when it came to ducking the awkward stuff. That's what he paid officials to do.

Regan, however, was a cop - a good cop - but a cop nevertheless and was obviously pretty much out of his depth in front of the cameras. Guthrie figured he'd better bring on the man whose well-known face would certainly feature prominently on the evening's newscasts, comforting people in their homes, explaining the inexplicable.

"Ladies and gentlemen, one of our most prominent citizens has been caught up in this tragedy. His aide, Dr. Liam Brannigan, was standing next to the group of priests when they were shot. He is at home just now under sedation, but retired Senator Joseph Lattanzi, has agreed to say a few words."

Back at the ranch watching the press conference live on television with Susan and her mother Liz, Liam smiled. "A couple of whiskies is *sedation* now is it?" he asked rhetorically.

Joe Lattanzi cleared his throat and spoke directly to the bank of cameras; a habit he'd picked up in Washington.

"The enormity of this act of terrorism is hard to put into words. One life lost is one too many. The life of a priest, a life given over to the selfless service of others, is precious and, when taken like this, is incomprehensible. That so many have perished is evil and barbarous. Nothing prepares us for this. This outrage cannot be tolerated in any civilised society."

Pausing to sip a glass of water, he went on. "This city, as Mayor Guthrie said earlier, prides itself on the safety of its citizens. But no city can be safe. No city can protect itself against this sort of mindless violence."

Lattanzi was getting into his stride when a newscaster more forward than his colleagues interrupted in a loud voice guaranteed to be picked up by every microphone in the room. "That's pretty pessimistic Mr. Lattanzi. Surely a man of your experience of government has a feel for policies which can put an end to this."

Lattanzi hesitated. "I know it would stick in the throats of a whole lot of people but now that I'm no longer running for office, I believe that there is only one answer. Gun control. It would take years and I'm aware of all of the arguments against it but no one can deny that this kind of insanity, this obscenity, would not be perpetrated on our communities if folks just did not have access to firearms. This outrage has hardened my views. The sooner lawmakers address the issue of gun control with courage and conviction, the sooner we can all feel safer walking the streets of our own home towns."

**

Watching Lattanzi's performance on television from the comfort of his den, at home in Twin Falls, Idaho, just across the Nevada state line, Colonel Trent Wallis, Commander-in-chief of the local Militia, turned to one of his uniformed militiamen. "Seems to me we might just have found our man, Lieutenant."

Wallis eased himself from the barstool from which he'd been watching television and poured himself a shot of bourbon before sliding the bottle along the bar to his confidante Austin Radigan who accepted the bottle and topped up his glass.

"I thought that particular politician had backed off," said Wallis. "Now he figures he's got to do us all a favour and take our guns off us."

"He one of them liberals, Sir?" asked Radigan.

"Sure is, Lieutenant." Wallis directed his glass at the television screen which still covered the Vegas news broadcast. "If my memory serves me right he ain't from 'round these parts. He's one of them east coast boys. He sure ain't no friend of ours and he's got some gall to come out here and instruct us on how good Americans should live their lives."

The bourbon disappeared from his glass and was just as speedily replenished.

"Yes sir", said Wallis "I think we got ourselves our national incident."

**

Lattanzi and Guthrie fielded a few more questions and an aide announced the press conference over. A few journalists were granted interviews on background with Guthrie in the Mayor's office and Lattanzi took the opportunity to make a couple of phone calls from an anti room. His first was to Johnny Di Maggio, head of the Mafia families in New York.

Di Maggio and Lattanzi met only infrequently to discuss business matters but got on well together. As ever, a "Chinese wall" existed between the two men in that Lattanzi never asked, and was never told, of mainline Mafia activity. Other than social chitchat, all that was discussed was business growth and investment decisions.

Lattanzi was aware that he was not speaking on a secure line so the conversation was rather coded.

"Mister Di Maggio. I have a business problem which could benefit from assistance from one of your advisers."

"This is an unexpected call, Mister Lattanzi. You know I am eager to assist but I am not sure which of my business colleagues would be best placed to help you solve your problem."

"I was most impressed by your description of the performance of one of your associates last summer in Memphis."

Di Maggio's eyebrows rose. "Ah, Memphis! It sounds like an interesting problem you have." He mulled the request over momentarily. "Of course this will not be a difficulty. I will make the arrangements." His curiosity was heightened by the restrictions imposed by the lack of a guaranteed secure line. "Would it be helpful if we discussed your problem together at a later date?"

"That would be extremely helpful. I will phone you tomorrow from home."

Di Maggio replaced the phone on the receiver and reflected upon what kind of business problem required the use of the Mafia's most experienced and capable investigator. Not every mob soldier was a hit man or an enforcer. This most valuable operative was used for complicated investigations which required intelligence and sensitivity and was certainly not to be wasted on mere killings.

His identity was a closely guarded secret and his activities legendary within mob circles. He had become an amalgam over the years as tales, many apocryphal, spread. He was short and tall, Asian and Caucasian; some even whispered that she was a woman. Some said that he had never been involved in a violent incident, others that he was a ruthless killer. Whatever. His or her next task would be in Nevada.

Finishing his call with Di Maggio, Lattanzi then phoned the ranch and spoke to Brannigan inviting him to find out more about what had taken place in Ireland.

"No problem, Joe. I know a journalist in Dublin who's well connected. I'll get on to it straight away."

**\*\***

The roe deer lapped at the spring water, raising its head every once in a while to permit visual and scent confirmation that no danger existed. Dappled sunlight fell on the small brook and made the water sparkle like crystal. A few dusty paths between the pine trees on its banks signalled the importance of the water hole to the local wildlife.

A noise startled the deer just sufficiently for it to straighten its forelegs, bringing its body round to investigate further. Almost simultaneously, the crack of a rifle sped a bullet towards the animal, burying itself in its rear quarters and causing it to crash helplessly into the shallow pool.

"Jesus Christ, Edson, you are for sure the *worst* goddam shot in this man's army."

"I hit it, didn't I?" growled the hunter, knowing the ridicule he could expect upon his return to the collection of log cabins they called base camp.

"Yeah, right in the ass. Three feet from a kill shot."

"You sonofabitch. You snapped a twig deliberately. I had that deer right in my sights but you're just trying to make me look stupid in front of the guys. I've a good mind to…" Edson grabbed angrily for the lapel of his partner's camouflage jacket with his left hand only to stop short with a yelp as the twelve inch blade of a hunting knife threatened to separate his nose from his upper lip.

"Temper, Edson. Don't *ever* forget you're dealing with Sergeant John Burring. I could cut you up faster'n you could blink. Now you just know that, don't you?"

Burring pressed the knife upward into the soft flesh of Edson's upper lip, drawing blood. "I said, you just *know* that, don't you?"

Both men stared hard at one another but Edson's fury had given way to defeat and both knew it. "Yeah, right."

"Right, *Sergeant!*" said Burring, pressing his advantage.

Edson could taste the blood in his mouth. "Right, Sergeant."

The deer was still flailing around in the now red brook as Burring sheathed his knife.

"Gimme that before you hurt yourself," he said, taking the rifle from Edson's grasp.

"Now watch how it should be done."

Burring lay prone and aiming carefully, fired once, stilling the deer.

"Now, let's you and me get her back to camp."

\*\*

Edson and Burring trussed the deer and slung it along a pole on which they carried it back to their encampment. The two men were members of the 105th Idaho Militia -implying that at least one hundred and four other Militia companies existed in the state of Idaho and due to the high levels of secrecy and paranoia which surrounded these bands, it proved easy to imply that a great force of men stood ready to answer a call to action.

In truth, nothing like this existed. Across America, a view held popular in many a bar room was that the Government was out of control and that, if it hadn't already done so, was perilously close to contravening the Bill of Rights.

A year previously, Edson had been persuaded by his now Commander-in-chief Trent Wallis that he should throw his lot in with the 105th.

Wallis had been the local Sheriff. He'd served in Vietnam. He'd been around the block a few times and once, during a fishing trip, had introduced Edson to the notion that there were different ways a fellow could help his country in times of need.

"What you have to understand, my friend, is that this Government and all the ones that went before them, 'way back to Kennedy, especially Kennedy, are going far beyond the powers that the people of this great county gave them in 1776." He turned to Edson. "You ever read The Declaration of Independence, Edson?"

"Sure I have."

"Well, I guess you'll be able to quote that bit about us holding these truths to be self evident? You'll know all about our unalienable rights including life, liberty and the pursuit of happiness? Sure you do," said Wallis, answering his own question. "But do you know that it goes on to say, and I quote, that when any form of Government becomes destructive of these ends, it is the right of the people to alter or abolish it?" And they ain't talkin''bout no election, my friend. It goes on to say that it is our right, it is our *duty*, to throw off such a Government and to provide *new guards* for our future security. Now them's the actual words in the document. There's none of that made up."

"Well, I heard some of that stuff before Mr Wallis but you sure are some historian."

"I'm more than a historian, Edson. I'm a super patriot. I care about what's happening to our country and I am telling you today that we're livin' in a foreign country. Our ancestors didn't go through all they went through just so's Washington could take our money in taxes and give it all to the United Nations so's they could fix things in Africa or Israel. They didn't expect our representatives to try to disarm the population so's we could never provide the new guards for our future security. You ain't got a job since the mill shut and you know why? 'Cause the States is full of foreign people from foreign lands. And there's so many of them now they can force our Government to spend our taxes in the self same foreign lands they've just come from so's to help the families they've left behind. And they do it in secret, Edson. That's what gets me, the secrecy. So me an' some of the boys, we figure we got to fight fire with fire. Know what I'm sayin', Edson? We got ourselves a hostile Government."

Edson's eyes narrowed as the full realisation of Wallis' analysis dawned on him.

He shook his head in appreciation, "You sure are some historian, Mr Wallis. And a patriot too, just like you say. A super patriot."

**

Edson and Burring entered the hutted encampment and took the deer over to a wooden shed which abutted the building used as the cookhouse.

The door opened and an attractive woman dressed in similar fatigues to the two hunters emerged. "Venison for supper! Why, Sergeant Burring, you're just a regular Davy Crockett."

"Couldn't find no quail's eggs ma'am. An' Edson lost the trail of some caviar we was followin'."

"Aw, better luck next time, Edson. That caviar can be a difficult critter."

Edson knew he was being made fool of but wasn't sure quite how to respond.

"We got you a deer, didn't we?" he muttered.

"Course you did, boys. Now why don't you hoist it up on the table and I'll try to make it taste like somethin' you ain't never tasted before. Then you better go freshen up. Colonel Wallis just phoned. He's gonna be up here within the hour and he wants a word."

**

A station wagon pulled up outside an isolated and antiquated rural gas station. Trent Wallis leaned against the window of the office in which he was waiting and offered a half-hearted toast with his coffee mug to the passenger who'd just emerged from the car.

Todd Tyler had completed his return leg from Dublin without further event.

Wallis spoke to his two companions without averting his gaze from the forecourt.

"Men, I will speak with Lieutenant Tyler alone."

As Tyler entered, Wallis was pouring him a coffee.

"Bank tells me the money transfer went through okay," said Wallis.

"That was the agreement. It was meant to trigger as soon as the shipment was delivered safely. I did my job." Tyler accepted the coffee.

"Our Irish friends called. They were pleased with the shipment. Matter of fact they want more. Good money too."

Tyler shrugged his shoulders, smiling to himself thinking, *what'ya expect, I'm a professional.*

"What'ya expect, I'm a professional."

Wallis looked at him coldly. "Sure you're a professional, Tyler. A professional idiot! You're such a professional that our Irish customers tell me that if you're the man I send over with the next consignment they'll shoot you dead before you step out of Dublin Airport. What in God's name possessed you to shoot a priest?"

"Is he dead?" Tyler asked in a surly voice.

"We don't know. But we do know that shooting anyone - far less a priest for Christ's sake - did not comprise your orders. We know that don't we? I mean I don't have this thing *wrong*, do I?

"I had to take him out."

"Why, for Christ's sake?"

"He was asking too many questions."

"What? Did ya go to confession or somethin'?"

"Me and my Irish minder got talkin' to him in a bar. I had too much to drink. We got talkin' bout Irish politics an' American politics an' he seemed to agree with what I was sayin' 'bout the Feds. So one word borrowed another an' anyway it just seemed to me he started gettin' suspicious. So I waited till the next day when he was alone an' blew him away."

Wallis drew a gun from his waistband. "You dumb bastard." He pointed the end of the barrel at Tyler's forehead. "You tell me right now what you told him or I swear to God you have only seconds to live."

"Hey, calm down man, I didn't tell him nothin'. We only talked in generalisations."

Wallis pressed the gun hard against the bridge of Tyler's nose. "I'm going to shoot you dead."

"Stop this," shouted Tyler. "Okay, okay. Maybe I shouldn't have shot him. He probably had no idea I was involved in anythin'. Look, I was drunk, man."

Wallis lowered his gun as if relenting but just as Tyler began to permit himself to relax, he drew his arm backwards across Tyler's face, the heavy gun smashing into his cheekbone.

"You ask me to consider you a professional. Then you tell me you get drunk on an assignment. Then you tell me you discussed your orders with a stranger. Though he *probably* didn't understand them. But you shot him anyway. Now you don't know if he's alive or dead. You don't know if he talked. You're a goddam liability, Tyler. No wonder the Irish want you shot."

Wallis raised his voice. "Collins! Baker!" The two men reappeared in the garage office. "This man is to be the subject of a Summary Court Martial. Secure him and take him round back."

Tyler was pulled roughly to his feet, still dazed from the blow to his head and dragged ignominiously out of the back door and thrown to the ground where Wallis addressed him.

"Lieutenant Tyler, this is war. You have been found guilty of disobeying your orders. You have placed colleagues at risk. You have jeopardised the success of our mission. But I'm going to shoot you dead, here and now, just because you're a *dumbass*."

Tyler lay sprawled on the ground his hands tied behind him. "Noooooooooh", he heard himself shout as Wallis levelled the gun at his head. His screams were drowned out by the crash of several shots and he slumped back.

**

Smoke swirled for a few moments and Tyler opened his eyes looking for the telltale signs that would indicate the ferocity of his injuries. There were none.

Wallis stepped forward. "Lieutenant, as far as I am concerned you are a *dead* man. You are alive right now only because I say it should be so. Your ass is mine. Do you understand?"

Tyler, still shocked, nodded.

"We're all goin' back to base camp right now. I got work for you. But first…." He stepped back and nodded at his two companions. "Baker. Bruise him. Collins. See that it's painful."

# Chapter Four.

Jimmy St James coaxed his car over a small hump backed bridge on the single track road leading to Joe Lattanzi's ranch. He'd qualified as an attorney almost forty years earlier and had majored on criminal law pretty much throughout that entire period. Early on he'd defended a small time racketeer charged with armed robbery and had gotten some publicity after winning the case only to find his photograph on the front page of the Boston Globe with an excited Alfredo Del Piero planting a kiss on his cheek.

Mr Del Piero's employers had been impressed by his abilities and over the years had come to rely on his lawyer's gifts of forensic cross-examination and oratory. After a while, Jimmy St James had a thriving law practice and a reputation as a real gentleman. He was, by the late fifties, the principle legal adviser to the Mafia on the west coast.

Like Joe Lattanzi, he benefited from the mob's need to go respectable. He fronted the negotiations for the Mafia when all that was sought was a good business deal. Increasingly, the vast amounts of money raised by the nefarious activities of the Mafia were being used to invest in legitimate businesses. Profits rolled in. Taxes were paid and a gigantic portfolio of companies was developed with no obvious relationship to the mob other than the original set up money.

For this strategy to be successful, an entire new army of people had to be brought in to oversee the growth of these new ventures. Only a very few senior people were aware of the interconnectedness of the network and Jimmy was one of these.

Every so often, an embarrassment occurred when a Mafia shake down was perpetrated on a legitimate business owned by the mob. Sometimes it went ahead, sometimes St James was asked to arrange for it to be called off.

But Jimmy was no ruffian. Like Lattanzi, he never saw the violent edge to the Mafia. Unlike Lattanzi, however, he was an adviser. Granted, he was hugely respected. His loyalty was not in doubt. But he was a paid employee, if an extremely well paid employee.

As he pulled up outside the security doors guarding Lattanzi's ranch house, St James was aware that he was visiting one of his bosses although only he and five other men knew of Lattanzi's covert role as head of legitimate operations.

The powered ranch gates swung back noiselessly admitting St James' purring Mercedes.

Joe Lattanzi stepped into the warm sunlight as he awaited Jimmy St James removing his briefcase from the trunk of the car.

"Jimmy, it's good to see you," said Joe warmly.

"And you, Joe. How's your gorgeous wife and your gorgeous daughter?"

"Both still gorgeous, Jimmy. And looking forward to seeing you. It's been too long."

Both men entered the house and were greeted by Liz who embraced St James.

"Jimmy, it's so nice to see you again. Where's Helen? Last time we spoke you promised you'd both visit with us."

"I know Liz but this is a professional visit. Just looking after your husband's interests. But I'll tell you this, once this business is over, Helen and I are going to spend a couple of weeks in Florida with you and Joe. Of course, that depends upon your husband behaving as if he's actually retired instead of continuing the slog. How building a hotel on the Strip can be construed as retirement is beyond me."

After some further pleasantries, both men were alone in Joe's study.

"We any further forward with the airport shootings?" asked Joe.

"The police appear to have found the vehicle used in the attack but have not yet reported on those who were driving it. It would appear, however, that none of our people were involved."

"I sure as hell hope not," growled Joe. "You know, apart from the callous nature of this act, it sure has the capacity to dent the take at the tables."

"I suppose so," said St James, "but I suspect that this kerfuffle will die down once someone is apprehended and matters will soon return to normal. We can live with it."

"That said, Joe, I thought you really were going to take a back seat on business matters. I received a call from our Chicago friend who expressed surprise at seeing you on prime time television. He seemed faintly riled that you were 'now a leading crusader for the anti-gun lobby' as he put it."

Joe smiled and shook his head. "That's why I was the politician and not Luigi. There is absolutely no down side to the position I took. I'm just the conscience of America. An old soldier playing to the gallery. Further enhancing my reputation as a wise ancient. Plus, my views will strike a chord with many Americans who will be reviled by the shootings. If I didn't say what I said, someone else surely would have and anyway, it helped get Nick Guthrie out of a hole so I don't expect any problems with the new hotel."

Jimmy St. James nodded. "Almost word for word what I told Luigi. But maybe you should give him a call. I had the feeling that he saw it as an act of betrayal to his side of the business that one of his own should call for gun control. As if all of the weapons he deals with are registered and legal."

"Yeah, I'll give him a call," said Joe "but like I said, there's absolutely no down side."

The door opened sufficiently for Susan Lattanzi's head to edge around it. "Jimmy, I was in the pool. Sorry I missed your arrival. Dad told me to expect you."

"Susan, how delightful," said St James, rising. "Your father was just reminding me how gorgeous you were. As ever, he remains the master of the understatement."

"And you, Mister St James, remain the master of flattery," said Susan embracing her father's friend.

In the doorframe behind her, Liam Brannigan appeared carrying a set of floral curtains in both arms. "Sorry to trouble you, gentlemen, but I'm supposed to be recovering from a trauma and this young lady has me engaged in interior decoration."

Lattanzi smiled. "Liam, this is an unconscionable intrusion on your rehabilitation. But my daughter is completely outwith my control in these matters." He motioned at St. James. "Jimmy's been telling me they've found the taxi but not the gunmen."

"Lieutenant Regan was good enough to call earlier and tell me," said Brannigan.

"Does he and Sergeant Bilk still want to speak with you?" asked St. James.

"I suspect that Sergeant Bilk would only be happy interviewing me with his foot on my neck." He handed the curtains to Susan who accepted them with a pretended scowl. "They don't need me at the moment but they'll doubtless want me to finger the people involved when they bring them in."

"You've been identified on television as a witness, Liam," said St James thinking aloud. "Do we feel that you might be in any danger?" He posed the question to the room.

"Certainly not while he's staying here with us",

interjected Lattanzi. "An army couldn't get close without us knowing about it."

"But suppose it was just two assailants. Like the two who shot the priests?"

Lattanzi shook his head. "This place is a fortress, Jimmy. I wouldn't put Liz and Susan at risk. Liam will be all right as long as he's here and anyway I can't believe that the police will take much longer to track these people down."

"If Susan puts these curtains up they'll maybe think I've been punished enough," laughed Liam dodging Susan's amused glance. "And Joe's right. Butch and Sundance couldn't get in here."

"You young folks run along now and finish your home decoration," said Joe. "Jimmy and I have some business to conclude. Apparently, one of our business associates has taken umbrage at my stance on gun control."

**

Bilko almost leapt from the police car before Regan had slowed to a stop and walked purposefully towards a yellow cab which had been coned off and was bathed in arc lights.

"It's nothin' short of ridiculous that we gotta come down here and show people how to do their job. They found this thing ages ago," said Bilko, more or less to himself.

He shouted at an officer who was engaged in recording some notes "Hey, Sherlock, you found out who owns this thing yet?"

"Looks like false plates, sir. And all the I.D. has been removed from the engine and the chassis."

"What about the prints?"

"Car's clean as a whistle, Sergeant."

Regan interposed himself between Bilko and the cop. "Any witnesses?"

"No sir, just those you spoke to at the airport."

Bilko intervened. "Somewhere must have reported a cab stolen. Somethin' must be on record somewhere. You tellin' me I got this wrong, Sherlock?"

"Nothing's showing up, sir."

"I heard tell you found some slug casing in the rear seats," said Bilko, still pugnacious.

"Yes sir, they're at the lab right now."

"Jeeee-sus," exhaled Bilko giving vent to his frustrations.

He and Regan walked to one side of the car. "This whole thing is beginnin' to look *not* like an accident boss," announced Bilko somewhat unnecessarily.

**

Paul Kinsella was an investigative journalist with the Irish Times. Some ten years older than Brannigan, he'd worked at the paper since leaving University and had established himself as an award-winning journalist focusing mainly upon political matters. Brannigan and he had met when Liam worked at the Times as a general factotum during study breaks and had introduced him to an uncle of his who was able to offer Kinsella the insight he needed into Republican intentions in one of the many  attempts to secure peace in the North. Over the years they had become friends and drinking partners when their various obligations permitted. Although they had seen little of one another since Brannigan had gone to the States, his early involvement on Capitol Hill had provided Kinsella with very useful information and he was happy to make a few enquiries now on behalf of his friend. Crime was not his speciality but his colleagues on the Times had the police contacts to write comprehensive accounts of the shooting. Kinsella had been told of the young Priest's penchant for a glass of beer in The Liffey

Bar just round the corner from his church. Rather than fax Brannigan the news articles from the Times, he figured he'd add a bit of colour by visiting the bar in question.

Kinsella sat in the back of a taxicab.

"The Liffey Bar, please." He settled into his seat, allowing a silence for a few minutes and permitting the driver to find his bearings. Eventually the journalist in him took over. Taxi drivers often provided him innocently with free information. "That was a terrible affair, that young priest being shot," Kinsella volunteered to the driver.

"It was certainly that all right. Especially him being in the church at the time."

"And who do you suppose done it?" said Kinsella lapsing into the vernacular.

"Well, some of the boys are saying it was the UVF being provocative. But I think it's more likely than not tied up in drugs money."

"Really?"

"I mean, everyone's takin' these drugs nowadays an' I'll bet that the priests are involved just as much as any other group in society. Especially young priests an' particularly especially young priests who worked with other young people. They're all at it. An' there's money in drugs you know. An' I don't just mean for Chemists."

Kinsella broke the flow of the driver's invective. "So this priest worked with young people then?"

"Accordin' to one of the lads, that's right. He was to be found regular in this Liffey Bar you're goin' to right now, talkin' with all and sundry although if you ask me it's not fit and proper for a priest to spend so much time in a bar. I mean, no one's going to stop a man havin' a glass. To be honest I have a few meself from time to time. Although not when I'm drivin'. I'm almost as pissed off with those people who drink and drive as I am with them priests that take drugs. They're all an affront to a civilised society. And as for them priests who drink and drive *and* take drugs…."

Kinsella called a halt, weary of the driver's conversational leaps. "Maybe you'd just drop me at the Liffey Bar." And before the taxi driver began his meanderings again added, "I see we're going a long way for a short cut. What with all our blethers, I almost didn't realise we're maybe adding another third to our journey."

The driver's eyes smiled in the rear view mirror, acknowledging his mischief. "Ah there's road-works all over the place but seein' as you've mentioned it, I'll deduct an appropriate amount from the bill."

**

Wallis drove his station wagon along the isolated, winding woodland road which led to the base camp of the 105th Idaho Militia. Beside him sat Baker and Collins. Tyler lay stretched out in the back where every bump in the road reminded him of the beating he'd just received.

The militia in Twin Falls, Idaho had sprung up over five years earlier when the local Baptist preacher, Norman Pellston had led a group of protesters to the front door of the Sheriff's office to complain about the Town Hall being let to a Gay Rights meeting. Wallis, who'd been the Sheriff at the time, took it upon himself to call in on the meeting and close it, arresting three of the participants in the process. His controversial actions found their way on to television screens and Wallis became something of a *cause celebre*. "Just for reflecting the views of the local community who don't much hold with these perverted people who are corruptin' the young men and women of Twin Falls," as he explained on network television.

He was suspended from duty and retired shortly afterwards, making a much publicised speech to TV cameras on how he intended dedicating the rest of his life to a new group he would form "in response to thousands of requests from well-wishers" called Wake Up America.

All sorts of people answered his call. Citizens who had beefs against liberal politics, gay, lesbian and other minority groups, blacks, immigrants, abortion providers and pro-choice supporters and those who held an intense dislike of the Federal Government and all of its organs of control.

Many of those who joined were white supremacists, right wing, gun rights advocates and those who supported *Posse Commitatus*, the County Rule Movement - which advocated the notion that the County is the supreme level of government, that the Sheriff is the highest elected official and that a new world conspiracy is underway, headed by the hated United Nations.

Over the years, Wake Up America spawned a number of special interest groups among which, in Idaho, was one of the most active Militias in the Patriot movement.

Wallis was held in high regard by all of the constituent parts of W.U.A. and was often to be found commenting in the press, pushing some right wing angle on whatever was under discussion. Still known as 'Sheriff' to many of his followers, he was Commander-in-Chief to those who served under him in the 105th Militia.

Wallis was an enthusiastic Militiaman. A base camp had been built deep in the mountains on the state boundary with Nevada comprising ten log cabins within a compound. Throughout the year, Militiamen and women lived in the camp, practising survivalist activity against the day when the Government moved finally against the people and had to be resisted with force. Wallis set up educational classes in one of the cabins as an offshoot to the work which was being done back in Twin Falls. Here was explained the unfair advantages which were given to blacks through the Government's affirmative action programs; how the World Bank was controlled by eight wealthy Jewish families and how the United Nations and the Federal Government represented examples of how taxes were being used by an Administration now finally and wildly out of control.

Wallis was fond of quoting from the Bible and from the Constitution of The United States. Interviewed on national television and asked to justify the growth of the Militia movement he spent a few moments excoriating the Federal Government and concluded …

"Finally sir, what you have to understand is that the people of our great nation are real angry. Too much attention is bein' given to the losers in our society, the perverts and the misfits. People are no longer goin' to watch their jobs bein' given over to foreign people. Americans will not be satisfied flippin' burgers for a livin'. Our forefathers expected us all to have the opportunity to achieve more than they did, to go all the way to the top of the heap. So we organise ourselves and we are fully aware of the Second Amendment to the Constitution of The United States of America which states that "*A well regulated Militia, being necessary to the security of a free state, the right of the people to keep and bear arms, shall not be infringed.*" That's not our justification, sir. It's just the goddamn law of this country."

\*\*

The station wagon took a bend in the road and stopped at a sentry post manned by two armed Militiamen. Both saluted Wallis and raised the log serving as a makeshift barrier admitting the vehicle to the parking area outside the compound.

Wallis nodded at his cargo in the back of the station wagon. "Men, take that injured soldier into the secure cabin. I will speak with him later."

## Chapter Five

One hour's drive south of Vegas on Highway 95 is the old mining town of Searchlight, home to only five hundred or so souls. Situated on its outskirts is the Golden Nugget Motel, a small shabby lodging which was only ever one third full but which provided its owners, Bill and Betty Huczynski with a home and a small income.

One of its windows had its curtains closed save for a few inches through which eyes scanned the approach road.

"Here she comes now."

A red Ford pick-up with a badly dented right wheel arch crunched over the gravel driveway leading to the hotel and sat, its engine running for a few moments while its driver collected some items from the dashboard and the passenger's seat. A slim bedenimed woman emerged and headed for Reception.

"Mornin', Mrs. Jones," said Bill Huczynski, long inured to the number of Jones and Smiths who had registered at his establishment over the years. Still, he preferred this to the guests who enjoyed a light-hearted approach and who required him to address them as Mr and Mrs Clinton or Sinatra or, memorably, Mr and Mrs Billy Graham. That just made him feel foolish.

Mr and Mrs Jones were the kind of guests he and his wife preferred. They kept themselves to themselves and had paid for four days' stay in cash and in advance. That said, their friend, Mr McCoy seemed a bit strange. There was nothing he could put his finger on but, so what, Mrs Jones took care of all of the payments and arrangements for all three of them so he didn't need to deal with him.

"Sleep well?" he enquired.

"Like a log, Mr Huczynski. Thanks for askin'," she said as she continued towards her room.

The motel room door was ajar as she approached it and was opened briefly by her husband to admit her.

"Any problems?" asked the man from his position at the window.

"Nah, although that hornet's nest we were tryin' to stir up sure is stirred up."

**

Julie (Sugar) Kane and her husband Matt along with Al Streikker were holed up in the Golden Nugget Motel awaiting further orders. Using assumed names, they had registered there the day before the airport shootings. In the quiet of the early morning they had collected the taxi from an old barn in which it had been hidden for the previous four weeks and which Streikker had fashioned from the entrails of a number of vehicles. Sugar Kane had followed the two men to Las Vegas then separated, heading for a disused car park which had previously served the needs of a warehouse situated just off the Maryland Parkway before its closure some six months earlier.

She waited there for around forty minutes while Streikker and Kane drove to nearby McCarran Airport and carried out their murderous orders. The taxi re-appeared on schedule and parked in a concealed alley behind the warehouse. Almost casually, the two occupants stepped out of the vehicle and briefly inspected the interior for any clues left inadvertently as to their identity. Satisfied, they removed their gloves and carried their weapons to the Ford placing them in the trunk before seating themselves. Almost as casually, Sugar Kane eased the car back on to the Parkway and all three headed back to Searchlight.

Back at the motel, Streikker still scanned the road outside. "Get through to the Pastor?"

"Yeah, we got our new orders. Two more hits and then report to Yancy up at Moapa Valley."

"Who we got to take out?" asked her husband.

"Just the top Rabbi in Nevada and an abortion clinic."

"Vengeance shall be mine, sayeth the Lord," quoted Streikker.

"I'm sure you'll help Him in His task but accordin' to Yancy, it'll be a piece of pumpernickel," said Sugar.

"When's the hits?"

"That's up to us but he wants the Rabbi taken care of as soon as possible. He wants the abortion clinic to get hit on Thursday."

Streikker had one last look out of the window before closing the curtains. "Well, Sugar honey, if you've got all of the details in that bag of yours, there ain't no time like the present to do the Lord's will."

Matt Kane shook his head. "No way, Streikker. Sugar's in charge an' these'll both take just as much planning as our last target."

Streikker laughed. "Some plannin'. We was meant to shoot up some Federal employees, not some Goddamn priests."

"Streikker, for a supposed man of God you sure have found it easy to shrug off the deaths of those priests. They were in the wrong place at the wrong time."

Matt Kane sprang to the support of his wife. "Shit happens! An' that's all the more reason to plan our next hits."

"Boys, boys, boys. Let's get sensible here. Sure we'll prepare but these look like real soft targets. I don't suppose it should take us too long."

Previously much less active than the 105<sup>th</sup> Idaho Militia and a much newer organisation, The Southern Nevada Militia had sprung from the loins of *Posse Commitatus*, a far right, secret, anti-taxation organisation dedicated to the same broad principals of the wider Patriot movement. However, *Posse Commitatus* was far more inclined to covert activity and direct action and these fundamentals were now to inform the activity of a newly formed cell of the Southern Nevada Militia.

The Kanes and Streikker were long standing members of the neo-fascist movement and were committed to changing America. Under the leadership of Pastor Mike Yancy, a local clergyman who chaired the High Command, they had been involved in establishing a Militia which was determined to take all necessary steps to bring America back from the brink. The movement was denied publicity because of its fascist character and so had decided to draw attention to its message by committing newsworthy acts. While other elements of the Militia were satisfied with publishing broadsheets, holding armed gatherings in public places or by encouraging survivalist training, frustrated members of the Southern Nevada Militia, at the behest of Pastor Yancy, set up a small, secret military unit  and returned to the original name and philosophy of *Posse Commitatus*.

Their main purpose was to secure information on groups in society which the Militia movement loathed and hated. Assassination targets would then be selected by the High Command and *Posse Commitatus* would carry out the hits.

One of the ironies of right wing, activist politics was that there was often a barely concealed contempt between active units such as *Posse Commitatus* and the equally right wing but less aggressive elements within the main Militia movement.

During that summer it had been decided to follow up on a newspaper article which reported on an anticipated golfing holiday to be taken later that month by a group of Federal employees. Sufficient detail was given to enable *Posse Commitatus* to plan an attack when the golfers exited from the airport following their return from vacation.

But this had been their first assassination. They were just learning. The priests had been a mistake.

**

Back at Police Headquarters, Regan thumbed quarters into a coffee machine with his right hand while supporting a collection of paper bags containing fast food in his left grasp. Stooping to pick up the plastic cup and balance it precariously on a nearby paper strewn desk, a dark suited man approached and asked gently "May I help?"

The Lieutenant eyed the man, confirming to himself that he didn't recognise him.

"Yeah, thanks, I'm takin' all of this stuff into that office." He nodded at the open door of his office within which sat Bilko talking on the 'phone.

The man obliged. "You're Lieutenant Regan, aren't you?" he asked.

"Unless I owe you money."

"I'm told you're the man I should be talking to. My name is Steve Montana….Special Agent Steve Montana, FBI." He held out his ID.

Regan didn't respond, searching the bags for his food and passing a coffee over to Bilko who ignored it. Regan took a bite and sipped at the coffee, grimacing at the pain of drinking boiling water. "S'pose I've been expectin' you boys."

"I'm not here about the shooting of the priests," said Montana.

"Right now, that's pretty much all I'm able to talk about, Special Agent Montana."

"Right now you're eating. We all got to eat. You could talk and eat."

"You come all the way from Washington, Montana?"

"Yeah, sure, Lieutenant," said Montana, tiring already of the banter.

Regan sensed the man's frustration and held his hand up as if signifying a truce.

"Okay, man, okay. You want a coffee?"

"It'll keep." Montana got down to business. "I was told you know your patch. You been around this place a while."

Regan shrugged his assent and nodded towards Bilko. "My partner and I been here since the gold rush."

Montana lifted a briefcase and opened it, removing a slim file. "We got information that the Militia movement here in Nevada are converging with some other far right boys and girls and they intend putting us all to the test."

"You think they were involved with the airport shootings?"

"Nah. There's more supposed men of God involved with these boys through the anti-abortion movement than you could shake a stick at. Looks to me like you're dealing with some common or garden crazies here. We believe that the Militia are still at the planning stage but our information is that they have the weapons and the manpower to cause quite a fuss. Frankly, these people could cause a fuss in almost every State in the Union but I've been ordered to spend some time around Vegas, to sniff around and assess the level of threat which we have here in Nevada."

"You mind tellin' me where you got this information?"

"You don't need to know that Lieutenant. You just need to know that you may have a police problem about to happen in the next while and I could probably make your life easier. Being honest, you and your partner could give me one or two pointers which would help me too."

Regan nodded. "So what you need to know?"

"Do you have files on the local Militia?"

Regan sighed. "Steve." He put down his coffee cup and folded his arms. "Can I call you Steve, Steve?" He didn't wait for affirmation. "There's lots of folks see these people as real American heroes. They've never done anything other than assemble peaceably, distribute leaflets, that sort of thing. They care about their country. We don't keep files on those kinds of people though I guess it'd be too much to expect that the Bureau takes the same approach."

"You got it in one, Lieutenant. We have to be prepared for whatever eventuality this country throws up. And right now we got ourselves an armed, secret society which threatens our government, Federal agents, health clinics and minority groups. We don't just wait around for them to attack us. *We* make the moves."

Bilko ended his telephone conversation and hungrily attended to the foodstuffs in front of him. Regan brought him immediately into the conversation.

"Sergeant Bilk, this is Special Agent Steve Montana, FBI. He's come to visit us telling tales of the mayhem we're about to experience at the hand of the local Militia movement. Apparently all hell's about to break loose 'less Steve here comes to the rescue."

Bilko talked with his mouth full. "We're up to our eyes in mayhem at present Mister. An' not just these killin's at the airport. We got outstanding murders, we got vice, we got drugs, we got the mob, we got all sorts. We don't just got the stuff you bin watchin' on TV. The Militia maybe just gotta join the queue."

Montana smiled. "Well, Sergeant, I'm going to be in your pocket over the next few weeks while you and the Lieutenant here go about your business. I've got my orders but that's not why I'm here. I just wanted to be around someone with such a sunny disposition. So, how about that coffee now?"

**

It was dark by now. The red Ford pick-up pulled up in a quiet alley. Sugar Kane turned off the ignition. The two men alighted and walked to the rear of the pick-up, each removing a rifle, unwrapping them from within two sacks. Wordlessly, both stepped across the alley, each slinging their rifle across their back as they did so. Sugar killed the car lights once both had reached a steel ladder fixed to the wall on the derelict building opposite. Silently, Streikker nodded to Kane who commenced his assent. Once he had climbed above Streikker's head height, Streikker stepped on to the bottom rung of the ladder and joined him on his climb to the top.

Matt Kane reached the roof first and inspected its characteristics before stepping on to its flat surface. Streikker joined him and both crouched down, each removing their rifle from their shoulder. Still stooped, they padded over to the far end of the building, slowing as they approached the ledge. A small wall ran round the circumference of the building and both men kneeled and peered over the top.

Across the street opposite was a house set back some ten or so yards from the sidewalk allowing an unkempt garden to hint at the probable condition of the rear enclosure. The road below was ill lit as was the house. Streikker and Kane could see the inside of those rooms in the building which were illuminated and observed that there appeared to be two men in the house, one writing at a desk and a second, a younger man, seated in another room apparently watching television or listening to the radio. On two occasions a woman entered the room occupied by the man in the armchair and, ignoring him, collected items and left the room.

"Housekeeper," murmured Kane.

"What you figure, the guy at the upstairs desk?"

"Looks that way."

Kane wiped some perspiration from his eyes. "Give it a second. We want to get this one right. It's got to be the guy upstairs. That one downstairs looks too young. There's no way he's old enough to be the top Jew guy in the city."

"We should just take out both of them," said Streikker. "The good Lord's not gonna miss another dead Jew."

Kane eyed him. "As you say, we're soldiers of the Lord, Streikker. We got our orders. The old guy gets it and that's it. No heroics, no nuthin'." He inspected his rifle and removed a silencer from inside his coat pocket. He screwed it on to the barrel of the gun. "This'll be a one rifle job. Just make sure there's no traffic or pedestrians, then I take him out."

"Since when did you become the best shot?" asked Streikker.

"Streikker, are you crazy? This is a military operation. It's a hit! We don't argue over who pulls the trigger!"

"So why ain't it me? I've been practisin' for weeks."

"I don't believe you, Streikker. You can't be serious."

"Okay", said Streikker. "We'll settle this straight forward."

Both men had left all of their small change in the hotel to improve their ability to move silently so there was no coin to toss. Streikker patted his pockets looking for a mechanism for a tiebreak while Kane looked on incredulously. Eventually he unearthed a motel business card from his pocket and tore a corner from it.

"Right then." He put both hands behind his back placing a piece of the card in each hand. "You choose. Torn small piece pulls the trigger!" He brought both hands, palm down between himself and Kane.

"Streikker, you are one crazy son of a bitch!"

"Choose!"

Kane slapped Streikker's left hand which he opened to reveal the damaged card.

Streikker smiled as Kane opened his other hand, revealing the torn corner. "The good Lord has revealed his blessings. I guess we do it like I said we should."

Kane's face revealed his irritation. "Let's get on with it."

Both men scanned the quiet street and waited while a barking dog was admitted to a house some distance away.

Streikker raised his rifle and levelled it. The crosshairs on the sights settled on the back of the man seated at his desk. Slowly they moved upwards until they centred on the Rabbi's skullcap. "Prepare to meet thy maker, Jew boy."

Streikker squeezed the trigger and in an instant his bullet had smashed through the window and into The Rabbi's head, precisely where it had been aimed. "Jesus loves you," said Streikker in his assassin's version of the last rites.

Kane looked anxiously up and down the street. Nothing stirred. Inside the house the man and woman had heard the crash of glass and were beginning to join one another in an investigation of the noise.

Streikker inspected his handiwork and seemed satisfied. "Let's move. This place'll be kinda busy in a couple of minutes."

Strapping their rifles across their back again, they scurried to the ladder and rejoined Sugar who illuminated their descent with her car lights. A few steps took them to the rear of the car where they replaced their rifles in the trunk. Seconds later they were heading back to Searchlight.

"Mission accomplished, honey," said Kane. Let's go home, get a beer and see how we got on on the television."

**

Trent Wallis picked up the hands-free phone in his cabin which, along with one other handset kept usually in the mess hall, represented the telecommunications system within the compound. His lips searched out a cigarette from a pack held to his lips and he ignited it with a flaring match before inhaling the smoke, coughing as the nicotine hit the back of his throat.

From his shirt pocket he withdrew a small notebook which he consulted before tapping out a series of numbers on his phone.

"I'd like to speak to Pastor Mike Yancy if you please," he said to the voice which answered his enquiry. "Sure I'll hold." He leaned back in his chair and put his feet on the window ledge. "My name's Trent Wallis," he answered in response to the next question.

Some moments passed. "Well now, it's been a while Commander."

"Been kinda busy up here in Idaho," said Wallis.

"Looks that way from my readin' of the newspapers. You're gettin' quite a name for yourself. All that speechifyin' on the television. I was talkin' to one of our people a while back an' he was tellin' me that you got yourself a fortress built in the woods up there so's you can hole up with your boys and keep yourselves out of trouble."

"Callin' you from there right now," said Wallis.

"I'm a privileged man. I certainly am."

"This is a courtesy call, Pastor. The Unit are about to commence an operation in your neck of the woods and I thought it would be neighborly of me to let you know."

"Well, now, Commander I would surely like to oblige," said Yancy with a new edge to his voice "but I just don't think I can help you out on this one."

"You don't say," said Wallis sarcastically. "You got problems with us operating on your turf?"

"It would compromise activity we already got on the go."

"Nevada's a big state, Yancy."

"So's Idaho, Wallis. I'd figure you had more than enough to be gettin' on with without troublin' your neighbors here in Nevada. 'Specially with all we got goin' on with our own people. What the hell you figurin' you're gonna get up to?"

"You know better'n that, Yancy. This ain't a secure line. Anyway, we operate only on a need to know basis an' you just don't need to know, my friend."

"Listen, Wallis, you're Commander in Chief in Idaho. You got complete autonomy in your patch. You call it like you see it over there, but you ain't got no call, talkin' 'bout comin' over here interferin' with plans we been workin' on for God knows how long. What the hell you thinkin' about? Lemme tell you, Wallis, you and your men step over that state line, there's no way I can guarantee your safety."

"We're meant to be on the same side, Yancy, so don't go gettin' all disputational on me now."

"Then you go through proper channels, Wallis."

"We have an opportunity. It won't wait for proper channels to clear. After that speech by Lattanzi on television we got to move quickly. We got a plan an' you know very well we're better organised and equipped than you are. The cause belongs to all of us."

"I'm warning you Wallis, we got powerful people in this state lookin' out for us. You come over here, you'll jeopardise military activity an' I'll make sure a whole heap of people will be lookin' out for you an' they ain't gonna be friendly."

"Sounds like my courtesy call ain't workin'."

"It sure ain't."

Wallis took a last drag from his cigarette before stubbing it out in an ashtray. "Well why don't you just do your worst Pastor 'cause we got business to take care of in your patch. We didn't plan it that way, but we seen the opportunity to advance a cause that a whole lot of people hold dear. So why don't you take your "proper channels" and shove them right up your ass. We're comin' in."

Wallis replaced the phone and walked to the open door of his cabin. "Collins, go bring Tyler over here. And tell Burring and Edson to come too." He turned and walked to the rear of his cabin where a map of Nevada was pinned to the wall. He spent some moments perusing the chart before being interrupted by Collins who had collected the three Militiamen out on the porch.

"Sir, I brought the men over."

"Thank you Collins. That'll be all for now." Collins turned and left, ushering in as he did so his three colleagues. Tyler's face was still bloody as was Edson's. Tyler held his arm across his ribcage as if to effect an easing of the pain he was experiencing.

"Men, I've just been on the telephone to our people in Nevada who have asked us to assist them in an operation which is top secret and dangerous," Wallis lied. "Now we been rehearsin' for a mission like this for some time and, for a regular job, I would normally ask for volunteers. But in the circumstances I'm goin' to order you men to volunteer because I need soldiers with certain skills. Edson, you're a loyal and good man. You're also the best driver I ever seen and that just might come in useful, though I hear tell you're no marksman."

Edson, initially exuding pride, looked stung at his Commander's closing comment.

Willis went on. "Burring, you're an excellent shot. Best we've got, handgun or rifle. Tyler, you blotted your copybook and you got a debt to pay in that regard. But you didn't get to be a Lieutenant in this man's army for no reason. You're a mean son of a bitch but you're experienced and 'bout as handy with a gun as Burring here."

He paused and faced the window, avoiding the gaze of his men before asking their involvement. "Now, any of you men feel you want out? 'Cause I'm goin' to start explainin' the plans we got an' you don't got no choice after I do that."

Burring and Edson assented immediately. Tyler, still bent slightly and holding his midriff looked hard at Wallis. "I think your goons busted one of my ribs. It's rest I need, not action."

"Oh, I'll make sure you'll get all the rest you need, Tyler. Ribs are funny things. There ain't too much you can do to fix them and the pain you have'll go away soon enough. But it'll stay around just long enough to remind you that if you get an order from me you make damn sure you carry it out immediately, without question and without deviation." Wallis pulled another cigarette from his pack. "Now, I can't afford to have a disgruntled soldier on this mission. You disgruntled, Lieutenant?"

Tyler held his Commander's gaze aggressively for some seconds before blinking his resignation. He spoke slowly and reluctantly. "No sir. And I'd be proud to serve at your command."

"Well that's good son, that's good. 'Cause let me tell you what the four of us are goin' to do for the people of this country. We're goin' to Nevada. We're goin' to apprehend an ex-senator and we're goin' to have him explain hisself to the American people for his views on gun control. An' if he knows what's good for him, he'll apologise to the American people. He took a deep drag from his cigarette and gestured the filtered end towards the three men. "An' there may be some gunplay."

Tyler smiled at the thought of action.

Wallis thumbed over his shoulder at the map on the wall. "Let's take a look at this map right now. We move out in an hour."

**

In Las Vegas, Pastor Mike Yancy was on the telephone to one of his colleague Militiamen who acted effectively as his personal assistant.

"Get me everything we have on Joe Lattanzi. The guy was Senator for one of the east coast states. Don't remember which. I want business interests, hobbies, his women. I want addresses, routines, favourite restaurants. I want everything and I want it now." The phone set was half way to the receiver when Yancy had another thought. "Before you do that. Make contact with Sugar. I want her to get in touch on a secure line. I got another piece of work for her."

# Chapter Six

Kinsella had visited The Liffey bar and had had a couple of beers without meeting anyone who could throw any light on the events surrounding the shooting of young Father Patrick Sheridan. This, a barman had explained was probably because he'd arrived after work when the bar was full of suits. The younger element didn't show up until much later.

Faced with the prospect of drinking alone for a few hours in the hope that something would turn up, Kinsella decided just to quench his thirst and to return later when Sheridan's charges were more likely to be there in number.

So it was later that evening that a wet and bedraggled Kinsella stepped into The Liffey Bar chased in by the inclement weather as much as by an undertaking to a friend. The same barman as was attending his needs on his last visit was hoisting pints of Guinness on to the top of the bar. He acknowledged Kinsella on entry, his eyes swivelling round the room in order to anticipate his customers' orders.

"A pint, is it?"

"Yeah, an' a good malt … eh," Kinsella scanned the gantry above the bar to identify and select his favoured whisky. "… give me a large Glenmorangie to warm me up.

The Liffey Bar was an old traditional pub. A polished oak bar dominated the centre of the large and spacious room swinging round in a horseshoe to provide the maximum elbow room. A few chairs and tables were scattered around, some congregating around a log fire at the rear, most clinging to the contours of the bar room in order to leave a large floor area in which the pub's clientele could drink and converse. The bar area was ablaze with light and the place was busy, warm and noisy. Other than the hint of an Irish slip-jig in the background, there was no other distraction to drinking talking, listening, arguing and laughing. The place appeared to have a significant number of regular customers given the pub notice board which listed a bewildering number of activities from quizzes to fishing and golf events. A collage of photographs grew in effusion around the board testifying to the good times which were regularly being had by all.

Kinsella lifted the malt whisky to his lips and allowed the amber fluid to flow unhindered. He grimaced and nodded a second from the barman, still waiting for his Guinness to settle in its glass.

He paid for his second malt and accepted the change. "It's pissin' down out there. God help us, the bloody Liffey will be flowin' through this bar if it doesn't ease up."

"Sure, it's been like this all day," said the barman, pouring another two pints of Guinness while wiping the bar and searching the gantry with his eyes for appropriate glasses to complete the next order.

Kinsella satisfied himself that his Guinness was now perfectly ready for consumption. "I spoke to you the other night about that priest who was shot."

"Yeah, I remember alright. Gimme a minute till I get rid of these pints."

Some moments later the barman returned. "I think you might have better luck tonight. There's a whole bunch of students over in the corner. Some of them were friendly with Father Sheridan. You'd do worse than speak to Tommy. He's the one over there wearing the white Arran knit."

Kinsella mimed a toast in thanks to the barman and wandered over to the group of students. "Tommy?" shouted Kinsella above the hubbub, "D'you think I could have a minute?" He gestured a smiled suggestion that the student extricate himself from the group by nodding in the direction of the door.

Tommy raised his eyebrows and pointed at his own chest asking non-verbally if he was the object of Kinsella's invitation. Pursing his lips in affirmation, Kinsella stepped back into a small recess cupping and swivelling his right hand miming an offer to the student to buy him a drink.

"No thanks, I'm fine," said Tommy holding up his glass of whisky as evidence of his needs having been attended to. "Do I know you?"

"Not at all, but I understand you know a friend of mine, Patrick Sheridan."

"Father Pat? He's a friend of yours?"

"I haven't seen him for years, mind."

"Listen, you're not a cop or a journalist are you? This place has been swimmin' in them ever since the shootin'."

"Well, to be honest, I'm a journalist but I'm a friend of Pat's on this one and I'm not lookin' to put anything in print."

"Look, Mister, no offence, but we've all told the *Garda* everythin' we know. Christ, the entire pub's been involved in interviews and everyone has been tellin' them that Father Pat hasn't an enemy in the world. I don't know what else we could tell you that might help. Everythin's been in the papers anyway."

"Yeah, I've read all that stuff all right but it's not takin' anyone anywhere. Do you know Pat well?"

Tommy finished his whisky and Kinsella, noticing this, raised his own half empty glass at the barman and shouted another round above the cacophony.

"He's more of a friend than a priest. A brilliant guy. I'm tellin' you he was shot by a bloody madman. I still can't believe he's lyin' there in intensive care on the point of death and his only concern in life is to help other people. It was either a mistake, sectarian or a madman. And my money's on the madman. I'm tellin' you, Pat could talk to anyone. We get a lot of young people in here. In fact, we get all sorts and Pat would make them welcome, he'd introduce them to other people, he'd make sure that if they had an interest in somethin' they'd meet the person who looked after that activity in the bar. The man was a bloody saint. And he was what, twenty-five, twenty-six? Jesus Christ, it would test your faith. It surely would."

"Was he a big drinker?" asked Kinsella.

"Oh, he enjoyed a glass like most of us but I wouldn't have put him down as a bloody dipso! He'd pace himself. Anyway he was always up early in the mornin' to handle his church responsibilities so he wouldn't want a hangover. At the end of the day he was pretty much a youth worker with a dog collar although we seldom saw him wearing the garb. Christ, we saw him more when he was wearin' fancy dress at one or other of the pub's outin's." Tommy stepped forward and leaned over the bar. "Hey Sean, have you ever got those photographs developed of us when we had that Karaoke competition that Pat organised?"

The barman stooped below the bar. "As a matter of fact, I got them this afternoon but they're pretty crap. I looked earlier." He handed them to Tommy who took them from the envelope.

"There you go. Look at him, the life and sole of the party and no dog collar in sight. And to think that the next evening someone nearly blew his head off."

Kinsella scanned the photographs. "Could I have one of these?"

"Not if they're headed for a newspaper."

"I promise you not." He continued his inspection of the revelry captured on film.

"Tell me, do you know everyone in these photographs?"

"I would expect so. Let's see them again and I'll soon tell you." Tommy went through them one by one, the slightest nodding of his head revealing confirmation that his confidence was well founded. "Oh, how could I forget about *those* guys?" He held up a shot of Father Patrick talking to a blond haired man in a brown leather jacket and an older man in a plaid shirt.

Tommy pointed at the man in the leather Jacket. "Pat spoke to him for a good while that night. He was American. A pretty drunk American. I talked to him myself for a while but I could hardly understand a word he said. I remember that he was over here on business and was due to return to the states a couple of days later. I can't believe I didn't remember to tell the *Garda*. Mind you I was a bit under the weather when I spoke to them"

"You remember a name?"

"Nah. He just sat at the bar all night downing pints. I only spoke to him when I was getting a drink in for Pat. All he said was some smart arse comment about our warm beer and then he ordered a chilled bottle of American beer…a Bud I think. But he didn't offer to get one up for Pat or me. Didn't much take to him mind you. He told us that he'd got into the gold and jewellery business after the Vietnam war. He was a scary guy. He said he got into the business by buying gold from the GI's who'd just returned to Saigon after a tour of duty. The Viet Cong used gold teeth like you and I would use a bank and these US soldiers used to pull them from the mouths of dead North Vietnamese soldiers with pliers and this fellah would buy the gold. He moved to Miami after the war but his business went bust because he couldn't compete with the Chinese traders. Said Miami was now a foreign country and that he'd moved back up north. Like I said, a scary man. I can't believe that I forgot he was in that night."

"How about the other fellah?"

"He was local all right but I don't know him." *Yes, but I do*, thought Kinsella.

"They been back since?"

"Just that night. But I suppose *they'd* be the last men who spent any time with Pat that night"

"Have the *Garda* seen this?"

Tommy called to the barman. "Sean, anyone seen these 'cept us?"

"You're first."

"Looks like we're the first,"Tommy said unnecessarily."

"Look, it would be helpful if I could hold on to this one of the American guy. Just for a short while."

"No skin off my nose," said Tommy. "But what should I do about the *Garda*?"

"I'd let them know about this couple, alright. But could you maybe remember to do that tomorrow instead of right away? I'd like to think it would be to Pat's advantage and I'll get the photograph back to the bar before lunchtime."

"And I suppose this conversation didn't take place?"

"That's about it." Kinsella slipped the photograph into his jacket pocket. "One for the road?"

"Thanks but I'd better be gettin' back over to my friends."

"You drink in here regularly?"

"Most nights I'm in for a while."

"Then maybe I'll see you again. You've been very helpful. Trust me, nothing will appear in the papers, I'm more concerned to figure out what's goin' on here. You have my word on that."

Kinsella shook the student's hand and made for the door, remembering with irritation that he was about to be soaked once again. The public telephone box he espied across the street had little shelter from the elements but it was quieter than the Liffey Bar. He stood in the light of the entrance to the bar and took out his little black notebook and thumbed through it looking for a phone number.

*Jesus this is getting dangerous. Perhaps I'd better start playing safe,* he thought to himself. There was no mistaking the Dubliner in the photograph. Eamon O'Farrell, one of the IRA's most trusted men. *How in God's name might the Provos be involved in the attempted murder of a young priest?* Especially one who was so obviously removed from the sectarian battlefields of the North of Ireland.

Kinsella turned up the collar of his overcoat and hurried across the street, splashing through the puddles of water until he reached the relative shelter of the telephone booth. Once inside, he perused again the inked numbers of contacts made from years of journalistic conversations. He pursed his lips. *Do I phone the Garda Siochana or make contact with O'Farrell?* His promise to his old friend Brannigan was to find out anything he could and let him know. He could just stop now and let other people investigate. But O'Farrell and he had dealt with one another before. *He was straight with me then, maybe he'll help me out now.*

He dialled the number and let it ring several times before it was answered. "Three one four seven!"

"May I speak with Eamon O'Farrell, please?"

"You're speakin' to him. Who's this?

"Eamon, it's Paul Kinsella of the Irish Times."

"Paul, Christ it's been years. I haven't seen hide nor hair of you since we got ourselves gloriously pissed in Johnnie Fox's bar up in Glencullen.  Now why would you be phonin' a lowly footsoldier like me? I thought interviewin' the Taosaich or members of the Cabinet was more in your line these days." There was a smile in O'Farrell's voice.

"It's something and nothing. I need some information and it wouldn't surprise me if you could help me. That said if you warn me off. It finishes there."

"Aye, you played straight with me the last time right enough. Can you give me a clue what you want to talk about?"

"Let's just meet. It would be good to see your ugly face again."

"We've very strict rules about meetin' with journalists. I'd have to clear it in advance. If I'm told no, then that's that."

"Yes, I know the rules. But I'm not really speaking to you as a journalist. Well, I am but it would give us both more freedom to talk if we just met for a beer. I promise on my honour there's no way I would compromise you. The last time we dealt with one another you'll agree I played it straight as a dye."

"You did that all right. I'll give you that."

"So what d'you say? A glass tomorrow at lunch time. Twelve o'clock, Riley's Bar. And no one knows about this but you and me?"

O'Farrell allowed a silence to hang in the air for a moment. "All right. But this is a big favour you're askin', Paul. If it goes adrift, I stand to be on the wrong end of a beatin'."

"I'll see you tomorrow. And thanks again."

Kinsella replaced the phone and glowered at the torrential rain. His shoes were letting in water. *I'm off home before I catch my death of cold*, he promised himself.

**

Susan Lattanzi had brought her father a nightcap in his study and bid him goodnight with a kiss on his cheek. Returning to the lounge, she approached Liam Brannigan from behind and cupped her hands over his eyes "Guess my name and win a glass of brandy."

"I'm not a man who likes to drink alone."

"Guess my name and I'll join you."

"In that case, your name is Susan Lattanzi and you're the prettiest gal in town."

"Why Mister Brannigan, I do believe that's the closest you've ever come to giving me a compliment… unless, of course there's a sting in the tail."

"Well now, I wouldn't joke about a woman who was offering me a brandy. Especially if it was from one of your Dad's special reserve bottles which only see the light of day at funerals or celebrations."

"If *you* don't tell, I most certainly won't."

Susan stepped over to the bar and opened the drinks cabinet containing Joe's favourite malt whiskies and classic brandies. "Let's do this properly, Liam. Crystal glasses warmed over a candle's flame to bring out the bouquet."

"Sure, it would only be what the brandy deserves."

Susan busied herself with preparations while Liam set aside his book and joined her at the bar. Earlier he had been listening to a Dwight Yoakam CD as part of Susan's campaign to 'civilise' him and convert him to Country and Western music instead of 'that raucous Irish devil music'. Oblivious of his gaze, Susan hummed along to a slow ballad completely caught up in the delicacies of pouring the perfect brandy.

Liam watched in appreciation. She really was a beautiful young woman. Long dark hair framed an impossibly pretty face but it was her innocence, her lack of any pretensions which caught him sometimes. Her beauty made heads turn at her entrance to a room but she seemed to be possessed of an elegant serenity which transcended mere physical looks. Almost casual about make up and manicures, she was as happy in jeans as she was in more feminine attire. Tonight she was in leisure mode, jeans and a man's oversized shirt. *That'll be a left over from her year-long relationship with that eejit Ben Dalton. Never could see what she ever saw in him. All he had was money. That and the charm of a snake oil salesman*, thought Liam.

Susan had poured the drinks. She offered one to Liam. "This is very civilised. Let's sit over by the fire."

Liam moved over and sat in a comfortable armchair beside the fire. Susan sat on the floor cross-legged at his feet but facing him. She raised her glass. "I want to make a toast"

"You go right ahead," said Liam raising his glass in anticipation.

"I want to toast the good fortune of my family in having you around. We nearly lost you at the airport and it made me realise just what you mean to all three of us."

Liam read the seriousness in her voice and reconsidered his first instinct to tease her.

"You know Susan, you're a very special person. Just when I think I've got a handle on you, you only go and surprise me. Its not very often I see you share a worry. But that's a very nice sentiment you express. Your dad is very important to me, and not just as a boss. He's a lovely man. And your mother's just the most elegant and delightful person west of the Pecos. You're fortunate. You've got wonderful parents."

"There's *three* people in the Lattanzi family," teased Susan.

"The third Lattanzi," mused Liam. He held the brandy glass to his face and breathed in the intoxicating bouquet, closing his eyes in appreciation.

"The third Lattanzi." He paused, unsure in which direction to take the conversation. "Well, I imagine she doesn't know this, but she's probably my best friend." He took comfort in speaking in the third person but found it difficult to meet her gaze. "She's the most uncomplicated person I've ever met. I respect her and if circumstances were different…."

"What circumstances might these be?" asked Susan.

"Drink your XO brandy. It's just magnificent."

"I asked you a question, Liam Brannigan."

"Oh, but I don't need to answer it!"

"If you don't, I'll tell my father you've been drinking his best brandy."

Both laughed.

"Listen, Susan. Sometimes I have to pinch myself to remind me that I'm not dreaming. Sure, I'm bright enough. *Doctor* Liam Brannigan! Isn't that very grand. But most of my contemporaries are sitting in research labs or lecturing students who only want to do enough to get by before heading for the nearest pub and here am I working with Joe in Vegas and being befriended by his family who are composed of the three nicest people in the world."

"You were saying about the third Lattanzi?"

"Susan, the third Lattanzi is my boss's daughter."

"And if she wasn't?"

"She *is*!"

Susan placed her brandy on the hearth and shifted her position so she was kneeling in front of Liam, her arms resting on his knees. "I'm embarrassing you."

"Drink your brandy."

"Liam." She cupped the brandy glass and held it again in a toasting gesture. "After my father, I can't think of any man I feel closer to." She sipped the brandy, "To the men in my life."

"I think I'm more comfortable when you're making fun of me but I'm more proud than you could imagine that you hold me in that kind of esteem. You're like a little sister to me." Liam clinked Susan's glass in response to her toast. "To the men in your life."

Standing just outside the lounge door having stopped *en route* to his bedroom, Joe Lattanzi overheard the concluding elements of the fireside chat. A mixture of guilt at his eavesdropping and pride at his daughter's love for her parents fought for supremacy. He smiled and continued quietly on tiptoe towards his bedroom. *Well now! Who'd have thought? I think this justifies waking up Liz.*

# Chapter Seven

The guest room in which Liam was accommodated whilst a guest of the Lattanzi's was lit by a shaft of sunlight which caused Liam to shield his eyes upon awakening.

He lay, organising his thoughts and orientating himself. The clock showed eight thirty, probably time to get moving. After stretching and yawning, he rose and headed for the shower-room, absent-mindedly hitting the TV remote button to listen to the news in the background.

The shower was piercing. Hot needles of water rid any remaining sleepiness and Liam enjoyed the sensation before stepping from the shower. Urgent knocking on his room door caused him to pause his towelling and use it instead as a wrap for modesty. He opened the door to admit Susan who rushed past him dressed only in the shirt she'd been wearing the previous evening.

"Liam, have you seen the news?"

"I wasn't listening. What's happened?"

Susan sat on the edge of Liam's bed and started to flick through the channels until she found CNN which was reporting on the assassination of Rabbi David Goldstein.

"There's been another shooting. Another religious shooting."

The news team covered the murder from every angle, interviewing Lieutenant Regan who said very little but was diplomatic despite the baiting and persistent quizzing of the reporters. *Just as well they don't let Bilko loose on these interviews; there'd be fist fights*, thought Liam.

"Liam, what's going on?"

"There's some pretty sick people out there."

"Is it the same people who shot the priests?"

"Possibly, or copycat killings, who knows. Jesus, its just madness."

Liam suddenly became aware of his semi-nakedness as the television news broke off for adverts. Simultaneously he became aware of Susan who was quite obviously oblivious to the fact of her scanty attire as she began again to use the remote to search for another news program covering the murder of Rabbi Goldstein.

*God help us, she's a stunning creature*, he thought.

"Susan lets get ourselves dressed and organised. Your father will want to discuss this and I'd rather do that with some dignity."

The sudden realisation of herself sitting on Liam's bed wearing only a shirt with one button fastened galvanised Susan.

"Oh my God, look at me. Father would have a fit. I'll go and get dressed." She rushed from the room.

*Whew! What a woman,* thought Liam. *Was that a tease or was she just caught up in the news of the murders. Maybe one day when both of us have had too much to drink, I'll ask her.*

**

"Venison stew's just gonna have to wait, honey," said Burring to the camp cook, whose slim figure was curiously enhanced by the bulky military fatigues she was required to wear. "I gotta go save America."

"Well Sergeant, you take care of yourself and I'll cook you up a mess of stew when you get back."

Tyler entered the cabin. "Everythin' loaded, Sergeant?"

"Yes sir. We're ready to go."

"Well, let's get movin'. We've got a long drive ahead of us and we ain't gonna get there any quicker if you're gonna fraternise with Private Carter."

Outside, Edson had checked the powerful and spacious Chrysler Cherokee off-road vehicle that would drive them to their base in Henderson, some ten miles from Lattanzi's ranch outside Boulder City. In the rear of the Cherokee were several containers containing clothing, food and fishing equipment; their cover, however flimsy, if challenged. Two of the boxes, however, contained an assortment of handguns and rifles, some semi-automatic, and a box of explosives. Edson decided to store the detonators under the driver's seat. *Best not to have them too close to the dynamite. Better safe than sorry.*

Wallis appeared and called Edson and Burring to the side of the Cherokee.

"Did either of you two soldiers listen to the briefing session?" he quizzed.

Both Militiamen looked at one another, puzzled at the question. They had obviously done something wrong.

"Goddamn it. Have I got to explain everything to you in words of one syllable? This, may I remind you, my comrades in arms, is a Goddamn *secret* mission. We're not meant to be spotted. We don't want to arouse the suspicion of the police never mind Yancy's people. Do you think it will help or hinder our covert approach if we all turn up in Nevada in battledress?" His chiding tone changed to one of insistence. "Get out of these togs now. We're meant to a fishin' party for chrissake. You got five minutes, then we go."

A few minutes later, both Militiamen reported back to the Cherokee. Wallis and Tyler were seated in the front passenger seat. Burring climbed in behind them. Edson pulled himself into the driving seat and switched on the ignition. A reassuring, throaty growl emanated from the engine and Edson turned to Wallis. "We move off now, sir?"

"We got to get to Henderson just south east of Vegas. We'll go via Salt Lake City to stay out of Nevada for most of the journey. Now that's the best part of six hundred miles so we'll share the driving if you get tired but we don't stop for nothin'. So now you know the route, you know the destination. Get us there without we get jailed for speedin'."

**

Forty miles south of Henderson, the Kanes and Streikker watched television in their motel room in Searchlight. "Just like the song says, 'Fifty seven channels and nothin' on'," said Sugar, prodding constantly at the remote.

Behind her, Streikker sat at a table consumed by his task of assembling a detonation device. "When this baby goes up so does half the city."

"It'd better not. We got to plant it and get the hell away from the building without we get blown to bits ourselves," said Matt Kane.

"You don't need to worry too much 'bout that," said Streikker "I'm goin' to set this with a two day delay. We could be on the other side of the world watching the bang on television when it goes off. Pastor Yancy wants this to draw the attention of the world to Vegas on the 23rd when The Supreme Court passes judgement on abortion law on Thursday. We can plant this any time within that time frame so's there's much less chance of us being detected. But don't worry, it'll do just enough damage to take out the wing that all of them Godless doctors and nurses hang out in."

"I figure we done good so far," said Sugar. "We just gotta make sure we don't get complacent. This hit should be the easiest so far. Trust me, we ain't got no problem plantin' a bomb with a two day delay in an unguarded

Abortion Clinic. Our problems are goin' to start when we go after Lattanzi 'cause we'll have the cops, the Idaho Militia and all their friends to worry 'bout. Lattanzi might even have Federal protection, him bein' a previous Senator."

"I still don't get what Yancy's on about," said Streikker, "I always figured we was all workin' for the Lord. Why the hell he wants us to mix it with people who's just the same as us has gotta be some kinda bullshit."

"Pastor Yancy has already explained that," said Sugar. "We're a disciplined force. We got orders and we carry them out. These people are renegades who're operating on our turf. They get caught or get outa hand, it's us who take the flack."

Sugar and Matt Kane returned to their disinterested television viewing and all fell into silence. Around half an hour later Streikker leaned back and stretched his arms out, yawning "Well now, I think the good Lord would approve of His servant's work tonight. We got us a detonation system here that ain't nothin' gonna stop once it's armed. It's a piece of precision, a work of art and I don't need to stay without a drink for one moment longer."

Sugar smiled and slid him a bottle of whisky which she and her husband had been sampling throughout the evening. "You deserve it Ed. You're the best explosives man in the business. Just make sure that timer's set for two days and not two seconds. It'd make a bit of a difference."

**

After breakfast the next morning, the *Posse* members bid a cheery good morning to Mr Huczynski as they made their way past Reception to the red Ford pick-up which was to take them back to Vegas. This time, however they carried no weapons. Any police check would unearth only gardening implements. The three large canisters, if opened, would reveal chemicals which, to the untrained eye, would resemble weedkiller. The spare parts for the grasscutter would seem innocent enough. However, once assembled and detonated, the chemical concoction would be powerful enough to blow the average family home into the next county.

Sugar drove as usual. The journey into Vegas was uneventful. Police cars were much in evidence but there were no roadblocks and the good people of Las Vegas seemed to be getting on with their lives just fine.

"We're almost there boys. Now remember, this one depends mostly on our confidence. Ain't no one goin' to question two guys cuttin' the grass and doin' a bit of horticulture. Pastor Yancy is particular 'bout this job. He's got a real bee in his bonnet 'bout them abortion clinics, killin' little kids. These doctors and nurses are no more than murderers. Well, this is war and they're gonna realise that the Lord will smite them with a vengeful hand because of what they do. Just remember that, boys. We're doin' the *Lord's* work today."

"Praise the Lord," said Streikker.

The car pulled up twenty yards from the front entrance of the abortion clinic. Cars were parked all along the road although, being somewhat out of town, every third or fourth space was empty. The two men stepped from the car and began to unload the bits and pieces of gardening equipment they had brought with them.

The modern building had been operational for a couple of years and, every so often had been the scene of anti-abortion protests. Nevada however, with its legalised gambling and sex industries was not the hot bed of right wing opposition to abortion as was the case in many other states.

Modern building or not, Sugar noticed that scaffolding was still in evidence around much of the medical block which would host the medical staff. Still, no workers appeared to be engaged upon any remedial work on the scaffolding so the way remained clear for them to proceed. The grassed area they'd targeted earlier could not easily be used for much in the way of leisure purposes other than sitting in the sun due to the occasional bushed area.

Streikker took a shovel and began to dig a hole some four feet wide and three feet deep which would accept the explosive containers once the gardeners were ready to leave but which could have taken a tree had anyone asked for an earlier explanation. Ed Kane had fired the petrol driven engine of the grasscutter into action and was busily engaged in tidying up the lawn. Streikker dug the soft earth easily and soon had the housing for his bomb just as he required it. This was the main point at which danger threatened. He placed the containers into the hole as nonchalantly as possible attempting to guard against the possibility of being observed while trying to complete this part of his task as quickly as possible. Having located the explosives, Streikker set to the more delicate matter of ensuring that the detonation device would cause the ingredients to blast the Abortion Clinic to smithereens.

Satisfied with his work, he began the process of in-filling the hole and redistributing the spare earth around the neck of the bush at which he was working. Just as he finished he looked up to see Kane kill the engine on his grasscutter and engage in conversation with a traffic warden who was passing by and had asked a question of him.

Still crouched, he looked around to establish the presence of anyone else. There was no one there. He damned Sugar for not letting him bring a handgun with him.

"Hell, Ma'am, you're askin' the wrong guy," smiled Kane at her question. "Me and my partner ain't exactly no horticulturists. They send us out to cut the grass an' that's pretty much all we do. That bush could be a Christmas tree for all I know. I take it you're interested in gardenin'?"

The warden shook her head. "Not really but I see that bush maybe three, four times a day and I've always wondered what it was. It's very attractive."

"Well, Ma'am, I gotta apologise but we're on rates an' if I don't get this stuff cut I'm gonna have one very upset boss on my back an' I lose money. S'bin nice talkin' to you, though." With that, Kane pulled the chord, bringing a whirring stutter from the engine which roared back into action after a faltering start. He held up a cheerful hand bidding farewell to the warden who began to amble down the street - *thank the Lord, away from our car -* noticed Streikker gratefully.

Streikker's own ten minute exercise had been completed to his satisfaction but Kane continued to complete his mowing of the lawn. *Well, you gotta figure he's got balls*, thought Streikker. *I just want to get the hell out of here while the going's good.*

Moments later, Kane finished his task and brought the lawn mower over to the grass edge next to the pick-up before silencing the engine.

"Let's get that stuff in the back and get over to Searchlight before someone else asks us more gardening questions," said Sugar through the open passenger's window. "Everything go all-right?"

"Sweet as a nut, Sugar. That baby's going to blow at nine o'clock a.m. on the button on the 23rd. And there ain't nothin' anyone can do 'bout it now. Someone tampers with that device now they're gonna get blown to kingdom come."

Sugar turned the key on the ignition and headed back towards their motel.

Special Agent Steve Montana had been as good as his word. He'd stuck to Regan and Bilko like glue, asking questions which usually resulted in Bilko's short fuse being ignited. Montana infuriated the police sergeant because of his refusal to enter into an argument and his method of meeting every insult with a calm demeanour and another question.

Presently, peace had broken out as all three sat in Regan's office eating a sandwich lunch. Montana read documentation, Regan flicked disinterestedly through a car manual and Bilko had just ended a telephone conversation with his oldest daughter who saw him only sporadically but who called more frequently when she was a little short of cash.

"Sally a little short again?" asked Regan, who knew the background.

"Damn sure she is," replied Bilko who could never accept any criticism of any of his three daughters nor resist any request made by them. Indeed this also applied to his now remarried first wife - even although he would criticise her mercilessly when he and Regan got drunk, which was often. "It's hard for kids goin' through college right now."

"You have children, Sergeant Bilk?" asked Steve.

"What ya figure, Montana? Surprised they're not space aliens?"

"Just making conversation, Sergeant."

The door was knocked and opened simultaneously. A uniformed officer entered. "Sir, we got results from Forensic."

"Lemme see the file," said Regan leaning across his desk. He scanned the document. "They say these slugs are different from those used at the airport."

"It don't take a genius to work that one out, Boss. This weapon was a single shot sniper's rifle, not the automatic these guys used to hit those priests."

Agent Montana interjected. "Begging your pardon, Lieutenant, any news on the portion of that business card they found?"

Regan redirected the question to the officer by raising his eyebrows at him.

"Sir, no word on the prints just yet. As you know, all we got is the last three figures of a phone number. That's gonna take us a while."

"Guess so, officer." He closed the file and handed it back. "That'll be all. Let us know when anything else comes up."

"So, where does this all take us?" challenged Bilko.

"Nowhere far," replied Regan quietly. "We need a fix on those prints or a weapon linked with the cartridges. Until then, we wait and we hope we get lucky."

# Chapter Eight.

The complete darkness of the night had surrendered to the dawn of a new day and Edson still had the wheel while Burring and Tyler slept fitfully in the rear seat of the Cherokee. Wallis had been quiet throughout the journey, keeping his thoughts to himself while listening to his favourite Shania Twain country tape, murmuring occasional phrases from her songs as the heavy vehicle sped through the misty light towards Nevada. They weren't far from their destination.

"Home ain't where his heart is .... anymore," croaked Wallis tunelessly, finishing along with Shania. He fell back into his silence. "Tell me, Edson," he enquired after a while, "You worked since the mill shut?"

"No, sir. I'm forty-four now and I got laid off on my fortieth birthday. 'Course, the company didn't know that. It was just one of them things. I was one of the first to go 'cause I was one of the last in, so I couldn't complain too much."

"You know who owned the mill?" asked Wallis.

"Company called DDZ Holdings, sir."

"Run by our Jewish friends, Edson. You aware of that?"

"I was not, sir. I just figured they was straightforward Americans."

"Jews, Edson. Jews. They got this country in an economic stranglehold and they hide behind these big conglomerations so's nobody knows what's goin' on. They control the World Bank, least eight of their most wealthy families do, and the World Bank controls governments. Our very own government is at their mercy. Ain't nothin' happens 'cept they say it should."

"How come you don't hear 'bout all this on the news, sir?"

"'Cause they control the goddamn media too, son. They got tentacles everywhere an' the only thing we got to protect ourselves is our Constitution an' the right to uphold it. When I was Sheriff I swore to uphold the Constitution an' I had me a side arm to make sure I could do just that. But it's gettin' all too serious now. It's economic warfare what with them an' the Japs. An' people are lookin' for new leadership now 'cause we've been let down badly. We've been betrayed and sold out and when the people rise up they're gonna need every bit of good fortune the good Lord can pass their way 'cause these people hold a lot of the aces. But they need leadership, soldier, and they need to see that it don't need to be this way. There ain't no way we can allow them liberal politicians to finish the business for the Japs an' the Jews an' take our weapons away from us. Ain't no way."

He lit a cigarette and continued his monologue. "I mean what we gonna do then, ask them real nice if they wouldn't mind givin' us our country back? Guys like Lattanzi should goddamn know better. Who could believe we could be so stupid not to see through that? Well, let me tell you somethin' Edson, we're gonna do somethin' important for this country. We're gonna say, 'this far an' no further!' You're gonna be a real American hero, son. Blood might be spilled, but when the goin' gets tough' you'll be an American hero."

Edson shifted uneasily. "I'm more of a driver, sir. I never was much good with weapons. You'd be better with the Sergeant or the Lieutenant if it comes to shootin'."

Wallis eyed him. "You 'fraid, soldier?"

"I'm a Militiaman, sir. You convinced me a while back that I should join up an' I'm proud to serve you and the 105th. I'm just not one for shootin'. But I won't disobey an order sir. I'm a good soldier. It's just that my speciality is drivin'."

Wallis smiled despite himself. "Well, in my opinion son, you're the best driver in the business so why don't you get us to Glendale for breakfast an' I'll make sure that it's the officers who are doin' any gunplay that's necessary."

"I'd appreciate that, sir", said Edson.

**

Susan Lattanzi sat on the top spar of a fence which served as a corral for the horses which she and her father raised on the ranch. She watched intently as a grey mare continuously circled a ranch hand who had looped a noose over its head and was uttering soothing horse affirmations.

Susan was dressed in her ranch attire. A blue denim shirt would have hung loose had it not been tied at the waist revealing a slim, tanned midriff. Her tight blue jeans fed into her knee high leather boots. A red neckerchief offered some colour to the ensemble.

Her attention was broken by her mother Liz, who joined her on the fence although she had to stand on the first rung to avoid straining her neck upward in conversation.

"Hi, darling. That grey looks like it's coming on well." She nodded towards the horse.

"Mother! Hi, I thought you were going into Vegas to shop with Dad."

"Well, I was but he's so involved just now what with these shootings and the hotel, I don't know when I'll manage to get in. You know I'm not keen on driving."

"Heavens, you know I'll take you in. Just say the word. I've got nothing on today."

"Oh no! That wouldn't be fair on Liam. Dad's said he's to stay with us until all of this terrible trouble dies down and we can't just abandon a house guest."

"Mother, Liam wouldn't mind. He'll have his nose in a book somewhere anyway."

Liz placed her hand on her daughter's arm, smiling. "Darling you're the best daughter a mother could ask for. Your father and I are so proud of you. You've turned out to be a wonderful, caring woman. But you can't always put our needs and wants before your own and it would be downright inhospitable to leave our guest to his own devices."

"Hey, let's not get too dramatic here. All I've proposed is that I drive you to Vegas." She swung down and joined her mother who had stepped off the fence. Both folded their arms and faced one another, smiling. "Mother, is this leading to another 'you should really have gone to college' lecture?" asked Susan.

"No, Honey. You won that argument years ago. You were the brightest girl in your year and Principal Thomson thought you could have had your pick of any educational institution in the country. You chose to stay with us. Both your father and I have shed tears over your decision over the years … not because you're passing up an education, although you most certainly are, but because you seem to want to invest your time in our twilight years rather than follow your own interests."

"Whew, where's all this coming from?" asked Susan somewhat more seriously.

"Oh, nowhere in particular. I guess I'm telling you how much your dad and I appreciate your attentiveness. We absolutely adore having you around the place but you also need a life of your own. You spend all your time here on Boulder Ranch. You look after the finances, take care of all maintenance needs and make sure everything goes well on the stud farm.

"And I absolutely love doing what I do, mother."

"I know that darling, but forgive me if I'm being too blunt. It's just that if you looked after the stud arrangements for our horses the way you do for yourself, this farm wouldn't make much of a profit."

"*Mother!* exclaimed Susan, as amused as she was embarrassed. "What a thing to say! She placed both hands on her hips, a sure sign she was lining herself up for a tussle. "I'm not sure I know how to respond to that. I went out with Ben Dalton for over a year."

"He was dreary, dear, and as pompous as they come."

"Mother, what are you leading up to?"

"Like I said darling, absolutely nothing. I just wanted you to know how your father and I appreciate you as a daughter. Now let's not get this out of proportion. This all started with us discussing a shopping trip to Vegas without leaving poor Liam all alone."

Liz paused and made a theatrical gesture, slapping her forehead with the palm of her right hand as if to convey the realisation of a bright idea. "I know, why don't we ask him to come along. He could drive. In fact, I'll attend to that right now." Susan's mother gave her daughter a brief hug and pecked her on the cheek. "One hour, out front. No need to change." She turned and walked towards the ranch house.

Susan stood mouth agape with a quizzical look on her face as she watched her mother disappear into the house. *Well, what on earth was all that about. Is my mother engaged in matchmaking? With Liam? A man who thinks of me only as his little sister? God, this is going to be embarrassing.*

**

Joe Lattanzi sat at the desk in his study reading papers. The door opened and Susan's head appeared. "Busy?"

Joe turned towards the question, lowering his spectacles to see more clearly. "Susan! I'm catching up on the project manager's latest report on the hotel development. Keeping this thing on budget is a problem. Every report asks for additional work which was unforeseen by the architect."

"I thought you were taking mother into Vegas. You could have visited the site when you were in town. You've not been in for the last few days."

"I've already apologised to your mother and suggested that you two go in. I have a business associate visiting me here at the ranch in a few minutes."

"Hmmm," said Susan. "Mother and I have just discussed that trip to the city."

"Well, you go and enjoy yourself. Buy yourself a new dress."

"I have a wardrobe full of dresses. You know what I think I need? I think I need some fatherly advice."

Joe placed his papers on his desk and swivelled round to face his daughter. "You want to sit down?"

"Just for a moment." She sat on a leather chair at the side of her father's desk and rested her boots on top of a pile of magazines which had been piled neatly on a low coffee table. "I think I just might have had some kind of lecture from mother and I'm not quite sure what it was all about."

"A lecture?"

"Not really. It was a mixture of the old 'missed education' stuff combined with 'you need to get out more' advice and what appeared to be 'wouldn't Liam be just the person to take you out.'" She wagged her finger affectionately. "You two wouldn't have been discussing my future, would you, father dear?"

"Susan, your mother and I are always discussing your future."

Susan put her left elbow on the desk and cupped her chin in her hand. "Come on, Dad. I'm twenty three, I've got the most wonderful parents in the world, I'm happy, I love my work here on the ranch but it's hardly surprising if recently I've been a bit of a home girl. These killings really shook me up - especially since someone as close to us all as Liam could have been killed."

Joe reached out and touched his daughter's arm. "I think your feelings are perfectly understandable, darling. It's been a difficult time for us all, particularly Liam. I'm sure that your mother feels it would be good for you to get out more though. Try to forget some of the horrors we've been through and I'm sure that applies to Liam as well."

He removed his glasses entirely and bit gently on one of the legs. "I have to admit, it would be nice to see you out and about a bit more. It must get a bit stultifying here on the farm even although it's been nice having Liam stay with us. You know how much we like him. You're fond of him too, aren't you?" he asked, rather disingenuously.

Susan sighed and lifted her feet from the coffee table. Getting to her feet she said, "Dad, I think Liam's special, really special. He's got more intelligence, personality and wit than any of the boys I've gone out with but if you and mother are under the illusion that he's anything more than a friend to me, you're mistaken. I think of him as just that. A friend. As the brother I never had, but that's it. Now, mother has apparently arranged for him to drive us both into Vegas and that's fine and dandy but I'd rather you didn't encourage his interest in me. If you must know, and if it helps bring this to a conclusion, Liam and I have discussed this recently and we both agree that our friendship is important to us …. but that's all. So let's all get back to normal, eh?"

Lattanzi's phone rang. His secretary spoke. "Mr Lattanzi, there's a man here who says he's an associate of yours, but he won't give his name. He says he's expected."

"That's fine, Elma, send him up. I've been waiting on him."

He turned to his daughter. "That's my appointment arrived." He smiled his affection at Susan. "You know your mother and I love you dearly. But you're an adult now. A fully grown woman and it would be wrongheaded of us to act as matchmakers. Sure, we'd like to be sure you're happy and had lots of friends of your own age. But you run your own show. I just reserve the right, as does your mother, to check on how you're doing from time to time."

Susan stepped back into the study and kissed her father on the cheek. "That sounds fine to me."

Joe rose to his feet and brought her closer to him, hugging her tightly. *If I'm any judge of Liz and Susan, poor Liam's going to have his 'friendship' tested over the next while. One way or another!*

**

Susan left and Lattanzi set his paperwork in a semi-tidy pile on the desk, clearing his mind in preparation for his next meeting.

Elma knocked the door timidly and, without awaiting an invitation, admitted Lattanzi's guest before leaving as deferentially and noiselessly as she had arrived.

"Mister Lattanzi, it's a pleasure to meet you. I've followed your career over the years with interest."

They shook hands and Lattanzi gestured for him to take the seat just vacated by Susan. "You have me at an advantage. I've not been told your name. What do I call you?"

"I feel most comfortable when as little as is possible is known about me, for obvious reasons. I'm a much better listener than I am a talker but perhaps it would be useful if we cleared the ground rules before you tell me how you think I might help you."

"Sounds like a sensible idea."

"First of all, I am led to understand that in this particular task, if it seems sensible for me to become involved, there is no fee payable by you. That is being taken care of elsewhere. Secondly, if and when we both agree that I should become involved, all decisions on how best to prosecute the task in hand rest with me. I am to be known as your associate, a consultant assisting you with a security problem here at the ranch. The identification I have brought with me on this trip represents me as John Jackson, a security consultant from Kansas City. If it is checked out by the authorities it will be confirmed as genuine."

He paused and looked earnestly at Lattanzi. "I have two more conditions, neither of which is negotiable. Thus far, I have had a successful career which has been underpinned throughout by appropriate levels of secrecy. You will have been advised by our intermediary that you were to reveal my arrival and my purpose to no one - not even to your wife or closest companions. Have you complied with that condition?"

"I have."

"Thank you. I appreciate that. But I must go further. You will not be held accountable for my actions if I accept your task. I accept all responsibility at the point of that agreement. However, despite inevitable temptations, you will never speak again of my involvement - not even to our intermediary - unless you wish to register a complaint. I am aware of the fact that our intermediary made mention of my expertise in the first place. That has been agreed previously and is permissible between he and I but I regret it will not be extended to include anyone else - including you."

"Fair enough."

"Finally, and I apologise for speaking so much on our first meeting, I am not a violent man but I shall consider myself free to take a life if I decide it to be necessary."

He placed his fingertips together. "Let me summarise. We will speak no more of these matters when I conclude. You and I have no financial relationship. I make all decisions on how to handle matters. I am to be known as a security consultant. You will never speak of my involvement -ever -and if I decide to kill one or more persons, I will do so without comment from you."

"You are one hell of a talker for someone who proclaims himself to be a listener. However, you certainly seem to get straight to the point, Mister Jackson."

"Thank you. I do. Are we agreed?"

"I would certainly hope that there is no need to spill blood during this investigation but I accept your conditions."

"Good. I hope I can help you. Now, before we begin to discuss the scope and nature of your problem, I was advised by our intermediary that because the ranch was so far from town, it would probably be wise for me to make use of one of your guest rooms."

"You'd be very welcome, Mr Jackson, or can I call you John?"

"Either will be acceptable dependant upon circumstances. Would you mind if I freshened up? Perhaps we could meet again in an hour. This time I'll do all the listening, and I'll let you know whether my skills are appropriate to your needs."

"That'll be fine. Come on and I'll show you to your room."

Both men walked to Jackson's room. Joe opened the door. "Hope it fits the bill."

Jackson glanced round cursorily. "Perfectly, thank you."

The door closed and Joe Lattanzi walked back to his study, trying to come to terms with the brisk and businesslike approach Jackson had taken. And so civilised.

They could have been discussing life assurance. He shook his head and permitted himself a quiet chuckle. *Well, go figure that. The Mafia's number one Associate! And with all the Italian soldiers they have at their disposal, he's got the demeanour of an English butler with a PhD and he's as black as the ace of spades.*

**

The Sheriff of Caliente, Nevada was getting annoyed with Pastor Mike Yancy. "Look Mike, I see the problem. Your Idaho people are quite likely to come through our patch on the way to Vegas but you can't tell me when they're comin', you don't know how many there are, you can't even give me any descriptions, 'cept Wallis and you don't even know if they're drivin'. They could be flyin' down.

"I got people at the airport, Tom. You think I'm stupid?"

"No, Mike you know I don't think that but I've got to say it doesn't sit right with me to take Trent Wallis out of action. He's a real hero to a lot of folks down hereabouts. An' to be real straight with you, I don't see how the hell I'm likely to get a hold of him. It'll be like findin' a needle in a cornfield."

"Look here Tom, I'm aware of Trent Wallis and what he's done for the Militia Movement. Now I don't want no harm to come to him. He just got to realise that here in Nevada, it's people like you an' me who know what's goin' on. I wouldn't bull you Tom, he's stumblin' into a top secret operation and he could put everythin' in jeopardy. All I'm askin' is that some of your officers keep an eye on the traffic goin' through your town. If your men see him, just hold him over for a while. I'll come over and explain things to him. Ain't no need for gunplay."

"You don't know if they've even left yet."

"Come on, Tom, I've had several calls put through to him from a number of different people. He's always been 'away on business'. Trust me, they're on their way."

"Well…okay, Mike. Though I'm still uncomfortable 'bout all this. But I'll do what you say. Us Nevada boys gotta stick together."

"Thanks Tom, I 'preciate your assistance. If I don't see you before, I'll see you and Martha when I visit your church in two weeks time. You take care now!"

Both men could have saved their breath. By the time Caliente patrol cars were out looking for Wallis, he and his Militiamen were long gone and were almost pulling in to Glendale for breakfast. Edson had excelled himself.

# Chapter Nine

Regan, Bilk and Montana walked down the precinct steps and were almost immediately besieged by a news pack hungry for information and almost universally critical of the police for the lack of progress in respect of the airport murders.

Regan stopped at the foot of the steps and attempted to answer the cacophony of shouted questions whilst attempting to cope with the pushing and shoving which accompanied the questioning.

Montana stepped forward and assisted Regan by trying to maintain some physical space between the battery of cameras and microphones and the Lieutenant.

Bilk found himself edged out as the ferocity of the pack focused upon the individual who looked like he was going to answer their questions.

"Goddamn assholes," he murmured to himself, deciding to collect the car and bring it round front for his colleagues once they had run the press gauntlet. A crew who had found themselves at the back of the mob spotted Bilk heading away from the melee.

"Officer, officer…" shouted a man with a microphone, chasing after Bilk, closely pursued by his sound-man and the cameraman. Bilk ignored the intrusion, continuing to head for the car without breaking stride.

"Officer, would you care to comment on a view which is being expressed that your department is the most incompetent in the country?"

*Jesus Christ, these people are morons*, thought Bilk, determined not to respond to the provocation.

"Have you come across the slightest lead which would convince the people of Nevada that they can sleep safe in their beds tonight, comforted by the knowledge that an arrest is imminent?"

Bilk's temper rose with every step.

The reporter moved up a gear in his attempts to obtain a quote from Bilk. "Do you consider yourself personably responsible for the failure to make any arrests?" He paused, pondering the next escalation. "Can the Mayor expect resignations if this matter is not brought to a successful conclusion very quickly?"

Bilk stopped dead in his tracks and faced the trio of news gatherers. "Listen, sonny, I'm a police officer engaged in the line of duty. The news conference is back there on the steps. Now, I'm attempting to nail people who murdered innocent citizens and I'm about to get into my car and go about my business, so if you've got half a brain you'll get out of my way. I'm warning you now that if you impede me in my duty, I'm just going to arrest you and we'll let the judge decide whether my actions were reasonable or not. I will not answer questions. There's officers over at the steps doin' that right now."

The reporter pressed his point and offered the microphone up to Bilk's face as he opened the car doors. "But surely you can understand the concerns …"

He never finished his sentence. "Okay, sir, you're under arrest for impeding an officer in pursuit of his duties. You have the right to an Attorney. If you can't afford one, one will be provided for you. You have the right to remain silent but anything you do say will be taken down and may be used against you in a court of law."

Moving with surprising speed, he swept the reporter's hands behind his back and cuffed him. "You got warned, sonny. You're keepin' me away from my main responsibilities but you got warned. So now you come with me. We'll need to go in the side door of the station. It's less congested and we wouldn't want your reputation as an arrested felon to break too quick to the press till such times as you've got yourself legal guidance now, would we?

"You can't do this," said the reporter to an audience comprised solely of Bilko, given that his microphone was being held in his now cuffed hands behind his back. He didn't know whether to be outraged at his treatment or whether to be licking his lips at his luck at being arrested. *This recording will go national*, he told himself.

**

As Susan had predicted, Liam was sitting with his nose in a book. Liz entered the lounge and sat across from him. "Am I interrupting your reading?"

"I'm making my way through a book on the busts and booms of the American airline industry. Fascinating stuff. They're either making untold billions or losing untold billions but it's not exactly 'un-put-down-able'."

"I was wondering whether you'd mind driving Susan and myself into Vegas. I've a mind to do some shopping and that daughter of mine seems happiest walking around the place in an oversized shirt."

*Don't I know it*, thought Liam.

"If I don't make her visit some decent clothes shops now and again I don't know what would become of her. She'd end up looking like one of our ranch hands."

*Oh no, she wouldn't.*

"And it would also get you off the ranch for a while. Joe's got you cooped up here."

"Ah, that would be no problem at all. I'd enjoy it," replied Liam. "When would you like to go?"

"Within the hour, if that's all-right. I have some things to do first."

"No problem. Just give me a shout."

Joe Lattanzi entered the room accompanied by Jackson.

"Darling," exclaimed Liz. "Liam and I have been having a chat. He's going to help Susan and me out shortly."

"Honey, this is John Jackson. He's a private security consultant and I've arranged for him to assist in the enquiries regarding the airport murders. The police have matters in hand, I'm sure. But the hotel business wants to ensure that the matter benefits from a parallel investigation. He was kind of hoping to speak briefly with Liam. When do you need Liam's help?"

"Not for an hour. Would that be enough time?"

Jackson answered. "That would be more than sufficient, Mrs Lattanzi."

"I hope it's not too much of an imposition honey, but I've invited Mr Jackson to stay over in one of our guest rooms."

"Of course, darling, I'll have one prepared."

"It's okay; I've already fixed him up in the barn."

The 'barn' to which Joe referred was a conversion which extended the house and which they'd had done ten years previously to accommodate the many and various house guests who stayed over at the ranch. The ranch house itself had been extensively refurbished shortly after they purchased it and contained two extra bedrooms - one of which was currently occupied by Liam, the other was full of Joe's various paraphernalia which he'd brought over from his offices in Washington and his previous home in Newport for the memoirs he knew in his heart he could never write in any candid way.

Liam got to his feet and shook Jackson's hand. "I'll be happy to help you in any way I can."

Joe and Liz made their respective exits, leaving the two men in the lounge. Jackson had done his homework well and didn't trouble Liam with a request to give him a chronological account of events.

"Mr Lattanzi has been good enough to arrange for me to speak by telephone to police officers investigating the case. Much of what they will tell me will concern ballistics evidence and other such matters. My question to you is rather simpler. Tell me, if you would, of the demeanour of the assailant."

"Well the guy in the rear of the cab did all the shooting. He just pointed an automatic rifle through the open window and let loose at the priests."

"Yes, but his demeanour. Cold? Laughing? Crazed?"

"To be honest I was busy diving for cover but I saw both men quite clearly. The gunman didn't seem crazy. He just looked like he was going about his business. He didn't seem to be in a rush and after he had loosed off his initial shots he paused and then opened up again. It was the other guy who looked a bit more panicky - the driver."

"The gunman was in his late forties, a leather jacket, five feet nine and stocky according to news reports?"

"Well, I couldn't testify to his height. I mean, he was seated in the rear of a car but I imagine that height thing came from my description of the guy as resembling Frank Sinatra in 'Von Ryan's Express'. That's what I told the cops."

"No apparent attempt to conceal his identity?"

"Nothing that I could see."

Jackson continued in similar vein, attempting to visualise a mental picture of the men he was seeking. After twenty minutes, he thanked Liam for his forbearance and asked whether he could speak with him again once he had discussed other elements with the police.

Liam agreed.

Streikker, 'Frank Sinatra in Von Ryan's Express', crushed the beer can whose contents he'd just consumed and lobbed it into a bin which sat at the side of the television he was watching disinterestedly.

Sugar and Matt Kane were putting clothes into a couple of leather bags in preparation for their departure from the motel. Streikker had completed his task earlier and could afford to relax in front of the screen.

Sugar had been contacted earlier by Mike Yancy and had been informed of their next job.

"Take care of this one, Sugar, and I'll arrange for you and Matt to spend a well earned rest down in Miami. Ed can go visit his brother in L.A. Everyone can disappear for a while."

For many years, Yancy had access to an isolated old house owned by a member of his church close to Boulder City. Sugar's orders were to assassinate Lattanzi before Wallis could get to him. "And if an opportunity presents itself to teach these interlopers a lesson, just do it. They gotta understand that it's us who look after things in Nevada and I just know they're goin' to try to take Lattanzi out. Now I tried to find out things about him that might help you. He doesn't have much in the way of routines these days, spends most of his time on his ranch, Boulder Ranch, just the other side of the city from your base at the Elliot's old farmhouse -Streikker knows it. Anyway, Lattanzi lives there with his wife and daughter. Some ranch hands also live there but not at the big house. He has a few cars but the one he uses most is a large BMW with a distinctive set of plates - JFK. He's got an interest in a hotel which is being built on the Strip. Everything else you'll know from the newspapers."

Sugar quizzed him on some points of detail and turned her attention to Wallis. "Wallis is an All American Hero. You better tell me clearly what you want me to do 'cause I'll have to bring Matt and Ed along on this."

Yancy repeated his instructions saying that teaching them a lesson could mean whatever she wanted it to mean. "What you gotta remember, Sugar, is that he'll be looking for Lattanzi with some of his men. They're well trained by all accounts and you may have to defend yourself if you come across them. Sometimes, in circumstances like these, you may as well get your retaliation in first, if you know what I mean. Lattanzi may be protected by Federal people for all we know. I know he's retired but the government may still keep an eye out for their friends so you'll need to be careful is what I'm saying."

"Well, we'll see how it works out if needs must."

"Now, presently we don't know too much 'bout Wallis. He's missing from his camp in Idaho and he's probably on his way right now. He's pretty sure to have Militiamen with him but we don't know how many. Anyhow, I've got people out lookin' for him so maybe he won't even get to Boulder City."

**

Sugar pulled the zipper on the last bag and said "You two guys stay here for a moment. I'll go along and let the motel people know that we're going and settle up." Streikker sat upright in his seat as the news channel opened with the announcement that "a police news conference on the airport murders in Las Vegas ended in chaos today. More later."

"Sugar, Matt, check this out! Somethin's happened 'bout the airport."

All assembled around the television to hear the announcer inform her audience moments later that

"Police attempts to hold an impromptu news conference today ended in chaos when a journalist was arrested for asking questions. Norman Previn reports."

A face talking to camera appeared "A television journalist working for Channel 14 News was arrested today for enquiring about progress on what's become known as the airport murders - an event which shocked America. Sergeant Donald Bilk, a serving officer with the city's police force and who is working on the murders case, arrested TV journalist Bob Munroe after warning him not to continue his line of questioning. The following scenes are shown by permission of Channel 14 News."

Streikker slapped his thigh and let out a hoot of laughter as the screen showed the altercation. "The Lord, he works in *mysterious* ways! That's that sonofabitch Bilko", he exclaimed. "He busted me three years ago for possession and carrying an unlicensed firearm. I pulled three months. I hope he gets his ass kicked good."

"….. and may be used against you in a court of law." A muffled exchange followed as Bilko cuffed Munroe in a way which brought the microphone from his lips to his ass in the blink of an eye. The camera continued to shoot as Bilko took the microphone from his grasp and handed it to the sound-man before leading Munroe to the side entrance of the building.

Streikker could hardly contain himself. "Yes *sir*! He always *was* a mean little bastard. Praise the Lord and *jail* the little punk!" he shouted at the television, still laughing.

His noisy celebrations drowned out the apologetic explanation offered by Regan to the cameras some moments later when he referred to the fact that both men were merely trying to do their job in trying circumstances. "Mr Monroe has been released with a warning about crossing the line between reasonable persistence and hindering an officer in the course of his duty. Sergeant Bilk has been suspended until he is spoken to by the Captain tomorrow. That is all. No questions."

The news item changed and Sugar switched off the TV. "Okay boys, fun's over. Now we got one more job to do so let's get on with it. Matt, darlin', how about you clean all of the handles and glasses - stuff like that -for prints and Ed can take all the baggage down to the pick up. I'll go see old Mister Huczynski and we'll get on our way."

"If we're headin' up to the old Elliot house, we'd better pick up stuff like towels, sleepin', bags an' some other home comforts," said Streikker. "I holed up there before I got nailed by my little friend Bilko and the Ritz Carlton it ain't."

# Chapter Ten

Binoculars fixed on the road leading from Boulder Ranch at the point at which it joined the main road from Boulder City to Las Vegas.

"He leaves the ranch he gotta come this way," said Wallis, adjusting the focus.

"Accordin' to the map there's only one way in, one way out," confirmed Burring.

The Idaho Militia had been in place since mid morning. Edson had backed the Cherokee up a stony track and sat it atop a rise which permitted a distant view of Boulder Ranch and a good view of the roads configuration.

"When you gonna decide we gonna go in or let them come to us sir?" asked Tyler recalling his Commander's recent reminder that they were engaged as a military outfit.

"You itchin' for a fight, Lieutenant?"

"Just don't like waitin' around when nothin's happenin'."

"It'll be much easier capturin' him out in the open. We go in there, there could be a bloodbath. We got no idea what the strength of his defences are. We'll wait awhile. Just keep your aggression holstered."

**

The door opened in an ante room next to the suite that had been reserved for the Mayor's press conference later that morning. Lieutenant Regan had been waiting for the Mayor for twenty minutes when Nick Guthrie strode in with two aides, signalling Regan to remain seated on the sofa.

"Hi, John. Your friend Bilk arrested any other major celebrities I should know about?" He sat on the sofa opposite Regan while his two aides sat on chairs at a respectful distance from the conversation.

"If you want my opinion sir, Munroe was out of order. He deserved to be arrested and warned as to his behaviour."

"As a matter of fact, I do want to hear your opinion John. Particularly as I happen to agree with it. I must admit I've met more personable individuals than Donald Bilk but I hear he's a damn good cop. Tetchy, but lives for his work and incorruptible to boot."

"You hear right sir, he's a hard working, honest man. A good man who has put his life on the line on more than one occasion to protect the citizens of Las Vegas. He deserves a medal not a rebuke."

"Don't call me sir, John. Not when we're sitting having a conversation."

"I guess it's a respect thing …. eh, Nick."

"John, you knew me a long time before I got involved in politics. People voted for me as Mayor for a whole lot of complicated reasons. But I don't need to be here. I don't need to seek re-election. I'll go back to running my electronics company and I'd go enthusiastically. So, I get to be different from a lot of other politicians. I actually get to call it like I see it, I get to look after the interests of this city without paying much heed to special pleading and I get to earn respect, not pretend that I'm respected because people call me sir."

"I know all that, Nick. It just makes you kind of unusual in this business."

"Way back before I was ever invited to consider getting involved in politics, my philosophy was that if anyone really wanted power, they just shouldn't get it. Now John, I'm no angel and I do deals in the interests of this City which sometimes I'd prefer not to. But I'm a realist too. It's important we get things done like I said we would before I got elected. But right now, we need to sort this Bilk thing out and tell people some news about progress we're making on the murder of the priests and of the Chief Rabbi. Never in my wildest dreams did I think I'd be dealing with this kind of thing."

"If I could answer in the order you just asked, Nick, I think you go on the offensive with the press and pretty much back up my earlier statement. Tempers can get frayed in any job and we all got to be more responsible from time to time but this all don't make Munroe a bad reporter and Bilko's an honest cop trying his darnest to catch the bad guys. I think we should let bygones be bygones. We should shake and make up."

Guthrie turned to his aides with a smile on his face. "You hear that boys? The Lieutenant here wants us to take on the press. What d'you figure, are we feeling lucky today?"

"It's your call, Nick," replied one of the aides anticipating Guthrie's likely response.

"Okay, we go with your suggestion. Donald Bilk is back on line. You'll already have spoken to him sternly - at least that's what I'm telling the press. I'll make a little speech about the importance of good old fashioned courtesy. If I do it properly, it should blow over and might even help bring about more polite press conferences. Now, what about the murders?"

"I'm afraid that there's nothing more to report. We're looking at prints and we'll come up with something soon on that I hope. But I'd suggest we buy ourselves a little more time by saying that the leads we're following up might be prejudiced if they're made public. We don't yet know if there's any connection between the religious murders and it would be fruitless to speculate."

"When you leave the force, we'll find you a place in our P.R. Department," smiled Guthrie.

"Well, thank you, Nick, but I'm too old for a career change."

The Mayor laughed. "You could have taken a pension a couple of years back if you'd had a hobby other than police work."

"What you goin' to tell the hotel owners?"

"I'm seeing them now then I'm talking to the press core. If I can persuade the owners to go along with an 'every confidence in the police' line it should bolster my press conference. I'm going to play it straight but I'm going to play it just as we've discussed."

Regan nodded his head in approval. He placed his hands on his knees signalling his readiness to leave unless guided otherwise. "I must be keeping you. I'll tell Sergeant Bilk your decision …. and thank you."

Both men shook hands and Regan left.

Guthrie turned to his two aides. "Okay guys, let's see if it's as easy as I made it sound."

**

The hotel owners were jumpy and critical of the fact that progress seemed slow in being made. A few made the point that they were themselves expected to provide their own stakeholders of good news, to reassure them that the city wasn't about to implode in an orgy of religious violence. Guthrie pointed out that the information he'd relayed was just what he was about to announce to the press, that it was accurate and that a number of lines of enquiry were being pursued. They were all 'big boys', he told them and asked if they would prefer him to invent a storyline that let them sleep easier.

"Being honest, gentlemen, it would help if our collective line was that we have had a full explanation from the Mayor, we retain every confidence in our police force to deal with this and we remain aware that Las Vegas is still one of the safest cities in America."

Despite some measure of reservation, it did not prove too difficult to secure the agreement as he'd intended.

Shaking hands with everyone around the table, Guthrie promised to keep everyone abreast of progress and excused himself, heading directly for the press conference. Always a punctual man anyway, he knew better than to keep the press waiting.

Guthrie looked comfortable and in control of his brief as he set out the position he'd negotiated earlier that morning including his attempt at mediation between the police and the press as a consequence of Bilko's and Munroe's altercation.

"Mister Mayor, can you confirm that you retain every confidence in Sergeant Bilk after his error of judgement in arresting a journalist?"

"Jack, I hoped that I made my position clear but let me re-affirm. We are engaged in the apprehension of people who committed vile and murderous acts. Inexcusable acts of cowardice which resulted in the deaths and injuries of holy men. Mister Munroe went about his business with zeal, so did Sergeant Donald Bilk. I do not condemn either man but I do wish to put on record Sergeant Bilk's track record which is more than exemplary. He is a brave and honest man who deserves the support of the citizens of this city and as long as I am Mayor and as long as he continues to live up to the high expectations of this city's administration, he will get that support. Now you can ask me questions all day but I will not be moved on this subject. I will not bow to pressure because, having investigated matters, I believe my actions to be right. Now you go right ahead and run articles calling me arrogant or whatever suits your storyline but don't waste my time or that of my law enforcement officers on what is a distraction from our task."

"Do you find yourself in agreement with ex-Senator Lattanzi's call for gun control?"

"Ladies and gentlemen, I thought it appropriate to update you on police progress on the recent murders and that must be our central purpose today … however, I have to say that while I do respect the position of those who wish the right to continue to bear arms, it does seem to me that we're locked in a kind of constitutional time warp. We've all heard all the arguments but most civilised countries seem to manage just fine without its citizens toting guns. We all want to live in peaceful communities and the question I pose is; is that more or less likely with or without guns? Well, the answer is obvious. How we ever get to that utopian state defeats better minds than mine but we've got to start somewhere and I think that Senator Lattanzi was both brave and insightful in encouraging that debate from the standpoint he did. So, yes. I'd like to see controls. You bet I would."

Watching on televisions in different rooms in the ranch house, Joe Lattanzi and Liam Brannigan nodded their separate approvals.

**

"Liam, it's for you. It's your mother."

Liam had brought the BMW round to the front and was checking oil and fuel when Susan answered the phone and called him inside.

"Well now, it's good to hear your voice son. We've just been hearing about these terrible goings-on in Las Vegas and if it wasn't for your friend Mister Kinsella phoning us, your father and I would never have known to be worried."

"Well I must thank him for that the next time I see him," said Liam. "It was the one thing I wanted to spare you both. I know you don't watch much in the way of television and you never read the papers. I thought there was a good chance you'd never hear of this until I got back home for a visit."

"So we're to be blessed with a visit?"

"Of course. I need to hang around for a while, while the police complete their investigations but I'm having a lovely time here, holidaying on a real cowboy ranch."

The conversation continued along the usual lines, each asking how others were faring until Liam brought it to an end by telling his mother that he was keeping everyone waiting. Each wished the other love and Liam was asked to repeat his promise to visit his Irish homeland … soon.

**

"My parents just found out about my current newsworthiness and decided to give me a call. Sorry if I kept you both waiting."

"Not at all," said Liz seating herself at the wheel.

"I thought you wanted Liam to drive?" said Susan.

"I've decided that it's really silly of me to be so lacking in confidence and to be so uncomfortable behind the wheel so, if you don't mind, I thought I'd have a go at driving. You both sit in the rear so I can pretend I'm driving myself. It's Joe's fault, really. He always drives."

*Dear God, this is so blatant*, thought Susan as she drew her mother a knowing and disapproving look.

"Would it help if I sat in the front, Mrs Lattanzi?" asked Liam, innocent of her purpose.

"Absolutely not. I must conquer my inadequacies."

"Mother, why not just sign up for a refresher course with a local driving school? Are you not taking things just a little too far?" asked Susan, allowing her comment to drip with meaning whilst at the same time climbing into the rear seat beside Liam.

The large car's heavily tinted glass reduced the glare from the bright sunshine as Liz Lattanzi drove off towards Vegas along the smooth, newly surfaced ranch road leading to the highway.

"Sir, there's a car leaving the ranch. Too far away to make out the plates," observed Burring, squinting at the distant image through the binoculars.

"Wake Edson and start the engine, soldier. If it's our target we'll want to be on our way."

Burring moved smartly to obey his command, handing his superior the binoculars.

Tyler, alerted by the activity, strode over to Wallis who was engaged in adjusting the focus on the binoculars. He scanned the horizon until he located the car.

"Well, it sure looks like a BMW but the plates can't be seen until it turns towards us at the next bend." He continued to follow its progress. "Let's get the show on the road. I want to be able to follow them if they're leaving the ranch."

Tyler and Burring joined the newly awakened Edson in the vehicle, awaiting their Commander's assessment.

Back on the ranch road, Liz lightly turned the powered wheel of the big car taking it up and over the humped backed bridge that crossed a small stream which had water in it only occasionally and which at present, under the constant attention of the blisteringly hot sun, was as dry as dust.

As the BMW turned right over the bridge, it followed the contour of the road and manoeuvred foursquare in front of Wallis.

"It's JFK, men, JFK!"

Tyler whooped with delight at the waiting being brought to a conclusion and Wallis jumped into the passenger's seat.

"Okay soldier, take this thing to the bottom of the road. We should get there before they pass us. When they do, I want a positive ID on its occupants. We follow, but not so close that they'd notice and we'll work out what out to do then." He turned to Tyler and Burring. "Take the safety catch off your weapons."

Burring complied. Tyler smiled. "Mine's never on, Commander."

**

Had Joe Lattanzi been driving, the BMW would have powered its way towards Vegas at a pace that even Edson would have found hard to match. However, his wife was a much more relaxed and conversational driver. In consequence she both drove more slowly and paid much less attention to what was happening in her rear view mirror.

Four pairs of eyes were locked on the gradual arrival of the BMW with the JFK plates. The car drove past the Cherokee which was parked with the engine running, slightly recessed on the dirt road they'd just come down.

"What'ya make?" asked Wallis.

There was a mumbled chorus of "don't knows" and "couldn't sees."

"Okay, Edson, follow them at a distance. There's a straight up ahead about a mile. Take them at that point and leave them in your dirt. But nothin' fancy, we're still a fishin' party till I say otherwise. Don't pass them too quick. I want to know how many's in the car and if one of them's Lattanzi. Try and see if he's protected."

Up ahead, Liz Lattanzi was driving almost on autopilot as the luxury, air conditioned car purred towards the malls of Las Vegas. Inside, Liam was in his usual entertaining mode and Liz and Susan found themselves laughing easily at his lighthearted banter. The road ahead was clear. Liz hardly acknowledged the Cherokee overtaking the BMW and increasing its speed so as to disappear up ahead within thirty seconds of passing.

Wallis brought his gaze back from the rear view window and damned the tinted windows of the BMW. "Edson, take us a couple of miles up the road. Burring, here's your chance to prove you're the crack shot you're made out to be. When we get far enough out of sight, we drop you off. Take cover. As the Beamer passes you, shoot out the rear tyre from behind so no one sees a gun flash. Stay down and don't act unless you judge your comrades to be in danger. We only want to have us a reconnoitre, so stay cool. But get that tyre!"

A short while later, Edson took a bend and pulled up sharply at Wallis' command. Burring opened the door and leapt from the Cherokee. He took stock quickly and selected the cover offered by a large rock which itself was partly hidden by bushes. His rifle had already been prepared for use while in the Cherokee. Moments later the Lattanzis' car appeared about three hundred yards away. Burring manoeuvred into position so he could follow the trajectory of the BMW as it passed his position.

Wallis had Edson park the Cherokee some distance along the road. "Tyler, when Burring brings that baby to a halt, you visit them real neighbourly like and comfort them like any friendly fisherman would…on foot from this vehicle. Edson and me will wait here until you return. If they ask, we're both sleeping. For now, I just want to know if Lattanzi's aboard. Make sure you play it cool."

**

"Now my *favourite* country and western song is called 'If I'd shot her when I'd met her, I'd be out of jail by now.'"

Liz and Susan smiled at Liam's teasing. They both enjoyed country and western music which Liam always claimed was typical American plagiarism, stealing Irish and Scottish tunes, contorting them, adding maudlin lyrics and claiming them as their own.

"You know, Liam, you ..." In an instant Liz was wrestling with the car, pulling the steering wheel this way and that with no apparent effect on the direction of the car, all the while pressing her foot-brake to the floor. In the rear seat, Susan and Liam were thrown around, their heads clashing, leaving Liam's nose bleeding.

After slaloming along and across the road for a hundred yards, Liz brought the car to a halt in the dirt edging, a cloud of dust enveloping the vehicle. She took a moment to regain her senses then turned in alarm to see both Susan and Liam clutching their heads. Somehow, blood had been spilled.

"Susan," she screamed. "Are you all right?"

Frantically she tried to pry her seat belt from its clasp but her fingers wouldn't obey her intentions. Eventually, she freed herself and opened the car door, terrified of the condition in which she might find her daughter. Susan was still dazed and only partly aware of her mother leading her from the car to the side of the road where she sat down. Liam had emerged from the other rear door and had joined them both at the roadside.

"Looks like we had a blow-out. Everyone in one piece?" said Liam, examining the blood on the front and sleeve of his shirt.

Liz was still fussing over Susan but seemed now more sure that her daughter was only slightly shaken. "I think we're okay. What about you Liam, you're all covered in blood?"

"I've just bumped my nose. I'm fine although I suspect I may have messed up the interior of your car. Let's see now, is Susan alright?" he asked with concern.

"I'm fine," said Susan, now more composed.

Liam knelt on one knee and took Susan's chin in his hand, gently raising her head to hold her gaze.

"Are you sure, that was quite a blow out. Your mother here did well to keep us on the road."

Susan nodded. Everyone was relieved that no one had been injured. Liz had fished out some tissues and Susan helped Liam clean some of the blood from his face although his shirt still betrayed his misfortune.

"You folks need any help?"

Liam turned on his knee and squinted into the sun. He shielded his eyes and saw a man walking towards them, concern etched on his face.

"Had an accident?" Tyler repeated his implied concern.

Liam got to his feet and acknowledged his presence. "Hi. Yeah we've had a blow out but I think we just about survived it. We're all okay and the car's still in one piece by the looks of it."

"You bust your nose?" asked Tyler.

"It's nothing. I've had worse nosebleeds. Doesn't feel broken. I'll be fine once I find a washroom."

Tyler nodded his satisfaction and spoke to the two other passengers. "Ladies, you both Okay?"

Liz answered for both of them. "Yes, thanks. We're all just a bit shaken. We'll be right as rain shortly and we'll be on our way."

Tyler was enjoying playing the Good Samaritan. "You won't be going far on that tyre."

Liam nodded. He'd already checked it out and had seen it was holed and needed to be replaced. He smiled ruefully. "Before we left, I checked everything except the spare tyre." He moved towards the car. "I'll look in the trunk."

Tyler spoke again to the women. "That was some fright you must have gave yourself, ladies. I was sittin' in my four-by-four up ahead and saw it all in my rear view mirror. You covered quite a piece of road before you came to a halt. You did good to keep it on the tarmac."

"More luck than judgement, I'm afraid," said Liz.

Liam reappeared at the side of the car. "There's good news and there's bad news. The spare's there but the car phone's missing."

Susan put a guilty hand to her mouth. "Oh, Liam, that was me. I took it out this morning when I was out riding Trigger. It's in the saddle bag."

"Ah, that's all right. Once we get the spare tyre on we'll be rarin' to go."

"Lemme give you a hand with that," said Tyler, moving to help Liam to remove the wheel from the trunk.

"Thanks," grunted Liam as together they lifted the spare free.

"My buddies and me passed you a ways back. You came out of the Lattanzi's place, didn't you?"

"Yeah, that's his wife and daughter there. You must be local, then?" asked Liam.

"Eh, yeah. Boulder City," replied Tyler. "Mister Lattanzi's well known around here. A fine man. Given great service to his country, him bein' a Senator an' all. Just as well he wasn't drivin' case he was injured."

"Nah, he's safe at home on the ranch. This is just a shopping expedition for the ladies and I've been drafted in to do the driving. It's just as well we don't have a phone. He'd be beside himself with worry if he knew about this. He just lives for these ladies."

"Yeah," agreed Tyler. "Probably better he doesn't know until you all gets back safe."

Liam and Tyler tussled with the spare wheel until the car was road-worthy again.

Liz and Susan, now composed and more relaxed, ventured to the rear of the car to see the finishing touches being put to the damaged wheel now being tucked away out of sight in the trunk.

"Thanks for your help," said Liam shaking Tyler's hand.

"Wasn't no problem."

"Thank you again," said Liz. "Now we can resume our shopping trip."

"You not too shaken up ma'am?" asked Tyler.

"No, we're fine now although I think I'll let Liam drive the rest of the way. I'm no amateur shopper. When I go shopping, I don't come home until I've bought something. Anyway, we won't be long and there's a garage along the road a bit where Liam can clean himself up. Now, Liam, if you'll take the wheel, we'll be on our way." She turned to Tyler. "Can we take you back to your car?"

"No thanks ma'am, it's only up the road a ways. But thanks anyway. You just get on your way and drive safely."

All three smiled their thanks and climbed back into the BMW. Liam steered the car back on to the road and drove on offering Tyler a cheery wave of his hand as he did so.

**

Moments later, Tyler had rejoined his colleagues.

"Well, we ain't got Lattanzi but we got his wife and daughter and he just loves both of them to bits. They got a driver but he ain't no security. They're headin' for Vegas to do some shoppin' and they're comin' back straight after that. Don't look like they'll be long."

Wallis considered his options for a few moments, tapping his fingers on the dash. "We get *them*? We get *him*. He'll come to us. Won't have no choice." He turned to Edson. "Take us back an' we'll pick up Burring. We'll wait for them to come back along and pick them off then."

Edson did as requested and headed back towards Burring who'd stepped from his hide, awaiting uplift.

Passing the point at which the BMW had come to rest, none of them noticed that the jack and the toolbox used to such good effect in repairing the wheel, were lying at the side of the road.

**

Pulling in to the car park at Caesar's Palace, Liz turned to Susan. "Darling, I'm going to phone your father and explain what's happened. Jimmy St James has an office in the Flamingo Hotel across the road and I'm sure he'll offer me a gin and tonic if he's in. Now I want you to take Liam to see Alphonse in Armani's. Security might stop you at the entrance to the mall but I'm sure you can explain our predicament. Now, Liam needs new trousers and a shirt so use your plastic to buy him both items and make sure they're colour co-ordinated. I'm not walking around Vegas in something Liam chooses," she said chiding him gently. "And make sure that Alphonse throws these blood-stained clothes in the trash can. They're beyond recovery. I'll join you both presently."

Susan listened to her mother feeling the same resignation as she had shown at the start of the trip. Her mother was not a woman to be trifled with. She was clearly intent upon ensuring that she and Liam spent time alone in one another's company and Susan knew better than to offer resistance. It would be a futile waste of energy.

"Ah, now listen, it would just be as simple for me to head on up to a jeans store and get something respectable. Armani probably wouldn't suit me. I usually wear pretty straightforward clothes."

"Precisely," said Susan deciding she may as well go with the flow. "Mother's right. It's about time you wore something a bit more adventurous so let's do it. And be warned, I'm going to make you try on everything Alphonse has to offer before we decide. You'll drive us home looking like Liberace if I've anything to do with it!"

# Chapter Eleven

Kinsella sat in the snug of a bar he used now and again if he wanted a chat in privacy. Riley's Bar was quiet. Still in the inner city of Dublin, the old pub had seen better days. The shipping community it once served had long gone, leaving the bar as high and dry as some of the disused wharves which sat untended and unloved only yards from its door.

Nursing the remnants of his first pint of Guinness of the day, Kinsella started with surprise when a hand squeezed his shoulder. O'Farrell had come in the side door.

Both men smiled at one another. "You'll have a Guinness, Eamon," said Kinsella, shaking his hand and anticipating his choice of drink. "Have a seat and I'll get a round up."

He stepped over to the bar and ordered two pints. The barman invited Kinsella to return to his seat indicating that he'd bring over the drinks once the stout had settled.

"He's bringing them over seeing as how we're his only customers."

"Aye, it's quiet all right," said O'Farrell looking round the bar. "And tell me now, Paul, are you doin' okay? I read your articles sometimes but they're too clever for the likes of me, added to the fact that they can be hellish boring."

Kinsella laughed. "I'll give you boring! Maybe they just give me my journalistic awards for my good looks."

"Hell, they're certainly not for that. Maybe they're for your clever writing after all."

"Well, I don't know about that either."

Both men were delivered of their Guinness and each silently toasted the other, Kinsella finishing off his first pint in one huge swallow.

"So tell me then, Eamon, are you keeping out of trouble?"

"Sure why would I ever be in trouble?" he replied.

"The last time we spoke you had just walked away from twelve of your peers who had found you innocent of smuggling arms in from Libya. And you and me both know that you were as guilty as sin."

"Well I could never comment on that to you seein' as how I hardly know you. And who knows what skulduggery is goin' on around us that could pick up and record our conversation."

"This is no set up, Eamon," said Kinsella, with a more serious edge to his voice. "I've a better sense of self-preservation than that. You may or may not have cleared this conversation with one of the boys but I'm entirely sure that someone will know you're with me and if something goes wrong …. well, I'm sure they'd know where to look."

"Here, you're not a very trustin' man, Paul Kinsella," he smiled. "God, the way you talk, you'd almost think I was involved in the armed struggle up north or somethin'. And of course, that would be illegal."

"Eamon, let's cut to the chase. I would appreciate a bit of help. Now, like I said on the phone, if you warn me off, I'll step back and that'll be it. You will not be compromised whatever you tell me. Even if you could give me a steer it'd be useful."

"What would you like to know?"

Kinsella opened the leather filofax he'd had lying on the table, took out a photograph and pushed it over to O'Farrell face down. "Who's your pal?"

O'Farrell hesitated, then pulled the photograph towards himself his face draining of colour.

"Jesus Christ, where did you get this?"

"Who's your pal?" repeated Kinsella.

"Paul, you just might be in over your head on this one. This is serious stuff." He thought further. "You wouldn't happen to know where the negative for this is now would you?"

"Or whether there might be a dozen copies in existence?" countered Kinsella.

"Paul. I'm tellin' you. You can have no idea how much trouble this would cause people, particularly me, if this got out."

"Listen Eamon, you know, or at least I hope you know, that you can work with me. I'm a journalist and I won't reveal my sources. I'm not sure I even want to know what lies behind all of this. I write about economics, not terrorism or freedom fighting and I don't really want to inhabit your world."

"So why do you want to know?"

"I've a friend in America needs to know who shot Father Patrick Sheridan."

"Police?"

"An economist."

"A bloody *economist*?"

"And why does he need to know this?"

"It's complicated, but he's a friend of mine and he'd like to guide the Roman Catholic church as to whether this was a sectarian shooting although I dare say that young Father Pat would like to know too."

Both men fell into a silence, each with their mind in a whirl.

"Can this situation be rescued?" asked O'Farrell.

"How do you mean?"

"Just supposin' there wasn't any copies. Do you imagine there wouldn't be any copies of this photograph… hypothetically speakin'?"

"Would it help you if there were no other copies?"

"It would, if I could get my hands on the negative as well as this one. Does anyone else know about this?"

"No one official but they're likely to very shortly. Like in a matter of an hour or so."

"Why do you want to know about the fellah in the photograph?"

"We both know that Father Pat spent time with you in the Liffey Bar the night before he was shot. We both know that you were minding an American. We both know he was a spooky son of a bitch. We both know you've been mixed up in the Republican movement. Now I don't know where all of this takes us but I would like to know who your pal is."

"You don't, Paul. You really don't." He paused again, obviously troubled. We are in the shite, my friend. The both of us. I'm starin' a heavy jail sentence right in the face if I don't take a bullet first for talkin' to you. For sure, you're lookin' down the barrel of a gun just for knowin' what you know already." He rubbed his unshaven chin. "Is there no way we can help one another out on this?" questioned O'Farrell.

"What have you in mind?" asked Kinsella, by now just as apprehensive as O'Farrell.

"Look Paul, on the life of my poor dead mother, on the eyes of my five children, I was only mindin' that fellah while he was in town. Trust me, you don't want to know why he was here." He hushed Kinsella as he was about to speak. "How much do I need to tell you before you'd help me get the negative of this?"

"Maybe I'm wrong but both of us appear to have stumbled across something we'd rather not have stumbled across," said Kinsella.

"You can be bloody sure of that, Mister Kinsella." He paused again and took a large draught of his Guinness. "Seems we might need to work together on this or both of us could end up dead. And I'm not kiddin'," he added for emphasis.

"I'm unhappy about the prospect of ending up dead all right. What do you suggest we do?"

"What do you need to know?"

"Were you or this fellah involved in the shooting?"

"Listen Paul, if I tell you and if this goes belly up, I'll come lookin' for you if I escape with my own life," said O'Farrell nervously.

"Jesus, Eamon, time is getting shorter if we're going to pull this out of the fire."

"All right, all right." O'Farrell took a deep breath. "Your man is an American. I was his minder. You don't need to know why he was here. He's back in America now but he shot the priest all right." He sighed. "Listen I was not involved in any way with the shooting. The guy's a nut case and I was really pissed off at him for what he did. He's a bloody psychopath but he's away now and he won't be coming back. I'm the one who'll take the heat and I wasn't even there at the time."

"The only connection would be the photograph?"

"I think so."

"Tear the photograph in half. I only want a shot of him."

"What'll you do with it?"

"I don't know yet. But you won't be involved. All the action, if there is any would be in the States."

"Was it sectarian?"

"No. It was for no reason. Like I said, the man's a madman."

"Give me a name."

"There's no way I'll give you that. I want the negative."

"We'd better go now or we'll be too late. I've a car outside."

O'Farrell nodded. Both men drained their pints, stood up and left the bar.

**

Alphonse was perplexed. Young Miss Lattanzi had entered his designer boutique, elegant as ever but accompanied by a man whose shirt and pants were bloodstained. *My Heavens, whatever can be going on?* And almost as quickly. *What might my other customers think?*

He almost ran to her side in a flutter of mincing steps and flapping hands.

"My dear Miss Lattanzi. Have we had an accident?"

"We have, Alphonse. But it's Liam here who was damaged."

"But you must go to hospital immediately …"

"It's all right Alphonse," said Susan calming him down and offering her cheek for him to kiss. When it came to schmoozing, Susan could compete with the best of them. "It's all been taken care of. We're in here to get rid of these clothes and to replace them with some of your wares. Mister Brannigan here has a preference for something flowery and frilly."

Liam had been looking round at the array of gentlemen's clothing but was brought back into the conversation by Susan's comment. "Yeah, or a white sports shirt and a pair of jeans."

Satisfied that Liam was not about to assault him, rob his store or die on the spot, Alphonse had been looking him up and down in order to assess his sartorial needs.

"Mr Brannigan, I am delighted to be at your service. First we must get you out of these clothes. Would you care to step into the changing room with me and we'll fetch a dressing gown while Miss Lattanzi selects some initial possibilities." He took Liam's arm and ushered him towards the rear of the store. The uneasy look on Liam's face prompted a giggle from Susan as she wiggled her fingers at him in a gesture of farewell.

"Something in pink, Liam?"

"Yeah, if you're tired of livin'," said Liam over his shoulder as he was led from the floor.

Susan spent some time selecting shirts and pants for Liam who soon accommodated the situation, offering suggestions and even trying on a couple of garments which were outrageous, much to Susan's amusement. Soon, peals of laughter came from the room as was so often the case when Liam and Susan were together.

Alphonse was dancing around, offering suggestions and dismissing certain of Susan's choices even before they had reached Liam. An assistant approached and told him a telephone call had been received for Miss Lattanzi from Mrs Lattanzi and would he draw it to her attention.

Susan and Alphonse disappeared into his office and Liam surprised himself by choosing the items he was wearing which were Susan's preferences and which were rather more classy than the clothes he would normally wear.

For the life of him he could not understand how people could shop in places like this where no item carried any price tag. Nor did Susan ever ask Alphonse the price of anything. Although America had been good to him and he wasn't worried where his next dollar was coming from, he still retained the financial attitudes drummed into him by his parents and felt uncomfortable buying anything whose price he wasn't aware of in advance. However he was not about to permit Susan or her mother to pay for his clothes so he used his moment alone to offer his credit card to the assistant. "This'll be fine, thanks."

Susan groaned with exasperation at her mother, who had just informed her that Jimmy St James would give her a lift back to the ranch, as he had some matters to clear up with Joe. "So why don't you two just stay on for a while, do some shopping, have a meal? There's a new Italian restaurant opened on Harmon Avenue, just behind the University."

"Mother, this is ridiculous," she whispered, trying to conceal her irritation from Alphonse who lingered just outside the door of his office. "Don't you ever give up?"

"No, darling. And neither should you. Spend some time with Liam. He's a lovely man."

Susan reappeared to find Liam staring at his receipt, mouth agog. "Mother said I had to pay for these clothes," she said.

"You'd need to earn more than the gross national product of a small nation to shop here," said Liam. "Thank Alphonse, and let's get out of here before he finds another way to take money off me."

"You look great," said Susan suddenly realising that Liam had selected the clothes she had suggested. "Turn round."

"Hmmm, very nice. I approve. Let's go before Alphonse asks you into the back room again."

Liam drew her a look. "Okay." He took her arm and led her to the door fending off Alphonse's effeminate fawnings. They stepped out into the mall. "Have you any shopping to do, or would you let me buy you a beer? I'm parched."

"Ah, Liam, I'd love a drink. Especially with you looking like a million dollars. All the girls will be jealous."

"Well I should look like a million dollars, the amount they charged in there. And the girls can just get jealous if they want. I'm out with my favourite girl."

**

Kinsella had explained about Tommy and the photographs during the car journey to the Liffey Bar. He pulled up round the corner from the bar and turned the engine off.

"Okay, here I go," said Kinsella. "You wait in the car and I'll see if I can talk my way into getting another look at the photographs."

"I'm still not sure about this. If you mess up, both of us could wake up dead."

"Well I'm no expert, that's for sure but I don't see how we can get them any other way without drawing attention to ourselves."

"Okay. But be careful for Christ's sake."

Kinsella levered himself from the driver's seat and composed himself before entering the bar. As with Riley's, the bar was quiet. A few people sat, engaged in conversation at the far end. An elderly barman he didn't recognise was restocking the chiller. Kinsella realised that if the photographs had been replaced behind the bar in the position they'd been left the night before, he could lean over and pick them up if the barman wasn't looking. The other people in the bar couldn't see his movements either.

The barman got slowly to his feet and approached Kinsella. "What'll it be?"

Kinsella saw that the guest beer was Bellhaven Best which appeared to have only one pump, at the far end of the bar. *He'll have his back to me*, thought Kinsella.

"Eh, give me a pint of Belhaven, thanks."

The barman turned and walked towards the guest spigot.

Kinsella's heart was racing. What he did now could have far reaching, untold consequences. Just do it, he told himself. He leaned over the bar but saw nothing. The blood in his head was pounding and he could feel his hands shaking. He reached forward, feeling for something, anything which resembled the pack of photographs.

His fingers touched the edge of a paper container. Is this it? The barman must have almost poured the Belhaven by now. Kinsella looked up nervously but he was still concentrating on drawing the beer. One last stretch.

It was the photographs. What to do? *Have I time to remove the negatives? No, I'll take the lot. That would be safer.*

Kinsella panicked. He turned and put the photographs in his inside jacket pocket and stepped slowly towards the door, almost as if in a dream.

The Liffey Bar, like many establishments had taken steps to ensure that theft was minimised. A salesman offering a deal on close circuit television had recently been shown the door, the owner believing that mirrors, placed strategically were less intrusive and could be just as effective in observing miscreants at work.

As the barman finished topping off the Belhaven, he noticed a movement in a mirror above his head placed precisely so as to observe activity to his rear. He turned, leaving the beer standing and walked hurriedly towards the figure retreating towards the door. He lifted the heavy wooden bar lid and followed Kinsella outside where he put his hand on his shoulder from behind. "What the hell d'ye think you're about?" he asked.

Before a statuesque Kinsella could turn around, a rough hand grasped the barman's throat and pulled him back into the doorway, pushing his face into the jamb so he could see only the door with one eye and the sandstone wall with the other although, truth be known, he had both eyes shut.

"What's your name old fellah? asked O'Farrell.

"Sammy."

"Sammy what, but?"

"Hennessy."

"And where does Sammy Hennessy live, then?"

"Who wants to know?"

O'Farrell pushed the barman's face against the rough sandstone. "Listen old fellah, this is Republican business. You want no part of this. We have taken some photographs, not anything of value so you won't get yourself into trouble." He eased back on his pressing, but still keeping the barman's face in the jamb. "Now Sammy, where do you live?"

"Up Mountjoy way. But listen son, if it's Republican business like you say, you have no problem. I've seen nothing. I probably threw them photographs out in the rubbish without realisin'. You don't need to hurt me."

"Well Sammy Hennessy from Mountjoy, I hope you're after tellin' the truth because you're the only one who knows I've got them photographs and this is a serious business. You do not want to get mixed up in it or you or your children or your grandchildren could get a terrible beatin'. Am I makin' myself absolutely clear?"

"I've just told ye son. I've been involved in the struggle myself. Go on your way. We have no problem here."

"Sammy, I believe you. Now don't look round. Just go back into the pub as though nothin' had happened and I'm sorry if I was rough with you."

"No problem son, no problem."

O'Farrell looked around him. The side street was still empty. "Okay, on you go."

Old Sammy stepped back into the Liffey Bar and walked over to the door behind which hung his jacket with his angina tablets in one of the pockets. He'd better take one. All that excitement wouldn't have been good for him.

He poured himself a glass of tap water, sipped it and sat down. He chuckled to himself. '*Sammy Hennessy from Mountjoy*'…he could still think on his feet…'*Sammy Hennessy from Mountjoy*'. Old Denis O'Neil from Mulhuddart took his tablet with another sip of water and smiled. One thing was for sure, though. He was a Republican himself and no mention would ever be made of the photographs. Still, it was nice to put one over one that young fellah.

He threw the water into the sink and went back through to the bar. No one appeared to have been kept waiting. He poured the Belhaven into the sink and went back to restocking the chiller.

**

The late afternoon sun saw Susan and Liam hiding from its intensity in a small bar just off the Strip.

"Are you sure you don't want to do any shopping yourself?" asked Liam.

"After the embarrassments I put you through earlier, I'd be too afraid of what you'd do to take revenge. I could just imagine you taking great delight in helping me choose clothes which would make me look like Carmen Miranda."

Both had had three drinks. After his first Bud, Liam had stuck to mineral water due to his driving responsibilities but Susan had had three large glasses of dry white wine and was feeling mellow. Every so often they would lapse into an easy silence and listen to the music. In the background Don McLean sang a song about Vincent van Gogh.

Susan hummed along …"this world was never meant for one … as beautiful as you."

Liam complimented her. "You know you've a lovely singing voice. You'd go down well back home in Dublin. Everyone sings in pubs."

"I'd love to go to Dublin some day. You always make it sound so …. I don't know, so romantic."

"It's a lovely city all right but I've never thought of it as romantic. But you should go some time. You'd love it."

*Yeah*, thought Susan, *not **we** should go sometime, but **you***! *I'm wasting my time with this man.*

They fell into a brief silence and Susan's feelings, complicated and complex, surfaced.

"Liam," said Susan uncomfortably, "about last night …. I hope you didn't think I was coming on to you or something. You know, when I said I couldn't think of any man I felt closer to?"

"Oh no, of course I didn't …"

"Yes I know but ... all I meant was … you know, you're like a brother to me … I mean I hope you didn't think ..."

"Of course not … you were very clear …"

"Because … I mean, you know I love you … but as a brother … not as anything else … oh, God … does that sound insultin g… ?"

"Not at all … I feel the same way. You're my best friend and you're my boss's daughter."

"Dammit, Liam," said Susan, suddenly angered. "I don't give a good Goddamn about me being your boss's daughter. I'm Susan Lattanzi. Not Joe Lattanzi's daughter…Well I am Joe Lattanzi's daughter but I'm my own man … I mean woman. Dammit, Liam, would you get me a glass of wine. I feel like another drink."

"One for the road?"

"Listen, Bubba, *I'll* decide whether it's one for the road or not. I mean, I'm your boss's *daughter* after all, and if I want to sit here all night drinking with the staff, then that's just what I'll do."

Liam gathered himself. "You know, Susan, you're a lovely, wonderful, beautiful, complicated woman. I just wish I'd met you in Dublin. Or even Glasgow. But I didn't."

"I'd like a glass of chilled *Sauvignon Blanc*, Mister Brannigan."

Liam smiled, he'd never seen his best friend like this before. "Coming up, ma'am. Anything you say, ma'am."

**

Kinsella drove off and, after a few minutes, turned off into another side street. O'Farrell had been careful to check that the barman hadn't come back out to identify them or the car they were driving.

"I think we're okay," said O'Farrell.

Kinsella turned off the engine. "Let's see if we've got what we were looking for."

He took the pack of photographs out of his inside pocket and handed them to O'Farrell. The negatives were there, and Kinsella held them up to the daylight to ensure that the incriminating shot of O'Farrell was among them.

"Thank Christ, it's there," he said with relief.

"Let me see," said O'Farrell. He inspected the negatives and pronounced himself satisfied. In doing so, he put the negatives back in the pack with the photographs. "No time like the present."

O'Farrell looked around to ensure that the street was quiet and stepped out of the car. He headed over to an abandoned shop doorway and knelt down. From his pocket he took a match and, again checking to see that no one was watching, lit a corner of the pack. In seconds, the photographs and the negatives were ablaze. Once they had been reduced to ashes, he returned to the car.

He turned to Kinsella. "Paul, you and me were close to all sorts of trouble there."

"I don't remember the last time I was so afraid. I suspect I'm not cut out for your type of work."

O'Farrell grinned his agreement. "I'm going to walk away from this car now, Paul. When I do, we will never speak of this again. There's a lot of people I work with who would not be able to understand what we just did. They didn't have to deal with our American friend. If he was brought to justice it would be a service to humanity but I can't have it interfering with our work here in Ireland. What are you thinking of doing with the photograph of the Yank?"

"What would you like me to do?"

"Arrange for the bastard to be taken out."

"But you won't give me a name?"

"I'd like to, Paul, but it might compromise our activities here in Dublin." O'Farrell half opened the car door. "Listen, you've got a picture of the guy who shot Father Pat, you know it wasn't sectarian but the work of a psychopath and you will never speak of my name in this context. Look, the guy's back Stateside. Fix it so he's nailed. He deserves it. If you ever need to confirm an ID, phone me and I'll talk to you as long as our conversation is secure."

"Eamon, I started out just trying to get some information for a friend who was asked by the Church to check on the background of the shooting of Father Pat. I had no idea I'd be getting involved with Republican stuff. God knows, I don't want to become involved in all of your nonsense. I'm going to fax your friend's photograph to the States but, like I said earlier, I'll only tell them what you've told me and you know I won't reveal my sources."

"It's not your journalistic confidentiality which convinces me of your sincerity. More the fact that you were an accessory after the fact and that if you survived a bullet, you'd spend as much time in jail as me if any of this came to light."

"Take care of yourself, Eamon."

Both men shook hands and O'Farrell strode off down the road without so much as a glance over his shoulder.

**

Susan had finished her fifth glass of wine and was, by now, quite drunk.

"Leeem, slurred Susan. My parents haven't seen me this drunk. I don' drink much 'cause I get drunk kinda easy. Truth to tell, that's how I kinda got involved last year with that bastard Ben Dalton."

*That figures*, thought Liam.

"That was all a big year long mistake an' I knew it before it'd even started."

Susan started to weep. "I'm no good with men. I just can't"…. She hesitated, reaching for words to explain her feelings … "Leem, I'm drunk an' my parents … my parents…" She leaned her elbows on the bar table and cupped her chin in the palms of her hands eventually finding the explanation she was seeking …"I'm no good with drink an' I'm no good with men …"

Liam, who was sitting opposite and who'd seen Susan slide into her maudlin state over the past two drinks rose and sat beside her. He put his arm around her shoulders and used a napkin to dry her cheeks.

"Susan, you're quite the most precious thing in my life."

She looked up at him. "I love your shirt."

Liam ignored her comment. "I'm only glad you don't wear make-up. Your mascara would have ruined my shirt and we'd have had to go back to see Alphonse."

Susan squeezed Liam's arm. "My mother says you're a lovely man."

"Oh, she does, does she?"

"Well, so do I … think that … I think you're lovely … and today," she fingered the collar of his shirt, "you're handsome in your new shirt and pants that I chose …" Susan lifted her glass, intent upon draining it but thought better of the idea. She pushed it away and looked at her protector. "Leem … I think you'd better take me home … 'fore I make a fool of myself."

# Chapter Twelve

Joe Lattanzi sat by his desk entering comments in the margins of drawings his architectural team had submitted for his approval. The phone rang and instinctively he reached out and answered. His Secretary, Elma, who had been with him almost as long as his wife Liz would shortly give him yet another row for answering before she did. "It's not professional," she'd tell him, as she always did.

"Joe Lattanzi," he answered.

"I wonder could I speak with Liam Brannigan," said an Irish accent.

"I'm sorry, he's not here at the moment. Could I take a message?"

"No… well it's important I speak with him as soon as possible. Do you know when he might be expected to return?"

"He's gone into Vegas but I'm hoping he'll be back before nightfall. Could he perhaps phone you back?"

"It's okay, I'm phoning from Dublin."

Suddenly, Joe became interested. "Listen, Mr?"

"Kinsella."

"Mr Kinsella, I'm Joe Lattanzi. Did Liam ask you recently to undertake an investigation?"

"What kind of investigation?"

"Into the shooting of a priest."

"You'll forgive me, Mr Lattanzi, but I'd rather discuss the matter with Liam once he returns. That was our agreement. But I'm sure that if I've anything to tell him he'll pass it on to you if that's appropriate."

"All right, if you think that's the way to do it. But just so you know, it was me who asked Liam to arrange for a few enquiries to be made in Dublin."

"If you don't mind, Mr Lattanzi, and I don't want to cause offence, but I'll speak to Liam." Kinsella thought for a moment then relented slightly. "One thing, perhaps. I'd like to fax a photograph of a man to Liam. He is central to what I want to discuss with him. Is your phone number the same as your Fax?"

"It is. I'll make sure Liam gets your Fax as soon as he gets back. You'll probably be able to speak to him in a couple of hours."

"That'll be great. Thanks. I'll call later."

They both hung up.

Some minutes later, Elma came into the office and told Joe off for answering the phone before she did. "It just looks as if I'm not on top of my job, Mr Lattanzi."

"I'm sorry, Elma. I didn't think."

Mollified, Elma handed him a piece of paper. "This just came through on the Fax machine."

"Thanks, Elma. I'll be down shortly."

Joe took the paper and looked at the head and shoulders image of a man apparently somewhat the worse for wear. He was holding a bottle of beer. He doesn't look like a priest, thought Joe. I wonder what part he's got to play in all of this?

**

Burring was halfway through his fifteen minute binocular shift, monitoring traffic coming towards them on the freeway. Edson had parked the Cherokee just off the highway close to the road leading to the Lattanzi's ranch and Wallis had set his men in rotation to watch from a bridge so the BMW could be seen at a distance sufficient to permit the Cherokee to reach the ranch road first.

"Nothin' yet?" Wallis was beginning to lose his patience.

"No sir," said Burring. "We can see half way across the County from here and there's been no sign of them. But they gotta come this way. Ain't no other way."

Wallis left him to his observations and walked over to the four by four in which Edson and Tyler sat, Edson ready to gun the accelerator when the Commander said to.

"Everythin' ready?"

"Yes sir. Soon as you say 'go', we go."

There had been a couple of false alarms as BMWs had travelled along the freeway towards them. Both times it was Tyler on the binoculars who announced, much to the irritation of Wallis, "Not JFK. Not JFK," and the men had been stood down.

"Remember Edson, soon's we see them comin', you get us to the farm road first. That's your sole job. Burring jumps at the turn off and we wait until their car comes up behind ours. When it stops, we step out, armed. They try to reverse? Burring has them covered. Tyler and me seize their car. They drive and we direct the route. You pick up Burring and follow us. When we get to the cabin outside   Henderson, we call Lattanzi. He wants his wife and daughter back he'd better come over an' get them. Then we call the TV folk an' arrange for Lattanzi to make his apology. Thing about it is, we pull this off without gunplay, it's just their word against ours. But we get Lattanzi wall to wall on television across America tellin' the world how he supports the people's right to bear arms. And it all starts with you gettin' us to the ranch road first, soldier."

One of the vehicles they'd missed, not unreasonably, was Jimmy St James' Mercedes as it passed beneath them, its lugubrious power carrying the unsuspecting Liz Lattanzi back along the freeway to the ranch.

Susan was still much the worse for her over indulgence. Exposure to the afternoon heat didn't do much to help and she clung to Liam's left arm with both hands as they walked - she unsteadily - back to the BMW. Liam had initially attempted to support her by putting his arm across her shoulder but she'd protested.

"Hey, hey, listen, Leem, let's not … y' know. I can look after m'self mister … Your li'l sister doesn't need the help of any man, never less a big brother. We wouldn't want people t'think there was anythin' untoward goin' on here … If you don' mind, I'll just steady m'self in my own way." So saying, they made their way to the car, Liam having to rescue her every so often when her knees buckled, giving her a gait not unlike a dance movement Liam had first come across at a Ceilidh in Scotland, where dancers entered a grace movement into a routine in which they dipped mid-step.

*Go figure women*, thought Liam, grimacing. *One minute we're great pals. Then she hints at a closer relationship and then she treats me like a hostile enemy… Go figure women all right!*

As they approached the car Liam suddenly remembered the missing tyre lever, jack and toolbox. He helped Susan into the front seat with some small difficulty and strapped her in. *My God, old Joe'll give me hell for bringing her back in this state*, he anticipated.

Once Susan had been safely ensconced in the passenger's seat, Liam went to the rear of the vehicle, lifted the trunk lid and confirmed that he'd left the tool box and accessories whilst at the roadside earlier. *There must be a sporting chance they're still there if I head back for them now*, he thought.

He returned to the driver's seat and looked at Susan, sitting beside him, now asleep. She was quite unforgivably beautiful even with her head lolling to one side and her mouth open. Liam stroked her cheek affectionately with the back of his fingers but she didn't stir. *I take it all back*, he thought, *she wouldn't enjoy Dublin.* He looked again at her in her drunken sleep and smiled. *She wouldn't last ten minutes in an Irish pub!*

Amused at the thought of Susan drinking pints of Guinness in O'Donoghue's Bar in Dublin - not so much a tradition as a compulsory activity for all visitors - he directed the car towards his missing toolbox and the ranch house.

The BMW coasted quietly along the freeway, leaving Las Vegas in its wake. Liam was relaxed behind the wheel, his earlier driving mishap now almost forgotten. Susan still slept. *If she's not used to the drink, she's going to have a sore head when she wakes. I only hope I can smuggle her up to her room when we get back. If Joe sees her like this he's not going to think much of me as her guardian angel.*

The miles slipped by easily until Liam came within a short distance of the place where the BMW had been forced from the road on the way in to Vegas. He slowed and pulled halfway on to the rock strewn shoulder partially blocking the road and flashing his hazard warning lights in compensation as he did so.

By the grace of God, he intoned, stepping from the car to see if the toolbox was still behind the rock where he now knew he'd left it. "Good," he breathed quietly to himself as he spotted his tools sitting as he'd left them.

**

Some way ahead on the same road, converging on Liam's BMW from the opposite direction, Streikker was driving the red pick-up towards the Elliot's place, just outside Boulder city where they proposed to gather themselves before working out how to assassinate Joe Lattanzi.

Up ahead he noticed a large car with flashing lights halfway on and halfway off the road.

"Looks like an accident," he said to Matt Kane who sat beside him.

A heavy truck rumbled towards them and Streikker dropped a couple of gears, reducing his speed as he prepared to pass the BMW once the truck was safely behind them.

Moments before this was possible, the driver of the BMW raised the trunk of his car and balanced a toolbox on the rim of the trunk. His attention momentarily diverted while he picked up a tyre lever, the toolbox fell on to the side of the road, spilling its contents around the rear of the car.

"Dammit," said Liam as he stepped out on to the road and waved at the driver of the pick-up which was now stationary while its driver considered the propriety of going on without offering assistance.

Liam tried to convey in his wave that everything was all right and that he apologised for inconveniencing those in the pick up.

The reaction in the pick-up however, was spontaneous as Streikker and Kane both recognised him immediately as the Lattanzi aide who featured so prominently on television as having witnessed the airport shootings.

"That's that Brannigan guy who saw us at the airport," said Streikker.

"You sure?" asked Sugar. "I didn't get a good look."

"The Lord has delivered him," said Streikker.

"It's him all right," said Kane, confirming the identification.

"Drive past him kinda slow like. Both you guys keep your faces hid. I'll have a look as we go past him."

The pick-up moved into first gear and drove alongside the BMW behind which Liam was still attempting to collect all of the tools and replace them in their box.

Again he fashioned a wave attempting to convey his apologies, smiling as a female occupant of the pick-up returned his salutation.

Sugar was satisfied. "Okay boys, change of plan. It's him all right." She thought for a moment. "Ed, drive on up ahead awhile till we're out of sight then turn around and we'll follow him. Pastor Yancy wants a hit on Lattanzi but we got us a chance here to be led right to him and take out the one guy who can identify the both of you."

Streikker was beside himself with glee "We *have* a friend in Jesus."

"Now remember, we haven't prepared for this. Usually we prepare. Lattanzi might be in a safe house, he might be protected by Federal Agents. So we play this real cautious, real careful like. Ed, keep your distance. Make sure we're not spotted. If he's in radio contact we could be surrounded by the Feds before we know it. We armed?"

Streikker smiled. "To the teeth, Sugar, to the teeth."

**

Liam finished putting everything back in the trunk and returned to the driver's seat. He checked that Susan appeared to be comfortable and, satisfied, killed the hazard warning lights and, with a glance over his shoulder, regained the highway.

He travelled at a regular fifty-five miles an hour, in no great hurry. He was escorting a beautiful woman and enjoyed the feeling of being in her company while she was asleep and unaware of the many sideways glances he stole as the car closed gradually on the ranch.

The red Ford pick-up kept its distance. Streikker was delighted at the sedate pace of the BMW. Had the driver put his foot to the floor, he wouldn't have had a hope of keeping in touch. Sugar was still cautious. "I didn't get a look inside the car when we passed. There was real heavy tinted glass in them windows. He could have an army in there."

"No way, Honey," said her husband. "If he'd had people in there, they'd have been out fixing the car 'stead of him."

"Well, I thought I saw someone in the passenger's seat, so that kinda blows your theory out of the window," argued Streikker.

"Keep well back, Ed," said Sugar. "Just keep him on the horizon."

**

Burring held the field glasses. "I might be wrong," he said quietly to Tyler who was standing beside him, "but I think our ship is comin' in."

Tyler shouted over to the Cherokee where Edson and Wallis stood. "Stand by, sir. This might be our target."

Edson started the engine and awaited confirmation. Wallis shouted over to Tyler to join them while Burring awaited a sight of the plates.

"Jay ... Eff ... Kay ............. JFK, It's them."

Burring raced towards the Cherokee which was already moving, if only slowly, to permit Burring to climb aboard. Edson took off at speed, clipping down the on ramp in an attempt to ensure that the four-by-four reached the farm road before the BMW.

He too was assisted by Liam's leisurely pace and they arrived at the ranch road without Liam seeing anything due to his view of their race being completely obscured by a clump of trees and a bend in the road.

As the Cherokee pulled into the road, Edson drew it to a temporary halt to allow Burring to leap off and then drove the vehicle forward only another twenty yards before positioning it diagonally across the width of the road, thereby prohibiting progress by any other vehicle. Wallis looked at Tyler. "No showboatin'. No gunplay. I want this over in seconds. Leave the rifle and use your revolver."

# Chapter Thirteen

*Almost home now.* Liam decelerated and indicated a left turn. He turned the powered steering wheel with the palm of one hand and was only slightly surprised when he saw the road blocked immediately ahead of him. Things like this happened not infrequently in the more rural areas as farmers saw to the needs of their herd, their flock or their land.

He was reassured when he recognised the figure who stepped out from behind the vehicle as being the person who had helped him change the tyre earlier. Liam was untroubled as his earlier assistant held up his hand, palm forward, indicating to him to stop.

"Hi," said Liam, greeting the man through the driver's window which was still opening electronically.

Tyler produced a revolver he'd kept behind his back whilst halting the BMW. "Do not make a wrong move or you watch your two women friends getting their pretty heads blown off."

Another man appeared from the rear of the car, opened the rear door and entered, sitting behind Susan. "Do precisely as we say, you won't get hurt."

Tyler joined Burring in the back seat. "Reverse the car back on to the freeway immediately."

Liam decided, in his state of fright, that these men were serious and did exactly as he was requested. Still Susan slept.

Wallis had monitored every move from the Cherokee and had ordered Edson to follow the BMW and to overtake it as soon as possible once both were back on the main road.

In a matter of fifteen seconds or so, both vehicles were back on the road they'd left only moments before.

Edson swung round in front of the BMW immediately and both cars set off for the isolated cabin Wallis had commandeered, in the midst of the one and a half million acres of the Kaibab Forest outside the township of Williams.

**

Streikker was sufficiently surprised that he cursed out loud when he rounded the corner and found that the half-mile gap Sugar had insisted on had been reduced to a few yards.

"How did that happen?" he asked his companions, each of whom were equally puzzled.

"Be careful, Ed. They could be trying to get a look at us or check our plates."

"Ed, you were right, I definitely made out people in the inside of that vehicle. Looks like they do have protection," said Matt Kane.

**

"Where the hell is Lattanzi's wife?" asked Tyler, roughly.

"She went back to the ranch earlier with a friend," replied Liam, now thoroughly frightened.

"Why?"

"She just did. We stayed on in the city for a couple of drinks."

"What's up with your girlfriend?"

"She's had one too many. And she's not my girlfriend."

"That's right. You're the hired hand and she's Lattanzi's precious daughter."

"Look, what the hell's this all about?" asked Liam, his curiosity overcoming his fear.

"Drive the car. Do as you're told and I don't mistreat your girlfriend."

"She's not my girlfriend."

"Maybe she'd be *my* girlfriend," leered Tyler.

"You *wish*!" replied Liam, regretting his response immediately as the point of Tyler's gun barrel pressed against the nape of his neck.

**

Liz Lattanzi was beginning to wonder what her daughter and Liam were up to. She was in the lounge with Jimmy St James and Joe who had started discussing the hotel but who had included Liz in the conversation upon her later arrival which soon resulted in the topic being changed to something else, anything else. Liz was not enthused about her husband's commitment to this long term project now that he was past retiral age.

"I wish Susan hadn't forgotten the mobile 'phone. Now I don't know how many to cater for at dinner tonight. Will your Mr Jackson be joining us?"

"I'm not sure. He's up in his room reading some papers I've given him and making some phone calls. I'll ask Elma to contact him."

"Thanks darling. But I wonder what I should do about Susan and Liam?"

"Well, *love of my life*, if you hadn't abandoned them in Vegas hoping that cupid would strike, perhaps we'd know." He turned to Jimmy in amplification of his comment. "My dear wife has become quite fond of young Liam and is of the view that so too has her daughter. However, rather than let her twenty-three-year-old take such steps as she feels appropriate, she has chosen to intervene and encourage the relationship."

"Oops," said St James. "I've always stayed out of affairs of the heart. I've discovered in a glorious legal career spanning decades, that my legal team have made a fat profit out of failed relationships which have developed out of mutuality never mind those prompted by a third party. That said, they do seem a good match and I share your assessment, Liz. They'd make a lovely couple."

"Jimmy, left to her own devices, my daughter will never find the right man. And I suspect that Liam's not entirely different in that regard. Anyway, I think they're both very close as it is so I'm not pushing them together, I'm merely offering momentum to a blossoming relationship."

Joe and Jimmy both laughed. "Darling, you're incorrigible!" said Joe.

"Well, we'll just see if I'm wrong."

"I must admit, I'm very fond of Liam myself," said Joe. "We've been together ever since he set foot on American soil when first he arrived from Ireland." The mention of Ireland prompted Joe's memory of his earlier conversation with Kinsella.

"Actually, he may also be quite resourceful in respect of his Dublin connections. I was asked by Father Frank Carlucci a few days back if I could help throw any light on not only the airport murders, but also the shooting of a priest in Dublin around the same time. The only connection I have with Dublin is Liam and, lo and behold, I get a call from a Dublin man this afternoon wanting to talk with Liam. He played his cards very close to his chest but it's obvious that he has something to tell him. As a matter of fact, he said he'd phone back this evening. Any time now, actually. He was very professional and wouldn't tell me anything but he did send me a photograph of someone by Fax."

"How interesting," said St James. "In all the hubbub here in Vegas, I'd quite forgotten that another priest was shot in Dublin. No wonder Father Frank's concerned."

Joe stood and walked the few paces to a cabinet and lifted the Fax. "For sure!"

He handed the likeness to Jimmy disinterestedly. "Doubtless we'll find out more when Liam's had a chance to speak with him."

Liz intervened and picked up the enlarged and copied photograph raising her hand to her mouth in horror. "Joe, it's him. This is the man who helped us change the tyre today."

Lattanzi heard the fear in her voice. "Are you sure? It's not a very good shot."

"It's him all right. My God, what about Susan? If that man's out there … this cannot be a coincidence … Joe, I'm scared."

Lattanzi and St James exchanged glances as Joe picked up the phone and dialled the guest room in the barn. He waited momentarily. "Mr Jackson, would you come down to the lounge immediately please, we may have had a development."

**

Susan awoke with a start as Burring shook her shoulder roughly.

"God help me, Liam, I'm never going to drink again."

"Wake up," said Tyler impatient to engage with the young and beautiful Miss Lattanzi.

Susan twisted in her seat, her face frowning in her attempts to make sense of what she saw. She looked at Liam for an explanation.

"Liam?"

"These two nice men have tricked their way into our car and appear to have another two of their colleagues in a four-by-four following us. They're armed, so don't do anything silly."

Susan looked round at her captors. "You … you're that guy who helped us this morning."

Tyler laughed. "At your service, ma'am."

She turned further to attempt a look at Burring who redirected her gaze by leaning the barrel of his automatic against her cheek and pushing her face to the front.

"Leave her alone, you bastard, or you'll have me to deal with."

Both Burring and Tyler laughed. "And just what'll you do, Mister?"

"Well, if I figure that you're going to kill us both, I may as well just drive all of us off the road and over the drop up ahead." As added emphasis, Liam put his foot further down on the accelerator.

"Slow down, right now."

Liam ignored the command. "I said slow down," said Tyler pointing his revolver at Susan's head.

"Calm down, Tyler," said Burring.

"I outrank you, soldier," replied Tyler.

"You mess this up, you'll answer to the Commander."

Tyler hesitated then drew back his arm, the threat receding.

*Soldier? Outrank? Commander? What the hell is going on?* Liam was puzzled.

"Listen, ain't no reason for anyone to get hurt here. We have no interest in you people. You're only a means to an end," said Burring.

"What's the end?" asked Liam, still speeding towards the drop about a mile away.

"Ain't no concern of yours. Just slow your speed and you and the lady don't get hurt."

Liam looked at Susan whose now pallid face betrayed the fact that she was quite obviously terrified. He cut his speed and adjusted the rear view mirror so he could look Burring in the eyes.

"I don't know who you are or what you're doing, but don't make the mistake of hurting her and letting me live. Because Mister, I'd dedicate the rest of my life to hunting you down and I would *not* forgive."

Susan felt a surge of emotion at Liam's gallantry.

Tyler laughed. "Pretty speech. And you say she's *not* your girlfriend?"

Burring closed the matter. "We hear what you say."

Susan sat in the front passenger seat, her mind in a whirl. *What the Hell's going on here? Why have these people picked on us?*

"Make a left at this road up ahead."

Liam decelerated and obeyed the command.

Susan looked at Liam who seemed grim and angry. Imperceptibly, her feelings modified slightly as she realised the import of the armed man's teasing comment. So now Liam's even telling crooks and gunmen I'm not his girlfriend?

**

Joe Lattanzi sat beside Liz with his arm around her, offering comfort in circumstances where nothing less than her daughter walking unharmed into the lounge with Liam would suffice.

John Jackson had attended on the Lattanzis within thirty seconds of taking the phone call from Joe and had listened patiently to Joe's account of events while Liz continued her anxious interjections.

"You may well have cause for concern. Liam is a material witness to a major crime and his inability to provide identification would suit the purpose of those involved in perpetrating the deed. If this lies behind the coincidence of their potential abduction, the prognosis would indeed be bleak. I was unaware of his proposed visit to Las Vegas. Had I been aware, I would not have recommended that he go."

He held up two fingers as did Winston Churchill when gesturing V for victory.

"Secondly, it is of course possible, that Mrs Lattanzi is mistaken and the person in the photograph is not the same person as the helpful individual you met this morning. This seems to me also to be quite likely."

Three fingers. "They may be late because they are dining or watching a movie. They may have had further problems with the car. Perhaps Liam has had a reaction to his earlier injury in the accident and is receiving treatment."

He thought for a moment. "Mr Lattanzi, how many telephone lines do you have in your system?"

"Four."

"Mrs Lattanzi, you might feel better if you were occupied. It would be helpful if you made contact with various medical facilities in Las Vegas and ask whether Liam has or is receiving treatment for his blow to the head. He may be concussed."

He turned to Joe. "Mr Lattanzi, you say that Liam is to expect a telephone call from Ireland this evening. I would propose that I answer all telephone calls this evening."

"Agreed."

"Other than that, I would not recommend any further action at the moment and would not propose that we involve the police. I wish to speak with Liam's friend from Dublin and determine whether his information is germane to our concerns."

Liz was still upset and anxious. "Mr Jackson, I'm sure that you're an extremely good security adviser. But I'm afraid we *must* involve the police. Liam is an important witness and it is my daughter we're talking about here."

Jackson caught and held Joe's eye, inviting him to intervene. Joe squeezed Liz's arm. "Honey, Mr Jackson is the best there is. The very best. You go and make your calls and I'll make contact with the police personally. Now let's get things moving. You go through to the office and start phoning around, I'll phone the police and Mr Jackson will await the call from Dublin."

Liz nodded and left the room.

"I don't like deceiving my wife, Mr Jackson. Would it hurt to phone the police in the circumstances?"

"I regret that it would and I prefer not to discuss matters further."

Jackson had had only a cursory introduction to St James when he had entered the room moments earlier. It was obvious, however that Jimmy was a close colleague of Lattanzi. "Mr St James, we haven't met properly and you might wonder at my approach but I must assure you that my record speaks for itself. Mr Lattanzi will confirm this." He turned back to Joe. "If you must deceive your wife then so be it but I must insist that my guidance be accepted."

Lattanzi pursed his lips and looked grave. "This situation may have taken on an entirely new dimension, Mr Jackson and I will not take chances with my daughter's life. Presently, I have to put my trust in your judgement. I hope it will prove to be a wise decision."

"Indeed so."

**

Streikker was finding it relatively simple to follow the BMW and the Cherokee in consequence of the dust cloud being created by both vehicles as they followed the winding dirt track to the cabin.

"Looks like they're heading for a safe house in the Kaibab Forest, up ahead."

Sugar was still apprehensive. "Keep your distance, Ed. If we can see their dust, they can see ours if they look over their shoulder."

Every so often, the vehicles up ahead could be seen as they passed an occasional gap in the pine trees apparently oblivious to the pick-up dogging their tyre tracks.

The road now wound in a clockwise direction around the side of a tree-covered mountain with a steep drop on the driver's side of the vehicle. Rocky outcrops fought with tinder dry pines and cedars for their space in the sun.

Streikker pulled up just before an exposed bend in the road. Matt Kane stepped from the pick-up and ran in a crouch to a position where he could establish the prospects of the *Posse* continuing safely. He'd carried out this manoeuvre on a number of occasions, always returning with news that they continue cautiously. This time he waited longer, observing the movements of those up ahead. After a couple of minutes he returned, still bent low to the ground.

"They've arrived at their safe house."

"Protection?" asked Sugar.

"There's six in all. I can't make out who's who but that guy Brannigan's there and I think one of them's a woman, though I can't be sure. Four of them's obviously armed. They took some boxes in. Looks like they'll be there for some time."

"If they're protected and they're in a safe house, we found our target all right. I say we go in tonight after dark," said Kane.

Sugar did not respond to her husband's suggestion and decided to take a look at their base gesturing to both men to join her. All three walked in a stoop to the bend and knelt behind a rock. Five hundred yards ahead on the dirt track, the BMW and the Cherokee were parked at the side of a wooden cabin, its paint dry and cracked. Obviously untended for some time, the house appeared to have two rooms at the front and an indeterminate amount at the rear although it looked as if perhaps an additional three or four could be accommodated within the general mass of the building.

Behind the premises stretched a forest which seemed to go on endlessly. To the right of the cabin a rocky edifice reached skyward, protecting their flank. To the left, the track continued and, from Sugar's vantage point, appeared to end behind the cabin. Across the track, a cliff plummeted downwards. *Any attempt to engage with these people will need a full frontal attack* figured Sugar. *But if **they're** going anywhere, they'll need to get past us first.*

# Chapter Fourteen.

Special Agent Steve Montana was really annoying Bilko.

"Greatest man who ever lived. Saved our country from Communism."

"He was a Godamn cross-dresser. A tyrannical bully. A nancy boy who liked dressing up in woman's clothes," countered Bilko, before going on. "Y'know, Montana, he was as all-American as the Queen of England. He denied the existence of organised crime … he blackmailed Presidents and, for all I know was responsible for the assassination of Jack Kennedy. The man was a Goddamn monster, so don't go givin' me this stuff about him bein' a saviour of our nation."

Montana shook his head sadly. "I was taught that police officers were instructed in ways which permitted them to view information presented to them with a healthy scepticism. That they didn't just believe what they read in the tabloids. It's not me, Sergeant Bilk, who accepts uncontested the left wing, liberal, bleeding hearts point of view peddled by those who would weaken our country and surrender it to the questionable politics of the United Nations. Frankly, I'm surprised that a man like you doesn't see through this conspiracy to impugn his good name."

"Jesus Christ, Montana, it's a matter of record. The guy was a fruit cake."

J.Edgar Hoover, former Director of the FBI, occupied the conversation of Bilko and Montana for some further minutes with Bilko becoming more irritable and Montana more certain of his conspiracy theory when Regan put his head round the door and waved a file at the combatants, inviting them into his office.

They both rose and followed the direction of the gesture.

"What we got?" asked Bilko.

"Edward James Norman Streikker. Know him?"

Bilko narrowed his eyes and thought. "Edward Streikker, Edward Streikker....*sure* I know him. Ed Streikker. A nut case. I busted him a few years back for firearms and drugs stuff. A weirdo. He talked like he swallowed the bible. Real religious freak. What you got him on?"

"His prints were on the card we found at the shooting of Rabbi Goldstein."

"Was he involved with any political groupings?" asked Montana.

Bilko looked uncomfortable. "Matter of fact he was. He was a member of *Posse Commitatus*, the right wing, anti-Jewish, abortion hatin', anti-gun control, anti-everythin', head cases." He looked at Regan. "It figures he was involved in this. You got up to date mug shots in his file?"

"Only what you arranged when you jailed him three years ago. He's been a good boy since he got out."

"That I doubt very much indeed. He must just have been lucky."

"Lieutenant, have we any idea where he might be right now?" asked Montana.

"Indeed we have, Special Agent Montana. Would you like to accompany me and Sergeant Bilk while we pay him a visit? It's beginning to look like we may have to apologise to you if *Posse Commitatus* is linked to the murder of the Rabbi. Maybe you Federal boys ain't as far off the track as we might have imagined."

"Thank you, Lieutenant. We are quite sure that the *Posse* is active and this could easily be an act of theirs. I'm ready when you are."

"Where is he, John?"

"The forensic boys have figured out the letters and numbers on the corner of the card. Seems it's from a motel out in Searchlight."

"You'll appreciate sir that he probably won't be there and may have merely touched a card which was already at the scene of the crime?"

Bilko remembered his dislike of Montana and his irritation that *Posse Commitatus* had been connected as Montana had implied. "You got a better idea, mister?"

**

No one felt like eating. Liz had phoned around every medical facility in the metropolitan area without any success. Now she occupied herself in the kitchen while her husband, Jimmy St James and John Jackson awaited a phone call from Dublin. Joe had informed Liz that the police had no information on Liam and Susan although he said the words through gritted teeth while staring hard at Jackson.

When it came, the trill of the telephone had the effect of a rifle shot. Everyone started, startled, with the exception of Jackson who leaned over and picked up the handset.

"Lattanzi residence."

"I wonder could I speak with Liam Brannigan?"

"Mr Kinsella?"

"Yes."

"I'm afraid Liam isn't here right now but it's important that you and I speak right now."

"And why's that?"

"Essentially because Liam told me earlier how much he counted on you as a friend," he lied. "And because he may by now be in great personal peril."

"How come?"

"You sent us a photograph, by Fax. Can you tell me the name of the person in it?"

"No, I can't."

"Because you don't know or don't feel able to tell us?"

"The former. Listen, who am I talking with?"

"My name is John Jackson. I am employed by Mr Lattanzi and Liam to protect them and the Lattanzi family."

"Why might Liam be in danger?"

"He may have been in contact with the man whose photograph you faxed to us. Can I ask you if that would worry you?"

"Jesus Christ. How could that happen?"

"Would that worry you, Mr Kinsella?"

"Look, I'd much rather discuss this with Liam."

"So too would we, Mr Kinsella, but the fact is that we fear that Liam and Mr and Mrs Lattanzi's daughter Susan may, at best, have been apprehended by this man. Now, would that worry you?"

There was a silence at the other end of the phone.

Jackson broke it. "Look, Mr Kinsella you may be concerned about confidentiality. Be assured, anything you tell me stops here. There has been no police involvement, nor will there be. We need to know what otherwise you would have told Liam."

Liz Lattanzi looked at Joe, puzzled.

"Okay. This better not be being recorded because people could get killed over here."

"This is not being recorded and you are speaking to me alone. There is no conference facility on this line."

"All right. ... That guy is a real villain by all accounts. He may have murdered someone here in Dublin. He's an American and he's recently back in the States. I can't see how he would be interested in Liam. Are you sure it was him?"

"It appears so. Is there anything else you would have wished to say to Liam?"

"Just that I may have put myself inadvertently in harm's way by following up his request for information."

"Are you in a position to cope with that?"

"I have a plan, as they say. I'll be all right, I think. But listen, I'm really confused by this. But if that man's involved with Liam, anything could be happening."

"Would you imagine yourself to be in a position to discover his name?"

"Liam's a friend, but further enquiries could seriously damage my health."

"In that case, I can only thank you for your assistance. Would you be prepared to leave your telephone number with me?"

"I'd rather not. I'll phone back tomorrow and hear how things are going. I'll speak to you then."

Both men replaced their handsets.

Liz had re-entered the room towards the end of the conversation, but had surmised that she had arrived during the phone call they'd been waiting for. She could not contain herself. "What did he say?"

Jackson had always had a facility for telling lies. "Everything appears to be all right, Mrs Lattanzi. The man in the photograph is Liam's cousin. Apparently he has lost a lot of weight recently and Liam's friend was merely drawing this to Liam's attention. His cousin is with Mr Kinsella right now so it would appear to be a case of mistaken identity. In conversation earlier you mentioned that Liam and Susan were encouraged to have a night together socialising?"

"Yes," said Liz weakly, beginning to trust that her daughter might just be having a meal with Liam.

"Well, I imagine we might well do the same. Everything seems to be all right."

"Of course, I'll rustle something up straight away." Liz left the room still confused and only partly reassured by Jackson's soothing tones.

Once Liz had left, Joe turned to Jackson. "The tenor of your conversation didn't appear to bear out the information you relayed to my wife."

"I thought she would *want* to believe me and took the view that we might buy ourselves some time whilst keeping her from making contact with the police."

"And the truth of the conversation?"

"He appears to be a very dangerous man. He's American and he's here in the States."

"So my daughter may be lying dead in a ditch?"

"Yes, that's possible. We may expect a phone call if there is a financial motive. If it is related to Liam's witnessing the murders, then we can expect the worse."

Jimmy St James intervened. "And your proposal?"

"We wait. And hope the phone rings. The police can not help."

The words had barely left Jackson's mouth when the phone rang with the same effect as previously. Jackson lifted the handset.

"Hello!"

"I'd like to speak to Joe Lattanzi."

"Who's calling?"

"You don't need to know that. I just want to speak to Lattanzi."

"You are," said Jackson.

"Well, you just need to know that your daughter is my guest at the moment and she'd like you to come and get her."

"Is she all right?"

"She is at present, but there's no guarantee that she'll stay safe."

"What do you mean?"

"Listen, asshole, you picked one fight too many when you took on the people of America. We ain't interested in your daughter, we're interested in you. You're going to appear on nationwide television and tell the world that you believe in the right of the American people to carry arms against a corrupt and incompetent Federal government, or you don't get your daughter back. It's that simple!"

"That sounds like a trade I couldn't refuse."

"You better believe it."

"And what happens to me after I make the broadcast?"

"You go home and your daughter is returned unharmed and within a couple of hours, but you don't get to retract your statement or we'll come back and finish our business."

"Is my colleague with her?"

"They're both here and unharmed."

"I want to speak with Susan or there's no deal. I'm not going to take the chance that they're both dead already and I'm just being lured into a trap."

Wallis had anticipated the request. He nodded to Tyler, who stepped forward with Susan, holding her by the elbow.

"Tell your father how happy you are to be here."

"Dad! They've got Liam and me ..."

Her voice trailed off as Wallis removed the phone from her lips.

"Give me the details," said Jackson.

"Goes without saying there's no police involvement. You come up here to our cabin in the forest first thing tomorrow morning and we'll talk about what you're going to say and do for the American people. You get to see your daughter. Maybe even speak to her. But one false move and she's dead along with your employee. And we can make it look like an accident. There's a real steep cliff right next to us. So come alone and we'll talk."

"I'll be there," said Jackson.

**

Bilko drove with four unmarked police cars trailing in his wake.

"We go in carefully," said Regan.

"Why don't we just phone the owners of the motel and ask if Streikker's there?" asked Montana.

"Because, Special Agent Smartass, how do we know that the owners of the motel are not in cahoots with Streikker? Forensic already told us there was more than one person involved at the scene of the crime. We'd all look kinda stupid if we phoned them up and gave them all a warning before we arrive."

"Good point, Sergeant Bilk."

"You find that with me. It's not uncommon."

The conversation lapsed as they got closer to Searchlight, the monotonous tone of the engine being enlivened intermittently by bursts of radio communication.

As they arrived in the town, the cars split up as prearranged with Bilko being the only driver to park in front of the motel. Montana had been dropped at the corner of the avenue, told to buy a newspaper and wait for further instructions.

Regan and Bilko strode up to reception where Mr Huczynski was sitting at his desk reading a novel.

"Got a couple of rooms?" asked Regan.

"Sure have, sir."

"You the owner?"

"Along with my missus."

Regan and Bilko glanced up and down the corridor. No activity. Bilko brought out his badge and warrant card. "We'd like a quiet word sir. In your apartment. Now, if you don't mind."

Mr Huczynski acceded to the request with only the merest suggestion that he was being inconvenienced.

"You recognise this man?" asked Regan, showing a mug shot of Edward Streikker.

Mr Huczynski put on his glasses and peered at the photograph. "Hey, is that Mr McCoy?"

"Where is he just now?"

"Checked out this morning. He was travelling with his two friends, Mr and Mrs Jones."

"When did they arrive?"

Huczynski checked his register. "Arrived five days ago. Didn't cause me no trouble. McCoy looked a bit funny but he kept hisself to hisself."

"We'd like a look at their rooms."

"No problem, officer. They're both still unoccupied. We haven't had time to tidy them up just yet."

Huczynski escorted Bilko to the apartments and Regan stepped outside and waved to Montana as arranged so as to stand down the officers in the other cars and have them convene at the motel.

**

"You harm my father, I swear by all that's holy I'll haunt you to your grave."

"Both of yous is tough guys, huh," said Burring. "Always threatenin' what you're goin' to do to us if we're bad to you."

"We won't harm your father, Miss," said Wallis. "We just want him to do what we said on the phone. He got no call tryin' to remove the right of the American people to bear arms, but if he puts matters right we'll have no further business with him. Or you two, for that matter. If everyone behaves, no one gets hurt."

Liam and Susan sat together on a couch which sat two people comfortably. Tyler was on patrol outside and Burring and Wallis sat in two armchairs, one on each side of the fire which they'd lit to take the edge off the coolness of the evening air. Dry-as-a-bone kindling wood was the only combustible material they'd had to hand so the fire sparked and crackled cheerily in contrast to the sombre mood of the room. Edson was in a room to the rear checking the contents of the explosives, arms and supplies which they'd brought in earlier.

Tyler came into the front room from his tour of duty around the perimeter of the cabin and leered at Susan.

"Care to sit outside with me awhile, Ma'am. Sunset's awful pretty out there. Bet it's been a while since you been with a real man. We could make sweet, sweet music." He grinned.

"I'd rather die first."

"I wouldn't tempt fate, lady," said Tyler, becoming surly.

"Soldier, you watch your mouth. We're here on a mission. And it's not to gratify your animal instincts."

Tyler looked at him sourly.

"You just bought yourself a second shift, Lieutenant. Get back outside for another hour and when you come back in, you have a little more respect for our guests."

Both men stared hard at one another until Tyler levered his shoulder off the wall of the cabin and went outside.

"What's all this 'soldier and lieutenant' stuff?" asked Liam of Wallis.

"Guess you'll find out tomorrow mornin' when your boss gets here." He picked up the automatic rifle which had lain on the floor at his side, ignited a cigarette he'd pulled from the pack using his lips as was his habit and settled back in the chair, inhaling deeply. "You're Irish by the sound of you, so you'll probably not know nothin' of our history. Back in 1775, the British were trying to enforce their rule over North America to the point where the colonists figured they were merely becoming coercive and domineerin'. For all I know, you Irish people were involved too."

"I doubt we'd be supporting the English," said Liam.

"Anyway, conflict started in Concord, Massachusetts, when British soldiers were ordered to take an arsenal that had been gathered by a local Militia, but one of our boys, a silversmith called Paul Revere, heard what was goin' on and rode to Concord to let the Militia know. That's when the American War of Independence started. We appointed George Washington as our Commander-in-Chief and, after a struggle, won our Independence. A while later, when the greatest minds in the world came to set out a code of conduct for the citizens of this country, they fashioned a document called The Constitution of The United States of America and we got ourselves a Bill Of Rights. These documents made us all free men and liberated us from tyranny. You understand what I'm sayin'? Now, one way it guaranteed our freedom was that it gave every man jack the right to bear arms against the day when the Federal Government itself became tyrannical and would not subject itself to the will of the people. Nowadays there's a lot of people who believe that that day has arrived. We got cities today that our founding fathers could not have foreseen. They've become foreign lands, inhabited by foreign people who don't belong here. They're Godless and corrupt. Spiritually and morally corrupt, full of homosexuals and Jews. We got a Federal Government that bows the knee to the United Nations, which permits the yellow man to humiliate us in battle, which turns on its own God fearin' people and which demands higher and higher taxes to finance its incompetence and corrupt practices."

"Sounds like you've got a real beef about corruption there, but why the militaristic stuff?"

"All across America people are rising up in opposition to the Federal Government, just like they did against the British Government. In every State in the nation, people are bandin' together and returnin' to the original concepts of them who designed our Constitution. They're formin' themselves into Militias, armin' themselves, an' trainin' themselves, an' educatin' themselves because the day's gonna come soon when the people will need to be prepared to move against the Government. That's gonna take determination, commitment and discipline. And that, my Irish friend, needs a military approach. I'm the Commander of an armed unit and I approach my task just as efficiently as I did when I was in charge of troops in 'Nam."

"You're a real John Wayne."

"I know you don't mean it, son. I know you're bein' disrespectful, but you just paid me a real big compliment."

**

Joe Lattanzi stood, eyeball to eyeball with John Jackson. "I don't give a good goddamn about what our deal was."

Jackson had asked Lattanzi to step into a nearby room to discuss matters, when he had announced to Joe and Jimmy that he would take care of matters personally. Joe had indicated that his daughter's life was in danger and that he would be at Jackson's side when he confronted her captors.

"With respect, Mr Lattanzi, we have an arrangement and I am not used to being challenged in my assessments of what requires to be done. You'll forgive me, but you're not at your fighting weight of some years ago. I imagine that you've never shot a gun in anger. It's important that you understand that you'll be a liability once I move into action."

"Well with the best of respect to you, Mr Jackson, you're forgetting two things. First, you have foreclosed on an option we may have to exercise. When we get up there, we might easily find that there is just no way that we can penetrate their defences. I might just have to comply with their demands and that's just what I would expect to do. You won't be able to exercise that option if I'm sitting here at the ranch. Secondly, Susan is my daughter. Nobody tells me how best to care for her."

Both men still stood nose to nose.

"And another thing. I was a Marine for a while."

"I could walk away from this."

"Then do so, but I'm going up to their cabin, with or without you."

After a silence, Jackson blinked first.

"Very well, but listen to me carefully. I know my job and if and when things start happening, I will act in accordance with my judgement and you will follow my instructions to the letter."

"Just so long as it doesn't put my daughter at risk."

"You are one stubborn man, Mr Lattanzi." Jackson sat on the edge of a table and thought for a moment.

"Okay, you say that cabin's about two hours from here?"

"Perhaps an hour and a half if we speed and the road's clear. I'm not sure of the last couple of miles. It's dirt track."

"If they're professionals, they'll have a man on point, hiding at the roadside and in contact with the main group but we're going to have to chance it. In my experience, Mr Lattanzi, you cannot take these people's word at face value. They could easily shoot you and your daughter once you'd made the broadcast. So we're going to have to go in. Quietly! And tonight."

Lattanzi nodded his agreement.

"We must be unhindered in our task. Tell your wife something to put her at ease. Tell her that your daughter's just phoned to say she and your employee have broken down in the city. She's borrowed a phone to call home and you and I are going in to help them obtain a second tyre. You may wish to confide in Mr St James if you feel he can help distract your wife but I cannot have the police involved."

"I presume we should be armed?"

"I remember you as a very gifted orator when you were in the Senate but I don't think you'll talk us out of this one. Weapons will be necessary."

**

Inside the bar, people were laughing and having fun. Joan Addison looked inside enviously and then shot a glance at her watch. Only twenty minutes until the end of her shift. She'd been on her feet all day, just as she'd been for the last six years. It wasn't a great job but it was regular employment and provided her with the income and the social contacts she needed to keep body and soul together. Being a traffic warden had its hassles but these seldom got out of hand and she much preferred giving warnings and helping people along. Not like her colleague, that bitch Norma Schwartz. It often seemed that she took pleasure in others' discomfort.

It was time to walk back to base and sign off.

The evening was cooling as Joan walked past the McArthur Abortion Clinic she'd passed on so many, many occasions. Unknown to her and to the rest of Las Vegas, the bush she'd just walked past and which she'd so admired the day before concealed an explosive device timed to go off in thirteen hours, just a matter of yards away from a wing in which doctors and nurses would be gathered together in conference, going over case files or having an afternoon coffee break.

# Chapter Fifteen.


It was dark now as Regan, Bilko and Montana sped back towards Vegas. They'd left Forensic to comb the place but before they'd left, they'd secured a positive ID on Streikker, knew they were looking for three people, one of them a woman - possibly married to the second man and that they were driving a red Ford pick up with a damaged wheel-arch on the passenger's side. The place had obviously been wiped and no prints were in evidence - except for a couple of perfect thumb marks on a beer-can which had been found in a bin at the side of the television, obviously overlooked by the departing fugitives. *Just wish we'd found those prints on the television itself or on a window. If these people get a good defence lawyer, they'll argue we brought the can with us to the motel. Goddamn lawyers!* Bilko vented his spleen to himself as he pondered the events of the day while gunning the car back to the city.

Entering the station, Regan took the clear plastic bag to the Forensic Department and asked that it be registered and that the prints be checked - particularly against one Edward James Norman Streikker.

Montana had hung behind, waiting on Regan. The administrative protocols completed, they walked together up the stairs to their offices.

"Doesn't Sergeant Bilk mind being referred to as Bilko, Lieutenant?"

"S'bin that way for the last twenty years. He doesn't seem to mind. He was called 'Duck' when he was a kid because his first name was Donald. I call him Don when I need a favour but he answers the phone 'Bilko' so he seems to be used to it."

"I'm not used to such informality in the FBI."

"If you don't mind me sayin' so, Montana, you don't seem to be in contact with them too often. Who do you report to?"

"My orders were to report to you and to assist in investigations relating to the airport murders insofar as they might involve the activities of *Posse Commitatus*. To be honest, I've not been in the Bureau too long, and I think I'm being allowed to see how the Police go about their work without too much interference from my superiors. The Bureau has a number of teams looking at various aspects of these murders, as you would imagine and I've just been asked to make myself as useful to you people as possible."

"Call me cynical, Agent Montana, but why do I get the uncomfortable feeling that you're a spy in the camp, put here by your bosses to make sure we don't do anything you disapprove of and to relay anything back to them that you feel might be of interest?"

"I can assure you, Lieutenant, nothing could be further from the reality of my mission. My role is to consider the possible involvement of the *Posse*."

"Well, I gotta tell you," said Regan as they arrived at his office door, "I don't give a shit whether this matter is resolved by the FBI or Las Vegas Police Department! My namesake, President Ronald Regan, had a sign on his desk in the Oval Office which read, 'Man can accomplish anythin' if he doesn't mind who takes the credit.' Now that's a bit sexist but it's somethin' I actually believe in. If we catch the bad guys, good enough but I'm just as happy if it's your people. That said, if I think you're hindering our investigation, you won't even realise you're being sidelined. Either that or I'll have 'The Duck' look after your education."

Inside the Lieutenant's office sitting on his desk, Bilko was speaking on Regan's phone. "Put out an

APB on Streikker. Get his photograph circulated and have everyone keep an eye out for red Ford pick ups, no registration available, damaged off-side wheel arch."

While Regan and Montana awaited Bilko finishing his call, another phone on the Lieutenant's desk breeped for attention. Regan picked it up and listened. Both he and Bilko laid their phone sets down at the same time. Regan spoke first. "We got a positive ID on Streikker's prints at Searchlight. We're closing in."

**

Streikker and the Kanes had driven through the vast Kaibab. and sat atop a pine-clad hilltop overlooking the cabin. They'd parked their pick-up in a small clearing beside the dirt track leading to the cabin and had climbed above their quarry in order first to observe.

"Looks like they've only posted one guard outside," said Sugar.

"Five more inside," said Streikker unnecessarily.

"It's real dark now, we should go in," urged Matt Kane.

"Listen Honey, we got to remember that this is a detour for us. We're trying to take out Lattanzi. We're not sure he's in there. All we know for sure is that his aide is. We know that there's protection so we got to figure that either the Feds think he deserves protection in his own right or that Lattanzi's in there as well. I'm a bit uncomfortable about this. I figure that they would protect people in a safe house or in a hotel somewhere. I mean somewhere with a bit of comfort. Don't even look like they've got a TV in there."

"We can't wait for ever," argued her husband anticipating her proposed action.

"We wait until tomorrow morning when we see what they're up to. They can have no idea that we're here so we're still going to have the element of surprise."

Both Streikker and her husband demurred but Sugar held sway. "Let's get some sleep. Who wants to take first watch?"

"I'll do that if you want," said Streikker. "Should we light a small fire? It's gettin' cooler."

Sugar looked around. "If we make sure the wood's dry and keep it small, we shouldn't be detected as long as we step back down the hill a piece. There's no wind but if a breeze springs up, we better kill the fire. The smell of wood smoke carries like you wouldn't believe."

**

A thousand feet up on the mountain above the *Posse*, fifteen hundred feet above the Militia, a pair of binoculars swept slowly across the scene. A full moon in the cloudless sky permitted good unhindered vision and amplified by the powerful lenses, considerable detail was evident.

*Well, I wonder what's goin' on down there*, asked Charlie Brookes of himself. *Ain't seen that old cabin occupied in years. Maybe a huntin' party, up on the hills just like me.* He brought his field glasses back up to his eyes and focused on the figure seated on the porch of the cabin. *That man's armed like he's guardin' the place and those folks on the hill look kinda hostile.* From his perspective he could see the three vehicles; the Idaho Militia's BMW and Cherokee next to the cabin and Sugar Kane's battered pick-up in a clearing just off the track.

He looked at his watch. Nine o'clock. If he continued his journey he'd make his own car in around an hour, and Annie's Bar with a further thirty minutes driving. Still time for a drink and some chat with them nice waitresses. His day hunting on the hills had been unsuccessful but he'd enjoyed himself anyway. *Somethin' funny's goin' on down there, but it'd be better if I paid no heed.*

Scanning the scene below one more time, he struck out for his car and a flirtatious and drunken conclusion to his evening.

**

Joe Lattanzi had informed his wife of Jackson's story about the BMW having lost another tyre and that Mr Jackson had agreed to accompany him to offer help. Throughout the tale, told to Liz, alone in the kitchen, he couldn't look her in the eye. As he approached the point when it became evident she would be bid farewell, Liz stepped towards him, put her arms around him and laid her tear stained cheek on his chest.

"Joseph Lattanzi, you have been a wonderful husband and father to me and Susan. Now I don't know what's going on but I know it's something serious or you wouldn't be telling me this cock-and-bull story. In our entire married life you've never told me a lie except the one big secret you think I don't know about. But you're not a good liar."

She hugged her husband closer. "It's possible that my daughter's in some danger, otherwise you and your 'Mr Jackson' wouldn't be dealing with matters in this way. But don't worry, I won't be involving the police. I can't think of anyone I'd trust more to take care of any situation involving this family than you. So you go ahead and do what you and Mr Jackson need to do but let me tell you this, Joseph Lattanzi, you bring my daughter and Liam back to this house safe and well. Bring them back soon and you make damn sure you don't hurt a hair on your head."

They held one another for wordless moments. Liz uncoupled herself and wiped the tears from her eyes with the back of her hand.

"One more thing before you go. I love you, Joe, but when you return from this - whether Susan and Liam are sitting safely in a Diner in Vegas or whether they're in some trouble - you are going, very quietly, to *confess* your secret to me and you are going to step aside from it. Now, we both know what I'm talking about but I'm not going to go through this again and I'm certainly not putting my family at risk again." She pulled a kitchen roll tissue from its dispenser and dabbed at her nose as gracefully as the uncomfortably unyielding paper would permit. "I'm going to sit here with Jimmy and he'll look after me until you get back, safe and sound. I'm pretty sure that was going to be his job anyway."

Joe Lattanzi had a lump in his throat which rendered him speechless. He closed on Liz and held her tight. Both wept silently until Joe gathered himself and looked at his wife. "You and Susan are everything to me. I promise I'll address every issue you raised. I promise I'll bring them home safely and I promise I won't get hurt in the process. You're probably thinking the worst because I'm keeping you in the dark. You know I'm only trying to protect you but I'm only going to be involved in some delicate negotiations so don't fret too much. I've spent my life negotiating and I'm the best I've ever met. This time it happens to be rather more personal but that'll just keep me on my toes. Everything's going to be all right."

The door behind him creaked as Jackson entered the kitchen. "It's time we left or they'll be wondering where we've gotten to."

"Yes, I'll be right with you. I'll see you at the front door in a moment."

Jackson left and Joe kissed Liz on the forehead. No further words passed between them and he turned on his heel and followed Jackson to the front door.

His head was thumping. *Well, I'll be a monkey's uncle. She knows about my 'big lie', my supposed 'secret'. God alone knows how but she does but maybe it is time I put all of this behind me anyway. I'm not getting any younger!*

With the thought of his advancing years in the forefront of his mind, he stepped out into the darkness and climbed into the farm Jeep behind whose wheel sat Jackson dressed in dark clothing looking for all the world as if he were spoiling for a fight.

**

In the cabin, Edson had made everyone a cup of coffee, including Tyler who was now off shift but who sat sullenly in the corner of the room fixed on sharpening his hunting knife.

Susan was now more sober but the after effects of alcohol, the later hour and the silence which enveloped the cabin leadened her eyelids and she fell into a drowsy sleep, her head on Liam's shoulder.

Liam found it harder to follow suit. In eight hours it would be morning and Joe Lattanzi was due to show up. *These guys look mean. Their leader talked about discipline and although he protected Susan against the fellah with the knife, I'm not convinced things couldn't turn nasty once Joe shows up.*

Liam moved his arm slightly to make Susan feel more comfortable. She really was an exquisite creature. He felt very protective of her and spent some time considering a number of options he'd pursue in order to get her out of the cabin and into the forest if things looked getting out of hand. Sitting on a two-seater sofa as they were with the Militia people seated around them, no conversation had been possible beyond some reassuring noises and a request from each of them to visit the washroom.

Their requests were agreed to but both were accompanied on each occasion by Edson, who stood outside the door, keeping it ajar, much to Susan's loud protests and Edson's evident and acute embarrassment, even though he stood facing in the opposite direction, his hand on the door handle holding it slightly ajar at arm's length and murmuring apologies about how he was only following orders.

Liam had half risen to his feet at Susan's annoyed imprecations but had been motioned to sit back down by Wallis who reassured him that Edson was merely holding the door shut from the outside. "We're just being cautious, Mr Brannigan. Right now, you two are our ace in the hole. We lose you, we lose our deal."

As midnight approached and with Edson on guard duty outside and Wallis and Tyler sleeping, Liam and Burring were the only two awake. As he gazed into the dying embers of the fire, pondering the fate which awaited them in the morning, Liam joined the rest in slumber.

**

Jackson and Lattanzi had reached the farm track which, according to the directions given them by Wallis, would take them to the cabin. Jackson pulled the Jeep onto a grassed area at the side of the road and, killing the headlights, shone a flashlight on a map of the area.

"I've outlined the route we've been told to follow here on the map," said Jackson, his finger tracing a red pen mark he'd made earlier. "Like I said earlier, if they're professionals, they'll have someone on point. We don't know whether there's two of them or two hundred. Now we're going to have to make some assumptions here because time is not on our side." He returned to the map. "The road divides about a mile up ahead. Anyone heading for the cabin would have to use that route. Now if he's been professional about this, and assuming he has the manpower, he'll have placed someone around there to monitor traffic but we're going to have to take the chance that there's only a handful of them at best - and that's not an unreasonable assumption. If that's the case, I figure he'll have his point man up much closer to the cabin - maybe even in the zone itself, on the basis that he'll need all of his people around him if there's any rough stuff."

Lattanzi was engaged. "I agree your scenario. What do you propose?"

"If he has someone on point, we're probably facing professionals in numbers that we'd be unlikely to overcome so we'll have to trust in your negotiations. I think we should test them." Again his finger pointed to his penned markings on the map. "We drive slowly and openly to the junction here." He stabbed his finger on the map where he'd marked it. "Then we sit, with lights on in full view of anyone who cares to see us. We even get out and sit on the fender, quite openly. We wait for one hour. If there's someone there, they'll probably come and collect us. However, if they don't, then we figure there's no one on point at that position and head on up the track to the right. Now the advantage of that move is that that track has several spurs and they are most unlikely to have anyone in that neck of the woods. One of these brings us up around a mile from the cabin. We should be able to hike on over to the cabin in about an hour from there given it's dark and we'll need to be quiet. Are you up to it?"

"It all makes sense to me. What about weapons?"

Jackson reached behind the seat and lifted a rag. "I have two sidearms in here. One is automatic and can fire off twenty rounds." He unwrapped the cloth. "This second one you keep in your pocket or in your belt or something. It's a 'Saturday night special', only one shot but it's easy to conceal." He looked at Lattanzi and shrugged his shoulders. "You never know. It might come in handy."

"What about you? Are you armed?"

Jackson smiled. "And dangerous!"

Lattanzi put the small single shot Derringer in his rear pocket and felt the heft of his pistol before lodging it in his waistband.

"Now be clear about our mission. We need to reach the cabin by dawn. If we do that we're in the driving seat. We wait and we watch. They've given us a deadline and they'll be anxious if we don't show on time. We estimate their strength. We observe the disposition of their people. Then and only then, do we discuss what we do."

"You're much more democratic in action that I'd imagine you'd be," smiled Lattanzi.

"There's obvious synergy in putting ideas together at a planning stage but once we have a plan, we go for it and I'm the only one who gets to change it. However Mister Lattanzi, if we get picked up on point and are taken to the cabin under escort, we will be disarmed and it is I who will have to rely on your famed negotiating skills. So we're a team, eh?"

"One hell of a team," said Joe. "So, let's go get my daughter back."

# Chapter Sixteen

Annie didn't actually exist.

In the summer of 1968, Courtney Riley and her husband Harry had got lucky with a sizeable cannabis haul destined for the many *aficionados* in the Haight Ashbury district of San Francisco. Everyone in the commune had been stoned for the best part of the previous week except Harry who didn't smoke and who couldn't take a joint without throwing up. However, he achieved much the same end state as his companions by indulging in his *penchant* for beer. From time to time he sobered up, a condition which also set him apart from his friends and on one of these occasions he happened upon a large consignment of the weed which lay in a room awaiting distribution. Noting the condition of those who sprawled around the apartment asleep or on another planet, Harry collected Courtney from a bedroom and, lifting the sack of cannabis, quietly stepped out into the street.

Driving west to Las Vegas for the want of somewhere better to go, Harry and Courtney decided to wise up. They sold the contraband for what to them then was serious money and after a few weeks, put a down payment on a bar just off Interstate 40 near Williams and called it Annie's Bar.

Over the years, its popularity ebbed and flowed but it always did well enough to keep both of them reasonably prosperous and, after twenty-five or so years, they were running a profitable and popular roadhouse. Most nights they'd have live bands and years previously had realised the value of employing young, attractive and, in the case of the girls, buxom bar staff.

They catered for a young crowd, mostly. Teenagers and students who'd drive out from Vegas, Boulder City or Flagstaff to hear the band of the evening. However their experience also taught them that the middle-aged had money to spend so, in the rear, they'd a smaller, quieter bar used by an older, more local clientele.

Charlie Brookes was having a whale of a time. In the bar at the rear he was cackling at the repartee of Wilma, one of the more experienced girls whose chat he always enjoyed when relaxing after one of his hunting trips or on the many visits he paid just to get drunk.

"Honey, why don't you bring me another pitcher of beer and get yourself Bourbon while you're at it?" Charlie was having a great time. Seated at the bar alongside him were two stalwarts of Annie's, Sam Brady and Jerry Allen, who found their way to the same seats every night and criticised everything which found its way on to the televised news.

Tonight was no different. Charlie enjoyed Sam and Jerry's company and shared their perspective on life.

CNN News on the hour appeared on a television which hung from the ceiling. A pause in the conversation was all that was needed for the fairly regular request to be made of Wilma that she 'turn the goddamn bad news up'. The three men sat transfixed by the detritus of American life which found its way on to national television news.

Most items were commented on in a pejorative fashion by one or all of the men who could usually find something in the story to incur their wrath. Occasionally an item would tickle their funny bone and they would guffaw with laughter at someone's plight. The more alcohol which was consumed, the more outrageous their sense of humour. One night Wilma had to call them to order, as they found the complete destruction of a trailer park by a hurricane in Florida to be excruciatingly funny and were beginning to annoy certain other customers who found little amusing in the tragedy.

Charlie's interest perked up when the local news came on. After a lead story about a transport strike followed by a shooting in a bar in downtown Vegas, the newsreader turned to an item which derived from a police press conference in which a spokesman indicated that police were looking for someone called Edward James Norman Streikker and two others, unknown, who may be armed and who may be driving a red Ford pick-up with a damaged wheel arch on the passenger's side. No other details were transmitted and the broadcaster moved on to the next news item about a road crash on the Strip which involved a local sports personality.

"Well I'll be damned," said Charlie to his two drinking companions.

"Ain't *that* the godamned truth," said Sam to Jerry as they both convulsed over their wit.

"I saw that pick-up." said Charlie ignoring them for once. "Tonight, when I was on the hill, over at the old Milhouse place, in the forest. Sure as I'm sittin' here right now. I figured there was somethin' amiss 'cause somethin' just wasn't right."

The three amigos were all involved in black market transactions, all regularly drove home drunk as skunks, all cheated on their employers, but every night they sat at the bar and denounced lawbreakers and evinced great satisfaction when someone was brought to book. They saw themselves as law abiding citizens who would be doing a hell of a lot better thank you very much if it wasn't for the criminals who walked the streets unhindered. Charlie saw himself as the ultimate, law abiding, American Joe Blow and realised he had to act.

"I need to get me a phone."

**

Bilko and Regan slept at their desks. Bilko favoured an approach which involved him sitting squarely in his chair and leaning his head on his folded arms on the desktop. Although it was Regan's office, for his use alone, there was a second work desk and Bilko used it just as much as he used his own desk even although it was located only feet away in an adjoining office.

Regan's feet were crossed on his desk while his body was contained within a chair which leaned against the wall.

Montana sat at a desk in the open plan accommodation in the main office. He was reading a file through bleary eyes but would not permit himself to sleep whilst on duty.

The phone on Regan's desk rang, waking him and almost knocking him to the floor as he lost his balance reaching for the implement.

"Yeah! Regan."

The voice on the other end of the phone said that a news item on Streikker had brought in eighteen calls. Six recognised Streikker, alleging that they knew where he was holed up; the rest had claimed to have seen the red Ford. Regan and the desk officer discussed the various calls. Regan prioritised them in order of their probable importance and arranged that each be allocated a visit at some point in the next few hours.

"Bilko and me were goin' out to the Lattanzi ranch first thing so we can call in on that sighting near Williams; it's past the ranch a ways. Kill two birds with one stone."

Bilko had also been awakened by the telephone ringing and was pouring himself a coffee. "You want one, John?"

"Suppose so. We got a response to the news release on Streikker. I've put a chase on all of them, even though some of them are obvious false alarms. One of them might be genuine, so I've asked the Desk Sergeant to get them followed up right away while the world and its brother is still sleepin'. We've pulled a visit to a cabin, up in the Kaibab, near Williams. It's up by the Lattanzi ranch so I figured we should go over later on so's we can get there around dawn. By the time we've checked things out, it'll be just early enough to annoy your friend Liam Brannigan when we ask to speak with him at Boulder Ranch."

Bilko handed Regan the coffee he'd requested. "Do we take Montana?"

"Yeah, I suppose we should. He's a bit eager beaver but he's only tryin' to do his job."

"S'pose," said Bilko.

"Hey, cheer up. You get to fence with Brannigan later on. It'll make your day!"

**

Jackson's Jeep straddled the fork in the dirt road with its headlights illuminating the initial stretch of the twin tracks which ran in a 'Y' formation immediately in front of it. Lattanzi and Jackson had remained seated for the first fifteen minutes before emerging to parade in front of the lights in order to make clear their presence to anyone watching from their hide.

Both now leaned on the front fender of the Jeep and awaited contact if any was to be made.

"All I want to do is to drive up that track and take my daughter home."

"One way or another, Mr Lattanzi, you will take Susan home safe and sound … but later today … once we've taken her back or negotiated her return."

"You're very confident, Mr Jackson. I wish I was."

"Few things in this world can be guaranteed, I suppose, but I've not reached my middle years without developing a certain confidence in my ability. I'm not used to working with a partner but, given the prospect of this possibly ending up in negotiation, I'm actually quite glad you're on board."

"You flatter me, you really do. If you needed a Senate vote to go your way or wanted to develop an infrastructural project in the teeth of opposition, then I'd also have 'a certain confidence in my ability'. Faced with discussions which involve the safety of my daughter, I have no doubt other than that I will concede whatever is necessary. And if I know anything about the human condition, her captors will also be aware of this. A father's love for his daughter is pretty much universal." He paused and the conversation ebbed. "Have you got any kids, Mr Jackson?"

Jackson laughed. "You know that I am black, that I have the capacity to speak intelligently, that I am in my middle years and that I am six feet tall. You might discover that I have a proficiency with weapons and that I have other skills, but I don't expect that you will discover any more information about me. I will move on to other responsibilities in the fullness of time and although you and I have an agreement, and I know you will uphold this agreement, it would be unwise of me to provide you with information which is unnecessary. I don't mean to be discourteous …"

"Oh, you're not discourteous, but I suppose I just don't understand how you manage to live your life in compartments."

"Well perhaps I don't understand that either. I have an unusual job. As I believe you are aware, I am a detective, although I work only for one company, and I find it almost a natural state to lead my life as I do. Security permits a measure of comfort for me and I find it no hardship."

Both men continued their conversation and discussed Lattanzi's political career until Jackson terminated matters half an hour later by looking at his watch and pronouncing that it was time to go.

Jackson took the wheel again and drove the Jeep gingerly along the track leading initially away from the Milhouse cabin. He drove using only his sidelights and stopped on three occasions, to consult Lattanzi on which track to follow when he was presented with options.

After a slow drive of some forty minutes, Jackson came upon a further junction.

"This looks like where we get off."

Joe Lattanzi consulted the map one more time using the flashlight. "Yeah, this is the junction." He looked past Jackson into the darkness. "If we climb the hill to the left of us we should be able to view the cabin from above."

Jackson asked the question Lattanzi had been asking himself since first the phone call had been received from Wallis. "You able to handle this?"

"I won't pretend that I'm looking forward to it. I've not seen action since I was in the army. Didn't enjoy it then and I won't enjoy it now but that son of a bitch has my daughter and my young friend and that will see me through."

Jackson stepped out on to the track and lifted a small rucksack from behind his seat.

"Let's go!"

They both moved silently into the trees and began the steady climb which would take them to a position above the cabin. Under the canopy of the trees, much of the climb was undertaken in complete darkness. Occasionally, they would come across a clearing which permitted them to make easier progress as a result of the full moon.

Jackson's estimation of an hour's walk was short by fifty per cent. Lattanzi was breathing heavily and sweating profusely. *I'm really out of condition. Once this is all behind me, I'm going to have to take more exercise and eat less of Liz's good cooking.*

Up ahead, Jackson knelt on one knee and raised his left arm, noiselessly inviting Lattanzi to follow suit. He did so, grateful for the respite.

Beckoned forwards to join him some moments later, Lattanzi whispered. "What's up?"

"I can smell wood-smoke," replied Jackson in equally hushed tones.

Joe sniffed the night air. "You're right. We must be close to the cabin."

"From now on, no speech, no noise. Avoid breaking twigs if you possibly can. I'll take the lead and you follow about twenty yards behind. Just watch me for signals."

Joe nodded. "Okay."

Jackson moved off noiselessly into the gloom and, after crossing a clearing, disappeared into the forest again. Lattanzi shivered involuntarily, waited for a moment, and followed.

Some moments later he almost stumbled across Jackson in the darkness, kneeling at the base of a tree. Unable even to make out any of Jackson's features, Joe still attempted to convey a futile signal of apology by means of a facial gesture.

Jackson pulled at his sleeve and had him join him at ground level. Looking through the brush, Lattanzi could make out the flickering of a fire - the source of the wood-smoke. Nothing else could be seen. No movement was evident.

After what seemed like an age, but was only about five minutes, Jackson tugged Lattanzi's sleeve and they retreated back about a hundred yards into the forest.

Satisfied that they could communicate in whisper, Jackson said softly "I can only imagine that's the point man who's stationed above the cabin. What I propose is that we work our way around him until we reach a point where we can keep him and the cabin in view at sun-up. When we get there, I'm going to return and see if I can get closer to him in order to listen in to any communications with the cabin. It looks like they might be at least semi-professional," he conceded. "They've got a man on look out but he's in the wrong place and he lights a fire … Sloppy!"

Forty minutes saw them in position. They'd climbed rather higher than Jackson had anticipated initially but now had a good view of the campfire and the cabin. For all the relative isolation of the place, had they only but known, they were now standing in almost precisely the same place that Charlie Brookes had been standing at when he'd watched the activities of both camps earlier. Too dark yet for field glasses, the illuminations provided by the cabin lights and the campfire were all that was necessary to offer orientation.

"You'll be okay here?"

"I'll be fine."

"Good! Right, I'm going back to the camp fire. Don't leave your post. Just observe everything you can once dawn breaks." He took the pack from his shoulders. "There's a set of binoculars in here. I want to know how many people you spot. What they're doing. Where they're located. If anyone's hiding in the trees around the cabin. Do they look complacent? That sort of thing."

"No problem."

"I'll be back once I've checked on what's going on down at the camp fire. When I return, I'll do so silently. Don't shoot me. I'm on your side."

# Chapter Seventeen.


It was four thirty am. Montana sat in the rear of the unmarked police car stifling a yawn. Bilko spotted his weariness in the rear view mirror and couldn't resist a comment.

"Sure you're up to this trip, Agent Montana? I could pull into a motel and let you get some shuteye. If you desk boys see any action it sure tires you out!"

"I've not slept for almost twenty-four hours, Sergeant Bilk," said Montana wearily.

"Stevie-baby," mocked Bilko. "Us law enforcement boys regularly go without sleep for days at a time when we're chasing the bad guys, but you Bureau guys knock us into a cocked hat every time when it comes to administration and desk work."

"I know you're just trying to bait me, Sergeant, but I do have a measure of pride in the detailed forensic work and the huge amount of research which the FBI puts into its cases, sometimes. So I plead guilty to your charge."

Regan sat impassively as Bilko spurred the car on and gnawed away at Montana who merely returned inoffensive fire.

**

The three men sped through the grey light of sun-up, the headlights of the unmarked car still ablaze in order to accommodate the gloom. Montana had consulted the map in Regan's office and had announced that he had memorised the route. 'Not too difficult a task,' Bilko had announced, given the fact that this only involved four directional changes.

The first of these occurred outside Williams when the spacious Chrysler turned left into the labyrinth of

small roads and dirt tracks which meandered through the Kaibab Forest, and headed along the one which led to the cabin outside which Charlie Brookes had seen the red pick-up.

"Expect we'll find anything here, Lieutenant?"

"The call was left anonymously, so we've not been able to flesh out details but the report indicates three vehicles, one apparently like the one we're looking for and a bunch of people occupying a cabin and sitting around an open fire. We're going to wake up a hunting party, nothing's surer! If I'd've thought there might be a chance that this might be our quarry, I'd've had the place knee deep in cops."

**

Sitting on the front porch of the cabin, Edson watched as two squirrels scurried up and down the trunk of a tree. Fascinated by their industry, he'd been watching the squirrels for some time since the enlightening dawn permitted him to see more of his surroundings.

The throaty growl of a car crept into his conscienceness as it neared the cabin, fighting for Edson's attention with his nature watch. Eventually, Edson realised they were about to have company and withdrew with some haste into the cabin to alert a sleeping Wallis.

"Commander, we've got company. There's a car coming up the track."

**

Up on the hill, Sugar was also wakening her husband and Streikker at the sounds of activity on the road below them.

"There's a car headin' for the cabin." All three stepped the few paces up to the top of the hill where they could get a clear view of any vehicle arriving in the yard.

They watched noiselessly, transfixed by the activity as Bilko drew the unmarked police car to a halt on the tree lined track, a hundred yards from the yard outside the cabin where Montana had thought he had glimpsed red metal in the bushes and had urged him to pull up.

"Well, I don't see no red Ford pick up," said Bilko applying the hand brake.

"There might be somethin' in those bushes, though I didn't see a turn off," agreed Regan. "But there's certainly two vehicles up ahead at the farmhouse so apparently there's someone home."

"So why don't we go ask them if they've got a red Ford pick-up in their bedroom?"

"Let's do just that. Special Agent Montana, why don't you check those two vehicles. Visual check first, then call in their details, see if there's anything on them. Before that, step over to those bushes and see if there is a pick up sitting there. If there is, call in the details. Sergeant Bilk and I will go speak to the occupants while you do that. Is that straightforward?"

"Straightforward, Lieutenant!"

Montana stepped out of the Chrysler and headed towards the bushes. Bilko and Regan drove on towards the cabin and parked at the neck of the clearing which acted in the past as a turning circle for farm traffic.**

The Nevada *Posse* watched from the hilltop while the Chrysler pulled up at the cabin but were unaware of any activity around the pick-up. They observed Bilko and Regan emerge from the car.

"Is that taller guy Joe Lattanzi?" asked Sugar.

"Can't make him out from here," responded Streikker. "If it was, I could probably get a clear shot in from here."

"We're too far away. Shootin' that Rabbi was like shootin' fish in a barrel compared with this. You couldn't guarantee a kill shot and we'd have them people in the cabin up here after us in minutes." Kane was still annoyed at losing the opportunity of assassinating the Rabbi.

"The Lord watches over me. He would not have me mess up one of His missions."

**

Inside the cabin, Wallis had hurriedly had Burring take Liam and Susan into one of the back rooms. "Look after them real careful. Lattanzi is earlier than I thought he'd be." He turned his attention to Tyler. "There should be no violence here. When he comes to the door, just bring him in and search him for weapons and electronics. Edson, you take the window and keep lookin' case he's got people comin' after him."

Edson stepped up to the window and twitched back the curtain.

"Shit, there's two of them comin' out the car."

"They armed?" asked Wallis, suddenly concerned.

"No sir, they don't appear to be."

"Tyler! Behind the door." Wallis gestured his instructions and Tyler responded immediately.

Moments later, Bilko knocked on the door. "Anyone home? It's the police!"

Wallis and Tyler looked at one another. This wasn't part of the plan.

*Well, we're in now,* thought Wallis. He swallowed hard. "Come on in. Door's open!"

Bilko opened the door and entered with Regan close behind him, both men trying to accustom themselves to the gloom as a consequence of Tyler having extinguished the lights moments earlier.

"Well, we sure as hell ain't gonna find out what's goin' on if we stay up here on the hill, Sugar. We should get down there." Streikker was eager for action.

"We go when I say we go, Ed. We don't know if Lattanzi's there. We just know his assistant's there. We got to remember, this is not our mission. This is a distraction. I'm only prepared to go in there if I figure we can take out that witness, escape injury to ourselves and get the hell out of here so we can focus on getting Lattanzi. If he *is* in there it looks like he's got six people guardin' him plus his assistant now those other two have arrived. They don't call these things 'safe houses' for nothin'."

"Sure is obvious that guy can't pick *you* out of a line up, Sugar."

"You're talkin' out of line, Streikker. Sugar's right."

"Don't let's get fractious boys. Remember, we're the Nevada Posse Commitatus and we're here for a purpose. We'll move closer but we do not show ourselves until we are agreed that we can deal with things here and fulfil our mission. Let's get organised and move on down to that scrub behind the barn. We should be able to see what's going on from there a mite clearer without they see us."

**

"I'd appreciate it if you men would just raise your hands and take care not to make me pull this trigger."

Wallis levelled his rifle at Bilko's chest. "Tyler, check these men for arms, electronics and identification in that order. Edson, keep them covered till I read what their papers say."

Edson complied.

After searching the two police officers, Tyler handed two pistols to Edson who stuck them in his waistband. "No wires," said Tyler handing wallets and other items to Wallis who inspected them.

"Lieutenant John Regan. Las Vegas Police." He threw the badge and ID on the table. "And Sergeant Donald Bilk, also a law enforcement man. Well, boys what call you got comin' all the way out here?"

"I'm goin' to lower my arms, mister, but don't you go shootin' that rifle. We're unarmed and, so far, we don't have a problem." Bilko was well known for his hot temper but Regan and others who had worked with him were also aware of his calm under duress. Bilko looked round at the three gunmen to ensure that no one looked crazy enough to put a bullet in him and slowly lowered his arms to his side. "You guys sure are careful. But I guess I gotta respect that. You won't get many visitors up here."

"Well, why don't you tell us why you're up here, Sergeant?"

"Just clean got lost."

"Normally I am the most even tempered of men, Sergeant, but my people here get real annoyed when someone starts bullshittin' them." He directed his gaze to Regan. "You boys are in serious trouble, so why don't you tell it like it is, Lieutenant?"

"My Sergeant isn't bullshitting you, sir. Fact of the matter is that we were told that there was some kids rampagin' around the forest here firin' off guns and drinkin' hard liquor. But that was in another part of the forest, some way from here and we just got lost lookin' for the area."

"A Lieutenant and a Sergeant goin' out lookin' for some kids at sun-up? A job an ordinary patrolman would do? I don't think so. I just don't think so." He thought for a moment. "You got any other people comin' out here?"

"No, sir. You might think it odd, but we really are lookin' for some minors and you obviously ain't them."

"Obviously not, Lieutenant…" Wallis made his mind up and decided upon decisive action. They were in too far now. "Tyler, use their cuffs. Immobilise them and take them in to the back room with the others but make sure they're also tied to a chair or somethin', I don't want them messin' us around.

**

Montana had found the pick-up. It wasn't too difficult as it wasn't really hidden, just obscured by the trees and the bushes at the side of the road. *Why'd they run it off the road, though?* He pondered. There's more than enough space around the place. He approached the vehicle. Certainly fits the description. Including the damaged wheel arch.

Inside the Ford, Montana could see some luggage but nothing suspicious. In its rear was a tarpaulin which, once it was pulled back, revealed grass cutting equipment. Again, nothing suspicious. A farm vehicle which appeared to be used for farm purposes.

*Guess I'll check the other cars*, he decided.

Now at the passenger's side, he decided to test the door as a precursor to leaving. It opened, retaining his interest for a moment longer. Looking around the glove compartment casually, he turned over a piece of paper and felt the shock of an adrenaline start as he appreciated its significance.

Leaning back out of the Ford, he lowered himself on to one knee and looked around. He unholstered his gun and listened. Nothing stirred. Reassured, he hurried, bent double to a thick knot of bushes and satisfied that he was hidden from view, inspected the receipt he'd taken from the passenger's seat - which confirmed the details of a stay at the Golden Nugget Motel, Searchlight, Nevada.

**

Joe Lattanzi had been kept awake by the occasional mosquito and his anxiety over the fate of his daughter and Liam. From his watch up on the hill, he'd witnessed the appearance of the car and had seen three people appear on the hill below; seen them watch the two men enter the cabin and had observed them collect their gear and set off in what appeared to be the direction of the house below.

The sun was up now and Joe felt some warmth returning to his bones. The morning was still and airless, the only sound an occasional chirp or whistle. He took out the pistol given him by Jackson and felt for the reassuring bulge in his hip pocket where he'd hidden the second gun. He felt the weight of the larger gun in his hand and felt fear. Not since his brief service as a Marine had he had to deal with violence on a personal basis. People close to him might lose their lives in the next few hours.

He thought of his own mortality. He didn't want to die. He loved his wife and his daughter, his many friends. He was still young, certainly young enough to be spared another ten or fifteen years and he'd always wanted to be a grandfather. He'd wanted that. Now all of that was under threat. Everything could be decided by his actions in the next hour or so.

"Hope I didn't wake you."

Lattanzi gasped out loud as Jackson placed his hand on his shoulder. "You can probably put that gun away just now. We won't be needing it for a while."

"Jackson, you nearly scared the bejeesus out of me there."

"Sorry about that."

"Listen, Mr Jackson, I've been thinking …."

"I anticipated you would. It's one thing planning an event in the heat of emotion, quite another when you're facing its reality."

"Whatever action we take must be based on the least loss of life and must guarantee the safety of my daughter. I feel we should negotiate first and see how that goes. I have no trouble denouncing gun control if that's what it takes to save my daughter and Liam."

"That was always going to be an option once we'd assessed the situation, or indeed been forced into it had we been captured. However, I now fear we have to foreclose on that approach."

Jackson came around and sat in front of Lattanzi to add emphasis to his next comments. "From what I could overhear from the group on the hill, we're dealing with *Posse Commitatus*, the right wing group. They see their task as assassinating one Senator Joe Lattanzi. They are also looking to shoot Liam as he appears to have witnessed a crime they committed."

"The airport murders!"

"Quite! And they also appear to be responsible for the death of Rabbi Goldstein."

"You found out all that?" asked Joe incredulously.

"It's simply quite amazing what you can find out when people don't know you're listening. But it changes things." Jackson looked Lattanzi in the eye and entered a new note of seriousness. "We now know that Susan and Liam are being held by what appears to be four men. *Posse Commitatus* think you might be among them. I presume they were aware of your car's registration and merely followed it here. The Nevada *Posse* is intent upon killing both you and Liam. We know them already to be murderers. If they are in a position to shoot Liam because he was a witness to their crimes at the airport, they will certainly not hesitate to shoot your daughter who would almost certainly be a witness to Liam's death."

"Dear God, this is a nightmare. And why in hell would anyone want to kill me? And why would I have attracted the attention of *Posse Commitatus*?"

Who knows, but we now have little option. Two additional men arrived by car. They'll possibly be a relief shift but they might just be strengthening the force. That makes it a total of six men guarding Susan and Liam and three people from *Posse Commitatus*, one of them a woman, looking to shoot you and Liam. Not good odds."

"Impossible odds. We're going to need to get police help."

"I do not work with police, Mr Lattanzi, and I insist that we keep to our arrangement. Once the operation is underway, I make all the decisions. Now, I know that you must be apprehensive, but I am not. I know my job and I'm quite aware of the crucial importance you place on safeguarding your daughter. That will be complied with as it was part of the original bargain, but so was accepting my authority in these matters."

Joe nodded resignedly. "Very well."

"Now, it would be foolish to attempt to take all of these people head on so we must use intelligence and guile. The three who camped on the hill last night are headed on down to the barn as we speak so we must move soon. They see the six inside as adversaries, so presumably they are not *Posse Commitatus*. They believe them to be protecting Liam and possibly you, so we might use that to our advantage. I'll need to depend …."

The words froze in Jackson's mouth as the cabin door opened and a man strode across the yard towards the large Chrysler parked at its entrance.

"Pass me those glasses please."

Jackson held the binoculars to his eyes and focused on the armed man. He watched him level his revolver at the car. Two shots rang out as Tyler put a bullet in each of the two front tyres of the unmarked police car. That done, he walked around the car and opened the door. Reaching in, he grasped some wiring and wrenched the car radio from its mounting.

"Now, what on earth is going on down there?" Jackson was puzzled. "They appear to have disabled the car which just drove up and removed a radio or something. It's unlikely to have been a receiver so it must have been a transmitter. Or both. Now why would they do that?" He exchanged glances with Lattanzi. "We'd better get down there. This thing gets more curious by the minute."

**

Liam and Bilko looked at one another in disbelief. Each began mouthing the words "*What are you…*" in bewildered unison and stopped. Bilko looked uncomfortable, his hands cuffed behind his back, standing in front of an erstwhile verbal sparring partner but Liam didn't take advantage. Regan broke the silence.

"What are you and the young lady doing here?"

Susan answered for Liam. "We're being held here against our will by four men with guns and body odour. Who are you?"

"We're police officers, ma'am. Looks like we're in the same situation as yourselves."

Burring walked to the door, uncertain of his response to the conversation which was taking place.

"Commander, these folks are talkin' with each other. Do I let them?"

Wallis had gathered himself. "'Less they're bad-mouthin' the Lord or the flag."

Burring sat on a chair by the door as Liam and Susan recounted their mishaps.

"What about you two?" asked Liam.

Bilko answered quickly. "We just stumbled across these boys." He turned to Burring in order to change the subject. "You playin' with the big boys now, mister? I just hope you know what's goin' on here. So far you don't have a problem. You've just sat in here quiet like. You've not pointed that gun of yours at anyone. You can still step aside from all this. Matter of fact, so can your buddies 'cause me and the Lieutenant here, we're sensible people, we understand that deals have to be done sometimes. What d'you figure, think maybe your boss is sensible people?"

Burring looked ambivalent but his Militia background stood him in good stead. There was no prospect of betrayal. "Listen, mister, we didn't figure on there bein' no cops involved."

"Yeah, but you see, there *are* cops involved. What is it you boys want? Maybe we can help you."

Burring was a hard man, comfortable in the wilds, able to hold his own in a bar, at ease with weapons. At root, however, he was just an unemployed farm labourer, rapidly finding himself out of his depth. He stood up and backed up to the door. "Edson, get in here awhile, I need to talk to the Commander."

# Chapter Eighteen

Liz Lattanzi rubbed her bleary eyes and sat up yawning and stretching stiffly on the large armchair in her lounge. At the other side of the coffee table from her on a second armchair slept Jimmy St James. Liz remembered her predicament and moaned, covering her face with her hands, shutting out an inexplicably wicked world. Last night had been spent talking, and talking, and talking some more, in an attempt to come to terms with the trauma which surrounded her. Jimmy was a good friend. He'd listened and offered wise counsel and comfort. Liz knew that Jimmy was not only involved with Joe in business and legal dealings but suspected that he would be aware of, if not involved in Joe's 'secret life.'

At one point in the wee small hours, Jimmy had advised her to take a sleeping tablet and get some sleep and that he would wake her up if there was any news. Liz had refused, insisting that she wouldn't go to sleep until her husband and daughter were sleeping safely under the same roof. Sleep had overtaken her shortly afterwards.

A shower seemed like a good idea. Liz had only a hazy idea of when she'd fallen asleep but it hadn't been sufficient. A shower would refresh and awaken her. She'd need to be on her mettle to handle what this day might bring. She left Jimmy sleeping and, checking to ensure that the jeep hadn't returned in the early hours and that Joe and Susan hadn't disturbed her out of consideration for her, went upstairs.

Montana had skirted around the thick foliage which grew all around the cabin. He remained at some distance from the centre of activity, following the perimeter of the yard some twenty yards into the forest until he arrived at a point where he could glimpse the front of the building. He was becoming increasingly concerned about the non-re-appearance of Bilko and Regan when the door opened and a man with a rifle stepped out and walked outwith his line of vision. Moments later two shots rang out and the man reappeared and went back into the house.

Montana moved right and crawled underneath some bushes. He cursed the Bureau's insistence on its officers wearing sober suits, collars and ties. Fine for the deskwork Bilko was ribbing him about earlier but hardly appropriate for duties which involved scrabbling about in dusty undergrowth. He still didn't have enough information on which to act so, after waiting for a few minutes, he began slowly to make his way back around towards the police car, unaware that the radio he sought had already been destroyed by Tyler.

**

Wallis had joined the hostages in the rear room, leaving Tyler and Edson on window duty. Burring stood in the doorframe, glad that his boss had taken over the verbal tasks associated with guarding the prisoners, and acting as a conduit between his Commander and his sentries.

Susan had explained their plight further to the two police officers and had expressed her concern for her father. "I understand you're expecting Miss Lattanzi's father," said Regan to Wallis.

"Well, we were expectin' him any time now, so we could discuss the retraction he's goin' to make on television 'bout gun control. But I guess he did what we told him he wasn't to do, which was to involve the police. He shouldn't've done that 'cause now we got ourselves a situation."

"And how are we goin' to get all of us *out* of this situation?" asked Bilko.

"Ain't quite figured that out yet."

"If you just hand over your arms, no one gets hurt and you guys walk away from this with a slap on the wrists, most probable."

Wallis laughed. "Problem is, you see, we're kinda *in* this situation because we wouldn't hand over our arms. Can't see us doin' that now." He fell into a silence. "Suppose you've got this place surrounded?"

Suddenly realising their unexpected tactical advantage, Regan allowed the presumption to stand and returned to their line on securing a resolution to the problem without gunplay. "You wouldn't imagine that we'd just walk in here without figuring that we'd walk back out," asked Regan rhetorically before continuing. "Look, mister, I know that you have a beef about gun control. Lots of honest, decent Americans have, but you are not going to progress your point of view by having a shoot out here. This is only going to end one way and that's by all of us walking out of here. You can't win and you know that."

Wallis looked downwards and tapped the point of his rifle on his boot while he thought through his options. Eventually he spoke. "Lieutenant, I used to be a Sheriff myself. Thirty years on the job over in Twin Falls, and I appreciate what you're sayin'. But I believe our country is in peril and I have vowed to sacrifice my life, or what's left of it, to bring it back from the brink. People over in Twin Falls still call me Sheriff and I'm proud of that. I'm no bloodthirsty criminal. So if you boys hadn't turned up we'd have taken care of our business with Mr Lattanzi and the media and everyone here could've gone home."

"But we *did* turn up," said Bilko.

"So you did. So you did. Yes, sir. So you did." Wallis continued to think. After a few moments he looked up and sighed resignedly. "Maybe *I* gotta make Lattanzi's speech for him."

"I could arrange that," said Regan, sensing an end in sight.

"I guess you could, at that."

Standing at one of the front windows, Tyler opened the curtains to let in the morning light. Edson followed suit at the other and then began to open the window to permit fresh air to replace the stale atmosphere within the cabin.

Outside, lying prone in the brush at the far end of the yard next to the two Kanes, Streikker had Edson in his rifle sights as he struggled with a window catch which hadn't been used since the previous owner had left nine years earlier.

Streikker was a soldier of the Lord. He lived his life in a world that he knew was corrupt and evil. Fortunately for him, he lived also in the knowledge that God spoke quietly to him, helping him understand the frailties and wickedness that governed men's behaviour. He was also aware that the Lord had chosen him to carry out His will in damning those who flouted His authority and, although he acknowledged the position of Sugar in leading the group of individuals who worked alongside him to do God's bidding, he knew deep within himself that they were not chosen as he was - they were not guided by the hand of God as he was. *My God is a vengeful God,* thought Streikker as he squeezed the trigger.

Edson reeled back in pain as the bullet tore at his shoulder. Tyler dropped to one knee and loosed off a couple of shots at no one in particular, shouting to Wallis that they had incoming fire.

Wallis was quite aware of the shots that had been fired as all in the back room had ducked automatically at the first crack of Streikker's rifle. He was angry now. "Your people must be crazy, startin' a fire fight like this. Now I'm tellin' you, this was *not* necessary!"

Bilko and Regan looked at one another both thinking the same thing. *Has Montana taken leave of his senses?*

**

Montana had not managed to make his way back to the police car. Moving very deliberately, he had covered only a short distance when he heard the gunshots. Freezing where he lay, he calculated that the initial shot came from only about twenty yards on the other side of the police car.

**

Sugar was livid. "What in God's name did you do that for, Streikker?"

Her husband was equally furious. "You dumb sonovabitch! You're going to get us all killed dead. I ought to shoot you right now."

"We have God on our side. We shall prevail."

"We'd better have God on our side, you dumb ass, or we're gonna get shot up bad," said Kane, still in a rage.

"They can't know how many people we got out here so they'll be reluctant to come after us. Best thing we can do is keep them pinned down till we can work out whether to go in after Lattanzi and Brannigan."

She thought further. "Okay, Streikker, we just got involved, though we're gonna talk about this if we ever get outa here. You keep them occupied. Just an occasional shot if you see a target. Matt, you and me better cover the road leadin' in here. For all we know, there's a squad of

Federal Marshals heading up the track. These boys have got to be in touch with their people so we need a quick assessment. Either we take the pick-up and get the hell outa this place or we go in."

"I figure we go in, Sugar. Ain't no way back now." Streikker had had his instructions from a higher authority.

**

Montana heard another shot from up ahead as Streikker set to his task of sniping at the occupants of the cabin. There was no way he could calculate what was going on. All he could tell was that his two colleagues were in a ranch house apparently occupied by the people they were looking for. But who in hell could be shooting at them from outside the cabin?

He lay still, his mind racing. A twig snapped behind him and he half turned to investigate the noise but before his head had pivoted more that an inch he slumped into unconsciousness as the butt of a pistol rendered him limp on the ground.

**

Susan and Liam had not been physically restrained when they'd been moved through to the back room. Wallis was now more alarmed and had ordered Burring to tie the legs of the handcuffed police officers to their chairs and to rope the wrists of Susan and Liam.

"What I told you in the back of the car still holds good mister," said Liam as Burring tied a cord around his wrists. "I swear by all that's holy that if any one of you harms this lady, I'll follow you to your grave and, if you're not already in it, I'll see to it that you're buried alive if necessary."

Burring was by now operating at a high level of anxiety. He drew back his right arm and swung it backhanded across Liam's face, smashing his pistol into the side of his jaw and sending him sprawling unconscious on to the bed, on whose edge he and Susan had been sitting.

Susan cried out in horror, as the violence she'd been praying wouldn't happen began.

"Liam!"

"Leave him alone, lady. He's got a mouth that needs shuttin'. Give me your wrists over here."

Susan punched tearfully and ineffectively as Burring wrestled her for a moment before finally ending her unequal resistance by slapping her and tying her wrists behind her back.

Both she and Liam now lay dazed on the bed as Burring warned all of them as to the consequences of any further defiance. "This has all gone too far now so be aware. I will shoot any one of you who so much as moves an inch." He moved to the door-frame as another rifle shot from Streikker crashed through another pane of glass and splintered a wooden beam above their heads.

Tyler had located the area from which the shots were being fired, and was returning bullet for bullet.

Wallis issued instructions. "Burring, get on out to the back of the cabin and take a look. I want to know if they've got people out there. We've got a cliff face on one side and a thousand feet drop on the other. The only way they can pin us down is to have come a long way round to cover the rear."

Another volley of fire crashed into the front room of the cabin, missing its occupants as Kane joined Streikker in the attack.

Burring moved through to the rear, checking on the four prisoners before edging the rear door open slightly and scanning the forest hillside which, beyond the back yard, stretched for miles, as the mountain and the gorge parted company to provide for another neck of the substantial pine forest which covered the more than a million square acres around the cabin.

He looked back into the cabin where Wallis, Edson and Tyler were all kneeling around the front windows looking for further clues as to the number and position of their assailants. He made his mind up. Although there was no indication of any people out back, there could easily be some one hiding in the skirt of the pine trees. Shots continued to be traded at the front as Burring stepped into the back room and pulled Susan roughly to her feet.

"You come with me."

Still shocked and dazed, Susan could offer little resistance.

Bilko growled at the man from his chair. "You be careful with her, son."

Burring ignored him and, making sure his colleagues were still occupied by the rifle shots at the front, slipped out the back door using Susan as a shield, just in case.

# Chapter Nineteen


Jackson's muscular build was tested as he lifted the unconscious Montana's dead weight atop his broad shoulders. Crouching, he looked around to confirm his actions had not been observed then carried him the fifty yards back into the forest where he laid him at the feet of Joe Lattanzi.

"Search him and let's see who we're dealing with," said Jackson.

Both men patted him down and inspected the contents of his pockets.

"Oh my God, he's FBI," said Lattanzi.

"Check the FBI identification with his credit cards and anything else he's got."

"His name's Steven Montana, he's a Special Agent," said Lattanzi reading the ID. He rolled Montana over and checked his likeness against his FBI photograph. "His photograph matches. So does his Visa card."

Jackson had earlier taken Montana's pistol and put it in his waistband. "Okay, let's wake him up if we can and see if he can throw any light on what's going on."

"Well, let's hurry up about it. There are bullets flying around over there and my daughter's inside that cabin."

Jackson slapped Montana gently on his face inviting him to regain consciousness. After a few moments, he opened his eyes, blinked at the light and grimaced at his pain. His hand reached to the back of his head.

"Did you guys do this?"

"Who *are* you?" asked Jackson.

"I'm Special Agent Steve Montana, FBI."

What are you doing here?"

"I guess I should be asking that question of you."

"We don't have much time, Mr Montana. You will notice that we have the edge on you at the moment. Now why were you armed and hiding in the bushes? Who is involved in the shooting at the house in the clearing?"

Joe Lattanzi's patience had run out. "My daughter's in that building. I'm a retired Senator and if you're who you say you are, we need your help."

"Senator who?"

"Senator Joseph Lattanzi."

"Jeez, so you are. I recognise you from television." Montana's attitude changed although he still wondered why a retired US Senator had clubbed him unconscious. "Two police officers have entered the farm house to interview people I now suspect of being involved in shootings. I was checking a pick-up when the shooting started so I've no idea how it started or who's involved."

"Might these earlier shootings have taken place at the airport?"

Montana's suspicions were aroused. "What makes you think that?"

Lattanzi intervened. "Stop behaving like an FBI Agent until you can assist us practically. Now we're the good guys here. Do you have other colleagues with you?"

"Just the two in the cabin."

Jackson took control. "Okay, the people who are shooting at those in the cabin appear to be responsible for the airport shootings and the death of the Rabbi in Vegas. They seem also to be members of the Nevada *Posse Commitatus* and currently threaten the life of Mr Lattanzi's daughter and her friend Liam Brannigan who witnessed the murders. We must intervene to put an end to that threat. Do you agree, Mr Montana?"

"That seems to be about right. How do you know they're from the *Posse*?"

"I'll tell you later. Until this action finishes, you will work under my command. Do you agree, Mr Montana?"

"The hell I do. I work for the FBI."

"I hold all the aces, including your life and death. I'm a professional with more experience and ability than you or anyone you've ever worked with and you will take my instructions without question, or I'll leave you here unable to play the part your limited training prepared you for."

Montana pursed his lips, impressed by Jackson's businesslike approach.

"You better be as good as you say you are."

"I am. Do you agree, Mr Montana?"

"All right."

"Then let's get you to your feet and we'll go over and deal with the *Posse*."

Montana rose, still groggy. "If we can make it to the unmarked police car at the edge of the yard we can use the two way radio to get some more people out here."

"Too late, they've shot out the tyres and ripped out the radio."

"Then I guess it's down to us," said Montana, still rubbing the back of his head.

"Our first and prime task is to save Mr Lattanzi's daughter from harm. Nothing else will stand in the way of that objective."

"If these people were involved in the airport killings I'll want to take them alive, and I don't want to contaminate evidence, so let's be careful about that."

"I believe I've made myself clear, Mr Montana. Susan Lattanzi comes first. You will proceed on that basis. If I believe you to imperil that objective, I will shoot you."

"Who the hell *are* you?"

Sporadic shooting could still be heard at the cabin. Joe Lattanzi's patience snapped.

"Will you two get moving? The last thing we need is the perfect plan and no survivors."

Jackson nodded. "Let's go."

Burring threw Susan to the ground, irritated by her constant resistance as he led her into the forest.

"Listen, lady, if I need to shoot you dead, I *will* shoot you dead. Now shut up and, if you're good, I just might turn you loose in the forest for the critters to eat once I'm out of trouble."

"Why are you doing this?"

"Like I said, lady, you don't talk, you don't mess with me and you don't ask me no questions. Maybe you'll live."

He pulled Susan up and gestured that they continue along a path they'd been following since leaving the rear of the cabin. Behind them they could still hear the intermittent shots of the combatants.

**

Sugar had made her mind up. "Okay. Let's move in. We finish this quick. Our targets are Brannigan and Lattanzi but we probably don't want to leave any other witnesses. Matt, you move around left, Ed, go right. Did you hit anyone with your first shot?"

"I never miss, Sugar."

"Then let's go. No more shootin' until I fire, then we move in close."

**

Wallis was furious as Bilko confirmed that Burring had disappeared with Susan.

"I swear to Christ that I'll shoot that sonovabitch dead when I get him. All that goddamn Militia trainin' and he buckles as soon as someone takes a pop at us." He returned to the front room. "Edson, how's your shoulder?"

"It's fine sir. Just a flesh wound. But it's bleeding kinda bad."

"Okay, just keep pressure on the wound. Tell me if it's causin' you problems, but let's keep our eyes open. They've gone kinda quiet now but pay attention. They could just be re-positionin'."

Liam regained consciousness with a groan and levered himself on to his shoulder. "These boys are not takin' prisoners." He looked around. "Where's Susan?"

"The big guy's taken her as a hostage, it looks like," said Bilko. "Their boss was none too happy."

"Is everyone still firing at each other?" asked Liam as he rolled from the bed and on to his feet.

"It's gone quiet for the time bein', but they're still tradin' shots."

Liam looked out of the door and saw that the three Idaho Militiamen were still kneeling at the windows, intent on guarding their front. "Sergeant Bilk, I'll back up to you and you can untie my hands."

"You'll just get yourself in trouble."

"Help him out, Don," encouraged his Lieutenant. "We're not goin' to accomplish much if we're all trussed up."

Bilko sighed and lifted his chin, inviting Liam to come on over. Gingerly, Liam backed up to Bilko who fumbled for what seemed like an eternity with his bonds. Eventually, Liam was free. He rubbed his wrists. "Now which way did that guy take Susan?"

"We couldn't see. Out back. Now untie our legs."

"You'll just get yourself in trouble," said Liam as he slipped from the room and set off across the yard and along the only track he could see which led into the forest from the cabin.

Bilko looked at Regan. "You *do* know he's goin' to get himself killed."

**

Streikker was a happy man. He was doing God's will.

Rather than take up a position to the right of the house as Sugar had ordered, he crawled back to the pick-up and removed a bottle of Kool-Aid that he'd filled earlier with petrol. Pausing further to stuff a soaked rag inside its neck, he returned to the edge of the yard.

Sugar still hadn't given any signal but that was because the Lord didn't speak through her. *He speaks through me*, thought Streikker, and he wants those sinners to burn in Hell.

He ignited the rag with a match and, closing his eyes tight for a second in obeisance to the Lord, he stood up without fear of taking a bullet, and threw the device at the front door.

The bottle tracked a perfect parabola, tracing a flaming arc through the air before exploding on the porch, engulfing the wooden doorway in a ball of fire and sending the three Militiamen spinning backwards into the room.

"They're trying to burn us out," shouted Wallis. "Fall back to the rear room."

Streikker walked towards the front door firing his rifle in time with each footstep, making no attempt to protect himself from any return fire.

Sugar had lost patience with Streikker but decided that the battle had now been joined irrevocably and that she'd better get involved. She opened up on the front door area and waved to her husband to move in.

"Shit, there's hundreds of them out there," said Tyler, estimating from the internal hallway and becoming apprehensive.

"Let's go. Leave the prisoners. Move out into the forest."

All three departed the house, leaving the inflagration to the immobilised police officers and the incoming Nevada *Posse*, firing at the doorway they'd just left to give them the time they needed to reach the cover of the trees.

Sugar arrived at the porch simultaneously with her husband who restrained Streikker from attempting to step into the blaze.

"Streikker, be careful. We don't know what's in there."

Streikker looked at his fellow *Posse* member but was drawn back to his version of reality.

He smiled. "The Lord is watching over me. Let's go." He stepped into the flames firing his rifle without reply. Matt Kane groaned and followed, as did Sugar.

The flames were still contained within the porch area as Sugar took stock. Streikker had stopped firing and Matt was checking the rooms. He found the two officers handcuffed and tied to their chairs.

"In here, Sugar."

Sugar stepped beyond her husband and saw Bilko and Regan. "Supposin' you tell us right now who you are and what in hell you're doin' here."

"We're both police officers held prisoner," said Bilko.

"Matt, check their ID."

Kane searched their pockets, finding nothing until Regan advised him of their ID wallets which still lay in the front room. Streikker guarded the room door, more possessed of himself now. "They're cops all right."

Sugar assessed the situation quickly. "They ain't goin' nowhere. Leave them here. We got work to do. We'll come back and get them once we've finished if the fire doesn't get them first."

So saying, she made to go out the back door but stumbled over Streikker who lay in a heap behind her, a bullet lodged in his gut, courtesy of the retreating Militia.

"Ed! You been shot?"

The blood seeping through his clothing provided her with all the information she needed.

Streikker clutched his stomach and got to his knees before grimacing and standing up. "It's okay, Sugar, they can't kill me. I'll be all right." He stepped unsteadily towards the back door and recommenced his pursuit of the Devil's disciples. Sugar looked at her husband with a look which said '*he ain't gonna make it*', and followed him out of the door.

Matt Kane hesitated then turned back to speak to Bilko and Regan.

"Who are those people who just left the house? Was one of them Senator Joseph Lattanzi?"

Both officers looked puzzled. "Who the hell are you?" asked Bilko.

"Answer my goddamn question, damn it, or I'll shoot you dead right now and leave you to burn."

"So you're not cops, then?" said Bilko sarcastically.

"Don't push me, mister."

**

Jackson, Lattanzi and Montana had observed the *Posse* rush on the building and had followed in hard on their heels at Lattanzi's insistent urging. Montana's FBI training infuriated Jackson, who was intent upon a speedy, silent entry.

"FBI. Put down your weapons," bawled Montana.

Angry as Jackson was, he contained himself and dived through the flames, promising himself he would take care of Montana later. Joe Lattanzi came in at his heels, only to be felled by a loose shot from Sugar Kane as she exited the building. He fell back into the flames clutching his thigh.

Jackson's instincts told him to follow the source of the shot but his professionalism had him return to rescue Joe. Montana entered the room, pistol held in the proper manner - each hand supporting the other, the barrel pointing to the ceiling.

He realised Lattanzi had been downed and helped Jackson raise him to his feet.

"I've been shot in the thigh but I don't think it's hit a bone."

"You're bleeding quite badly. Let's get out of this room."

Jackson left Montana to assist Lattanzi and checked out the building. He noticed the two officers but visited the other rooms in the house wordlessly before returning to them.

"Tell me who you are."

"I'm gettin' *real* tired of this," said a now irritated Bilko.

"We're police officers," said Regan, trying not to annoy another heavily armed man unnecessarily. "Our ID's on the floor." He nodded at the badges and warrant cards that lay on the floor where Kane had thrown them.

Jackson checked them and nodded his approval. "We'll get you out of these chairs and out of here. He set to the leg bonds by slashing them with a razor sharp hunting knife he took from a sheath attached to his belt. "Have you got the keys for these handcuffs?"

Bilko was beside himself with rage. "They've taken the keys with them."

"Okay, outside. We've an injured man. He'll stay with you for the moment. Now was Susan Lattanzi with you? Is she hurt? Where is she now?"

"She was okay when she left ten minutes ago. Brannigan's gone after her but he's unarmed and that last group appear to have gone after everyone."

Jackson acknowledged the information. "You guys stay here with Senator Lattanzi. I'm going after the bad guys."

Montana was listening to the conversation. "We're both going after them."

Jackson re-focused his gaze. "I don't work with officers of the law."

Montana persisted. "You do now!"

# Chapter Twenty

"Don't use the track, keep within the trees," shouted Wallis to Edson and an onrushing Tyler. "Brannigan and Lattanzi's kid are up ahead somewhere. We don't need them no more, but if you meet up with that sonovabitch Burring, shoot him dead for desertion. Now split up. If we make it out of this, we make our own way back to Twin Falls."

"I need medical attention, Sheriff. I'm losin' a lot of blood."

Wallis looked at Edson's arm. "Keep pressure on the wound. You'll be okay. Now let's get the hell outa here."

All three disappeared into the cover of the pines.

**

Up ahead, Burring led a still recalcitrant Susan by the wrist, gripping it in such a way as to cause her pain if she resisted overmuch. The path was fairly well defined, obviously used in the past as a route through the forest. It wasn't wide enough for a firebreak. Susan continued to complain sporadically and frequently cried out in pain as Burring dragged her ever deeper into the forest. Every so often, he would stop and utter threats and imprecations demanding that she quieten down which she did, albeit temporarily.

Liam wasn't much of an athlete but moved along the forest trail much faster than Burring could drag Susan. He cursed his lack of foresight in not bringing a weapon. *I don't know if I could use it, but that guy wouldn't know that,* he mused.

Much of the path was grassed but every so often it was dry and dusty. In one such stretch, he knelt down and looked at a confusion of footprints where Susan had had one of her contumacious exchanges with Burring. There in the dust he could see quite clearly the large army boot impression made by Burring and the more petit mark made by Susan's heel. *There must be Apache blood coursing through my Irish veins*, he told himself, spurring himself on to greater effort.

**

Streikker was still on a higher plane as he trudged along the path, every step spilling blood. Sugar and Matt Kane had opted to head for the more reassuring cover of the trees and had kept together, silently picking their way through the low branches, sacrificing speed for safety.

**

By now the entire cabin was ablaze, endangering the tinder dry forest as sparks flew and smoke carried small pieces of red hot ash into the air. Bilko and Regan, although mobile, couldn't do much to help Joe Lattanzi as their hands were still pinned securely behind their backs.

"Put your arm around me sir. We'll step over to the edge of the clearing."

Lattanzi complied and the three men made their way to the relative safety of the tree line.

Lattanzi made to sit down.

"Sir," said Regan, "a few more paces. Some of those people might return. We'd be safer if we were out of sight. Let's move into the trees a little."

Lattanzi nodded and allowed himself to be supported by the policemen into the pines.

**

Liam stopped dead in his tracks in order to confirm his hearing. At first, all he could hear was the thumping of his heartbeat. Then, not too far away, Susan's voice. "You big ape! When Liam catches up with you you're finished. He's a karate champion. He's a Black *Master*!"

Liam groaned quietly to himself as Burring laughed. "That's a new qualification … a Black Master." He laughed again and continued pulling Susan along the path.

The last fight Liam had taken part in was in the school yard. He'd lost. This called for some thought. Stooping slightly he scurried forward until he could see the advancing Burring with Susan in tow.

Both were approaching the brow of a hill, Susan still being contrary. If that's the top of a hill, they'll have to start on a downward path. Perhaps that'll give me cover then the momentum I'll need, he thought. Liam waited until Susan's head had disappeared over the horizon and sped to the top of the hill. Both were only ten yards in front now. *Here goes nothing*, figured Liam as he accelerated towards Burring's back.

Burring detected the noise of Liam footsteps an instant before he was caught amidriff by 168 pounds of out-of-condition Irish muscle.

Susan was thrown to one side as Burring tried to regain his feet. He'd also lost his grip on his pistol following the collision. Liam's momentum had taken him through and over Burring. He too lay sprawled on the path, trying to get back on his feet before Burring. He failed. Burring's boot lashed out and caught him a glancing blow on the face, starting his nosebleed again. Liam rolled over, escaping a second swinging boot and half rose to his feet. Propelling himself forward he tackled Burring waist high and both fell backwards and into the bushes which lay on each side of the track. Liam was no match for Burring who threw him off easily and sat astride him, positioning himself to bring a flurry of blows down on Liam's unprotected face.

A heavy branch swung by Susan caught him on the side of the face and he reeled sideways freeing Liam who got to his knees and crawled towards Burring's discarded gun. Again Burring was too quick for him and leapt on his back crushing the air from his lungs. Yet again Susan wielded the log to good effect and hindered Burring in his aggression. Still the gun lay beyond the grasp of both men. Burring butted Liam in the face;, who lay back, dazed. Rising to his feet, he swatted Susan away with a backhanded blow, and picked up the pistol.

Doubled over to catch his breath, he pulled back the firing mechanism on the weapon and pointed at the couple, both of whom now lay spread-eagled on the path. "You pair been nothin' but trouble. Now you're in my way and you're goin' to have to die so's I can get me outa here."

The forest had become used to the cessation of gunshots following the various retreats from the cabin. Birds again flapped from the trees as the crash of two further shots pierced the stillness. Burring took a last look at the two young people lying before him before kneeling down and raising his gun to Liam's chest. An unnecessary third shot spat out and Burring's head blew apart like a ripe watermelon, given the two shots in the back he'd taken one second earlier.

Half a mile away, Streikker had strayed from the path and was staggering through the trees and bushes quite oblivious to the whipping motion of branches as he continually fell and righted himself. His glazed eyes began to comprehend the shape of another human being lying in a clearing.

Edson had decided that discretion was the better part of valour and had lost sufficient blood to set himself apart from his colleagues, sit down and attempt to make a tourniquet by tearing his blood soaked shirt into strips by using his teeth. *It always seems so easy in the movies*, he thought as little progress was made and blood continued to seep alarmingly from the wound in his arm.

He'd become aware of Streikker crashing through the undergrowth moments earlier and sat awaiting the appearance of whatever was causing the commotion. He placed his pistol underneath his right thigh and held it ready for use should it be necessary. He needn't have bothered.

Streikker staggered towards him and slumped to his knees. "Lord, I shall be with you if you accept me into your house. What is twisted cannot be straightened," he continued, quoting Ecclesiastes. "Salvation belongs to our God who sits on the throne and to the Lamb." A vision of Edson ebbed and flowed before his eyes. "Did you hear three trumpet blasts? I must meet my Maker."

Edson rose and laid him gently on his back. "The Lord your God wants to know why you were making use of a weapon against others."

"Why, they were sinners. They soiled His name and acted against His word. They are profane, they are sinners all. They would kill little children. But I have carried out

Your will, God. I have brought these killers to justice. No more will they rip the tiny bodies of Your unborn lambs from the bellies of wicked mothers."

"The Lord wants to know how you've helped him in this work."

Streikker laughed and coughed blood in doing so. "But the Lord already knows. For it was He who guided my actions. He it was who showed me how to visit great pain on those who would harm His children. At nine o'clock this morning they will all burn in Hell for the Lord my God is a vengeful God."

"Where will this happen?"

"I will exalt you, my God the King,… I will praise you for ever,… and ever."

"The Lord wants to know where this will happen," repeated Edson.

"The Lord … sustains the … humble … but casts the wicked … to the ground," said Streikker, uttering his last words on earth before he closed his eyes and, for all Edson knew, going to meet his maker.

**

Montana and Jackson had split up on leaving the blazing cabin. It was obvious that the quick way out of the clearing was to follow the track into the forest. Jackson nodded to Montana to take the track, and plunged into the forest until it got quiet and he could listen. Nothing. He moved on.

He moved like a cat, silently making his way through the forest, as aware as any deer of his environment.

Up ahead he heard movement. *Careful now.* It might be Miss Lattanzi or Brannigan.

He moved forward and slowly parted some branches to secure a better view. *Sure enough, it's a man and a woman.*

He watched as they themselves crouched, listening for any sounds which might guide their actions. Satisfied, they moved on as quietly as they could manage.

It took less than a few minutes for Jackson to circle them and await their arrival at a small clearing. When they arrived, they again stopped and listened for any sound of pursuit.

"Place your weapons at your feet immediately or I will shoot you dead." Jackson's voice carried sufficient authority to persuade both Kanes to comply just in time to avoid a warning shot.

"Raise both arms above your head and take three paces forward. Immediately." Now lie on your fronts with your face in the grass … Now!"

Both did as requested. Jackson's tone changed. "I'm afraid you've been most unfortunate. In the forest just now, we have representatives of the Federal Bureau of Investigation, Las Vegas Police Department and other good men and true. I regret to inform you that, although ostensibly we work towards the same ends at the moment, I happen to be self-employed. As I imagine you will appreciate, I work to a slightly different code of conduct. Accordingly I will ask you some questions. You will answer me immediately and honestly. If I believe you to be stalling or to be attempting to deceive me, I will simply shoot you."

Jackson pulled back the catch on his revolver. "What are your names?"

Matt Kane responded as requested. "Matt and Julie Kane. We're married."

"Where is Miss Susan Lattanzi at present?"

"If that's Lattanzi's daughter, we don't know. She wasn't in the cabin when we went in."

Kane screamed as a bullet smashed into the back of his right knee.

Sugar came to his defense, terrified. "He's tellin' the truth. Only people in the cabin when we got there was two cops. We didn't touch them."

"Why were you intent upon shooting Miss Lattanzi?"

"We wasn't, we were after Brannigan and old man Lattanzi."

"Why?"

"He made a speech against the right to carry arms. Our people wanted an example made of him. Brannigan witnessed a hit we made at McCarran Airport."

"Who are your people?"

"The Nevada branch of *Posse Commitatus*."

"The name of the man you report to."

Sugar hesitated. Her husband was still holding his leg and moaning in agony. She didn't respond quickly enough for Jackson.

A second shot broke Matt Kane's thighbone, causing a further series of screams from both Kanes now.

"His name!"

"Pastor Mike Yancy. He's got a congregation over in Vegas."

"We've got three knees left here. Anything else I should know about your operation?"

Again Sugar hesitated.

Jackson fired a third time. This time into the back of Sugar's knee.

"You crazy bastard," shouted Matt Kane. "Stop this shooting! We'll tell you everything! There's a bomb planted underneath a bush in the garden next to the entrance to the McArthur Abortion Clinic in Vegas, just behind the university. It's due to go off at nine o'clock this morning." Jackson looked at his watch. *Six forty.*

"My immediate priority is Miss Lattanzi. You can't help me further regarding her whereabouts?"

"We've no idea."

"Then thank you for your assistance. Regrettably, I'd rather you didn't testify to my interrogation techniques." Both Kanes were so agonised by the wounds inflicted by Jackson, it almost came as a blessed relief when two bullets, one behind each of one of their ears dispatched them from this life.

**

Susan had almost fainted in terror when the dead body of Burring slumped on top of her. Still groggy, Liam helped pull him off only to see another of his erstwhile captors, Wallis stepped out from the trees, rifle in hand.

"Oh my God this is endless," said Susan as Liam scrambled to pick up Burring's pistol.

"Hold still, young man, you're in no danger."

Liam did as requested partly because of the man's reassurance and partly because he still had a rifle under his arm and had just demonstrated what he could do with it.

"You bust your nose?" asked Wallis.

"I'm suffering less than your pal there. Why'd you shoot him anyway?"

"Well, in my business, you follow orders. You need a disciplined force. He was trained to cope with anything in defense of the flag but he let us all down. He deserted his comrades when they needed them most. Also, he looked like he was goin' to shoot you young people and that was not why we came here to Nevada."

"Why *did* you come?"

"Your boss, Mr Lattanzi? He was spoutin' off about how the people should have their right to bear arms removed from them. Now particularly when the Federal Government is actively workin' against the people, I figured he might be persuaded to go on television and withdraw his remarks if we held his daughter for a while as a sort of encouragement."

"So what happens now?"

A voice from behind Wallis answered the question as Tyler rose from a crouched position behind a bush, pointing his rifle at the back of Wallis.

"Why we're goin' to have ourselves another Court Martial right here in the field of combat."

Wallis half turned, recognising the voice of his fellow Militiaman.

"Put down your rifle, Lieutenant, it's all over."

"Not by a ways, Commander Wallis. You think you can criticise my actions in the field of combat, have your boys beat the shit outa me, callin' it a Court Martial and then you carry out a Summary Court Martial on Burring and you think it's all over? Ain't no way, Commander. Why, I think I'm just goin' to have a Summary Court Martial of my very own … but I want to spare you the hassle of you hearin' the case for the prosecution and I sure don't want to hear the case for the defense. So I guess that just leaves the verdict and the sentence. Well, let me see now I think I'm goin' to find you guilty as charged. And now I'm goin' to *shoot* your ass."

"FBI. Throw down your weapons - both of you." Montana stood, feet spread, pistol pointed in regulation style at Tyler.

Jackson watched the encounter behind and to the side of the group of people standing on the track. He sighed at the persistence of Montana in keeping to the book.

"Well now, the Federal boys are here. We *are* privileged. You goin' to shoot me in the back, Mr FBI?"

"Put your weapons on the ground." Wallis obliged, throwing his rifle in a ditch.

"And you," said Montana to Tyler.

"Anythin' you say, sir."

In a flash, Tyler reached out and swung Susan between himself and Montana, his rifle pointed at her neck. "What you gonna do now, Mr FBI?"

Montana was asking himself the same question when a silver blur sped from behind a bush and Jackson's hunting knife buried itself almost up to the hilt just below Tyler's left ear. Death was instantaneous. He dropped like a stone.

Susan felt safe enough to run the few paces to Liam who hugged her tightly. "Hey, hey, hey. It's goin' to be all right now. It's okay."

Jackson joined the group and pulled the hunting knife from Tyler's head, cleaning it on the dead man's shirt.

"Do you have to announce yourself in advance anytime you want to get the jump on someone, Mr Montana? You certainly try my patience!"

"I suspect we were taught in different methodologies, Mr. ...?"

"You don't need to know my name. Now let's get back." He turned to Susan. "Your father's well, as are the two police officers. We need to account for seven people, three of whom are here, two lie dead in the forest. That means two remain to be accounted for."

He removed a lace from Tyler's boot and secured Wallis' hands behind his back. "Agent Montana, we should make our way back. You head off some twenty yards in front of us. Mr Brannigan, take this gun and protect Miss Lattanzi." He looked at Wallis. "Your name?"

"Wallis."

"Then, Mr Wallis, you have an important duty. You will walk directly in front of both of these young people. If anyone wants to take a shot at them, your job is to get in the way."

He looked around almost as if to scent any trouble. "Any questions?" There was no response. "Then let's head off."

# Chapter Twenty One

The party travelled a few hundred yards along the path before Montana turned and signalled the main body to stop and take shelter by waving his hand at them. Jackson guided them behind a fallen tree and bid them all crouch down. Tempted as he was to follow in support of Montana, he knew he'd almost completed his mission and decided to stay protecting Liam and Susan until whatever drama which lay ahead unfolded.

Montana was guided through the trees by a soft moaning. His pistol at the ready, he tread softly until he reached the clearing where lay the body of Streikker and the almost lifeless Edson.

He approached gingerly, wary of a trap. There was none. "FBI, lay down your weapons." His sole concession to Jackson was to utter the warning softly.

Edson turned slowly and looked at him. "FBI? Show me your identification."

Montana could see the man was badly wounded and had both his hands empty at his sides. Placing the point of his pistol against Edson's temple, he felt for his badge and showed it to Edson.

Edson coughed. "Listen to me carefully. My name is Arthur Hamilton. I'm FBI too, working out of the Denver office. You can check…Two things. One, I need a proper tourniquet and blood transfusion quickly or I'm going to die. Two, I've been working deep cover inside the Idaho Militia for five years and I've got enough stuff on them to shut the whole thing down and prove links with the IRA in Ireland. Now listen, these people who attacked the cabin, whoever the hell they were, look like they've planted a bomb somewhere. It goes off at nine o'clock this morning. I don't know more than that."

"Who's the top FBI man in Denver?" asked Montana, seeking more confirmation.

"Elmer Schmeer."

"Who runs the New York office?"

Hamilton coughed. "Last time I heard, it was Benjamin Lieka."

"Well, you seem to know your way around the Bureau. Are you sure you can't tell me any more? Who else knows about this bomb?"

"No one, I guess but there's not much time to call it in."

"I'll take care of that okay. Have you got a weapon?"

"Yeah, a pistol. I couldn't be sure who'd appear."

Montana nodded at Streikker. "Who's the dead guy?"

"Don't know. He came wanderin' in to the clearing then died of a gunshot to his belly. He seemed a religious freak, kept quotin' the bible."

"Okay Agent Hamilton, we'd better take care of you."

Montana levelled his gun at the rear of his colleague's head and pulled the trigger, almost blowing the back of his skull off and covering himself in Edson's blood in the process.

**

Jackson half rose when he heard the shot and remained in that position until Montana re-appeared on the track up ahead. He walked back towards the group.

"It's all over. The last two guys are lying dead in a clearing up ahead in the forest. Let's get back."

"Why only one shot?" asked Jackson.

"One guy was already dead. Shot in the stomach."

Jackson nodded, satisfied. "Let's get back and see your father," he said to Susan who still clung like a limpet to Liam.

They walked back along the track, bloodstained, tired and emotional but less afraid. All the aggressors had been accounted for. All were dead except for Wallis, who was now restrained.

Shortly they came to the clearing where the cabin still blazed ferociously. No one was to be seen and Susan felt sick as her expectation of seeing her father immediately was not realised.

"Susan!"

She turned and her father was running the short distance towards her as fast as his limp would allow him.

"Father, you've been hurt!"

"Just a flesh wound. I'm okay. What about you?"

"Scared stupid, but I'm unharmed."

"Liam?"

"Every five minutes someone makes my nose bleed. I've just ruined my new Armani outfit. This means another trip to see Alphonse."

Susan hugged him. "Liam, you were so brave. I can't *tell* you how I feel about you." She turned to her father "Liam saved my life, Dad. He was wonderful!"

"I owe you a great deal, Liam."

"It's your friend here we need to thank. He's quite an operator."

Jackson stood listening and smiling occasionally. "Mr Lattanzi, a word please."

Both men walked a few paces while Jackson spoke earnestly about what the Kanes had told him. Joe looked serious.

He turned to address the group only to find Montana had collected Bilko, Regan, Susan and Liam and had ushered them into a tight group. He was pointing his pistol at the cluster. Wallis knelt, head bowed from exhaustion, some yards away.

"Sorry about this everyone. But business is business. I can't take chances about who knows what. Orders are orders." He beckoned Wallis to stand and join the group.

"Sheriff, I'm real sorry about all this. You've been a hero of mine over the past few years and I'm sorry you're caught up in all of this. I salute you as a genuine American and a great man. But America's got bigger plans for your memory."

"The FBI certainly appears to be a complex organisation," mused Jackson.

"You'd better believe it, mister. Times are I don't rightly know what's going on myself, so I figure the only sensible thing to do in the circumstances is to follow orders. So that's what I'll do."

Wallis rose to his height and spoke slowly. "Son, you put your pistol down. There's been enough killin' today."

Montana shook his head. "'Fraid I can't do that. I'm going to be the only one who walks away from this conversation."

Joe Lattanzi pulled his daughter tighter to him.

Montana's first shot hit Jackson square in the chest, knocking him backwards. Wallis was next as he ran at Montana aiming a kick which never found its target. A bullet in his neck saw to that.

"What the hell you doin', Montana?" asked an incredulous Bilko.

Montana turned to face him. "You just wouldn't understand, Sergeant. Higher orders."

He pulled the trigger and sent Bilko spinning back, a bullet wound in his shoulder breaking his clavicle.

Joe Lattanzi watched in horror, as a series of murders began to take place in front of his eyes. His first thought was to protect his daughter and he placed his left arm tighter around her, gathering her closer.

The blaze behind them had spread and was now burning fiercely in a room adjacent to the one which all had been held captive. Edson had used the room to store the explosives and the detonators they'd brought with them. The flames licked at the boxes and found them. The consequent explosion reduced the building to matchwood in a single ball of orange flame. All standing in the back yard were bowled over by the blast.

Joe Lattanzi was first to react. With his right hand, he felt in his trouser pocket for the small Derringer which Jackson had encouraged him to conceal about his person. Liam rushed Montana as all other alternatives had been exhausted but just as they were about to collide, a short crack signalled the dispatch of a single shot from Lattanzi's Derringer and Montana keeled over, blood spurting from his wound. Liam crashed into him anyway and helped him on his way to the ground.

Regan knelt next to Bilko and spoke to his wounded partner. "That looks like a shoulder wound. You'll be okay if we get you some attention." He shouted to Lattanzi "He's okay."

Liam checked Wallis. "This fellah's dead."

Joe Lattanzi knelt over Jackson who stared at him through eyes which were glazing over. "I want to thank you from the bottom of my heart," said Joe.

Jackson nodded and coughed up some blood. "One more thing, Mr Lattanzi. The bomb goes off at nine o'clock in the Vegas Abortion Clinic. You don't have much time left." His head turned sideways and the life left his body.

**

Joe Lattanzi stood slowly, the pain in his leg and the loss of blood making him dizzy. An emotion he didn't understand enveloped him as he stood over the now crumpled body of Montana. Slowly he raised his derringer and pointed it at the head of the FBI man. Squeezing the trigger repeatedly, he attempted to fire more rounds into the body of the man who had attempted to take the life of his loved one – just as had his Uncle Dino all those years ago in New York. This time however, the weapon would not comply and, realising the limitations of the Derringer, he lowered his arm, exhausted and let the gun fall to the ground.

Liam stepped forward and took his arm.

"Joe, we need to get out of here. This police officer, Susan and I are the only able bodied people we've got left. Let's get past this burning building before the fire spreads further and catches the cars."

Liam and Regan helped Bilko, and Susan supported her father as they tried, as best they could, to shield themselves from the heat from the fire. As Liam had anticipated, the grass had caught fire and was indeed threatening the BMW.

Liam raced towards it and jumped into the driver's seat. The engine kicked into life at the first time of asking and he swung it into reverse and away from the cabin. Sweeping round, he brought it to a halt at the side of the others. Susan helped her father and Bilko into the back where they were joined by Regan. She took her place in the front with Liam.

Lattanzi had surfaced from his fog as the import of Jackson's last words hit home. "Drive, Liam. We don't have much time. These crazies have planted a bomb at the Abortion Clinic in Vegas. It goes off at nine. We need to get to a phone and get some medical attention for me and Sergeant Bilk."

**

The Brookside Medical Clinic was going about its normal business. Medics and clerical staff had arrived for a day's work and were engaged in organising their day. Great bunches of flowers, gleaned from the surfeit presented to its patients, were everywhere.

Patients were abed or watching television in the several communal rooms. The decorators were still going about their job. Just another day.

**

Liam didn't want to drive recklessly. It was obvious that both Joe and Bilko were in a lot of pain and every bump in the road brought a groan from the Sergeant.

There was a garage not far along the freeway. They'd have a phone and he could alert the police as to the bomb and have the place evacuated. Regan would ensure that it wasn't treated as a hoax. Then they would ask for an ambulance and have one come out and meet them half way. Both casualties must have lost a lot of blood.

The BMW had only about half a mile of dirt track left before its wheels could perform on the concrete surface of the freeway. So far, so good, thought Liam.

Just as he was congratulating himself on getting to the end of the bumpy track without causing his passengers too much pain, the rear windshield smashed. Liam looked in his rear view mirror and saw the Cherokee racing up behind him with a bloodstained Montana at the wheel, a gun in one hand.

Liam pushed his foot down and shouted "Hold on, everyone," as he accelerated at speed towards the end of the track.

"I don't suppose anyone thought to bring a gun," asked Regan.

Those who were able to looked at one another sheepishly.

Liam turned on to the freeway and sped towards Vegas. "If he gets lucky and hits one of our tyres, we're all dead," pointed out Liam as the needle showed him to be closing on the city at one hundred miles an hour.

Unfortunately, the powerful Cherokee was closing at one hundred and three miles an hour and coming back within shooting range.

"He's gaining, Liam," said Susan.

"It won't go any faster. You should have had it serviced."

Another bullet spat from Montana's pistol, kicking up a chip from the concrete just ahead of the BMW.

Lights full on despite the hot, bright, sunny day, Liam found himself increasingly having to overtake cars as they neared the city. Fortunately for him, a driver in a Porsche took exception to being passed by an upstart in a BMW and decided to pull out and give chase.

No sooner had he done so than he became aware of the Cherokee on his bumper. "Je-e-esus, what the hell's the world coming to?" he asked his wife, who was used to his aggressive driving but who still got upset when he involved himself in a testosterone charged challenge on the freeway.

His manoeuvre had caused Montana to brake, and the seconds which passed between the Porsche driver feeling pleased that he'd blocked off a roadhog before showing the guy up ahead what driving was all about, gave Liam much needed distance.

Smiling with quiet satisfaction, the Porsche man looked in his rear view mirror in order to gloat. Instead, he saw the enraged Montana covered in blood, taking aim at his precious car.

In an instant he had pulled over. Unfortunately for Montana, the first act of the driver after consoling his distraught wife and attempting to pull himself together was to dial 911 and explain to the police that a homicidal maniac was heading for their city with murder and mayhem obviously very much on his mind.

Somehow, the BMW managed to outpace the Cherokee all the way in towards Vegas. Eight fifty-three and inside the city limits now, Liam drove slightly more cautiously. He could still see Montana in his mirror but the manoeuvring both had had to undertake and the greater numbers of vehicles between them lessened the opportunities Montana had to take pot shots.

Regan was directing Liam right and left as the BMW came ever closer to the Abortion Clinic. "Second on the left then first right," urged Regan. "It's almost nine o'clock."

Liam swung the big car around and over-steered on the last turn. He reversed, stalled and reversed again before bulleting the car onwards towards the Clinic.

Just as the BMW took the last corner and its occupants could see the clinic, the timer in the device beneath the bush clicked to nine o'clock and detonated the contents of Streikker's home made bomb.

A huge crash of orange and red flame blasted the scaffolding, reducing the wing it supported to rubble. Cars parked at the sidewalk also exploded, adding to the carnage. Debris showered down on the BMW and took out the front windshield causing Susan to scream.

Liam looked over his shoulder apprehensively only to see Montana pull up at the end of the road, observe the chaos and, steering the car towards a side-road, go on his way at a leisurely pace.

## Chapter Twenty Two

Within the car, blood was everywhere. Liam's nose had decided to resist all attempts to have its bleeding stop and his front was scarlet. In the rear of the vehicle, Joe and Bilko were pale and unconscious, their blood now staining garments and car interior alike.

"Liam, the hospital. Now!"

Liam looked at the Clinic, now engulfed in flames and decided that there was little he could do. He knocked the remaining glass from the front windshield and followed Regan's directions to the hospital.

After seeing her father admitted and having been reassured that he'd be okay once he'd received some blood, Susan phoned her mother.

Liz almost snatched at the phone, incurring the unspoken wrath of Elma.

"Liz Lattanzi."

"Mother, it's Susan." She wept.

"Susan, thank God. Where *are* you? Is your father with you?"

"Everything's all right, mother. We're all okay."

"And Liam?"

"*All* of us. That includes Liam. He saved our lives."

Now Liz was in tears. "What in God's name have you all been involved in?"

"It's a long story, mother. Why don't you bring a change of clothes for father?"

"Where the hell *are* you, daughter?"

"Harmon General Hospital. Dad's injured his leg but he's fine. We'll tell you everything when you drive over. But drive slowly. Better still, get Jimmy to drive you. Father told me he's staying over so I'm sure Jimmy'll want to come to the hospital as well. I'm stepping out with Liam for a while but we'll see you both when you get here, probably around noon."

**

Liam sat alone in a waiting room watching television. Bilko had been whisked away to the operating suite and Regan had insisted on going with him.

Susan returned, now much more composed and followed Liam's gaze to the television on the wall. A reporter was commenting on the explosion which had just taken place at Brookside Medical Clinic and was speculating on whether it had been occasioned by a ruptured gas main or a bomb planted by anti abortion protesters.

"In either event it was extremely fortunate that the Medical Wing which took the force of the blast was under reconstruction and no fatalities ensued. Some slight injuries were caused when cars parked nearby exploded. A Parking Warden was detained in hospital for minor wounds although Ms Joan Addison, who works for the City, is not seriously injured and is expected to be released shortly."

"How anyone could have survived that escapes me," said Liam.

"It was awful."

Susan changed the subject. She'd had enough of violence for one day. "I phoned mother. She's coming over to the hospital and she'll be upset and anxious enough without seeing you pretty much as she left you - all covered in blood. Come on, let's go back to see Alphonse before she arrives. There's nothing we can do here. Dad's fine."

"You're one to talk. You're covered in dust and your clothes are all torn. If you're selecting clothes for me, I'm choosing for you. Agreed?"

"I'm not sure about that. But I'll agree because Alphonse would never allow me out of his store wearing anything which he felt didn't make me look radiant."

"Susan, you could wear anything and you'd look radiant."

**

Jimmy St James and Liz drove into the hospital car park from which they entered Reception and were guided to the private room in which Joe was lying abed. Tubes fed him the plasma he needed and a nurse fussed at the side of the bed checking the monitors which told an increasingly promising story with each minute that passed. Joe's leg had been cleansed, stitched and bandaged. He'd been given an anaesthetic and was sleepy but brightened up when Liz and Jimmy entered the room.

Liz almost ran to his bedside, weeping. "Joe, I've been so worried."

"Well, I've been kind of worried myself, this last while."

"I want to know everything. Every single thing." She hugged her husband tightly.

Joe held her tightly and, raising his glance, acknowledged his old friend. "Jimmy, it's good to see you. I suppose you'll want to know what happened as well?"

"If you're up to it."

"Well, I suspect that it'll have to be done in instalments. They've given me a little something to help me sleep but I'll start and we'll see how far I get."

Joe gave them the main details, aided by Jimmy hushing Liz as she attempted to ask supplementary questions at every turn of events. "Let him tell his story, Liz."

Joe got to the point where he'd slipped into unconsciousness just prior to the bombing when Liam and Susan returned, both dressed in leather boots, jeans and denim shirts. Liz leapt from her seat and hugged her daughter. After a tearful reunion, she raised her hand in speechless welcome to Liam without letting her daughter from her grasp.

Liam tipped an invisible hat. "Howdy, ma'am."

Liz laughed despite herself. "You both look as if you're about to perform at a rodeo."

"We never made Alphonse. This time it was my choice," said Liam.

The nurse returned. "I'm sorry, Mr Lattanzi needs some rest and he'll be fine. Perhaps you could all return later."

"When would you suggest?"

"The doctor proposes to discharge him tomorrow after a good night's sleep. Why don't you all get some rest? Phone tomorrow morning and make arrangements to come and collect him."

"That sounds wise, Liz," said Jimmy. "I'll drive you all back to the ranch."

**

Liz decided that she'd have a welcome home dinner for Joe the next day, so asked Jimmy if he'd make arrangements to collect Joe from hospital. She also asked Jimmy to inform him that, upon his return, she would speak with both of them about Joe's 'big secret' and he should alert his friend, her husband, to this.

Jimmy agreed, anticipating the tone of the discussion.

## Chapter Twenty Three

It was late in the afternoon. Liam and Susan were helping Liz to cook the evening meal when Jimmy pulled up outside with Joe. Both joined Liz in welcoming him but were returned to their tasks when Liz indicated that there was to be an 'adult discussion' and that the children were to be relegated to the kitchen.

"Ohooo," said Susan pretending petulance, "we'd better make ourselves scarce, Liam. The grown ups are going to talk about things us kids wouldn't understand. Come on, let's go back to preparing this meal and you can burn something."

Joe was on crutches. He levered himself stiffly into the lounge and seated himself down tentatively like an errant schoolboy. Liz had been working on her speech for the past few days and was confident she'd carry it off with dignity, but before she could start she felt the tears welling up in her eyes and surrendered to her emotions. Joe set aside his crutches and limped over to her using the furniture as assists. He put his arm around her shoulders. "Darling, before I left with Jackson, you said you wanted to speak to me about something. You want to tell Jimmy and me what it is? It's not often you ask me to bring my legal adviser to a family discussion."

Liz wiped her eyes with a handkerchief handed to her by Jimmy. "Jimmy's here because he's our oldest friend ,and because I suspect you're both up to your necks in this together."

"Up to our necks in what, exactly, Liz?"

"Joe, I love you and Susan more than you could ever imagine. You are now sixty-five years old and I want you around for another twenty years. More if the Lord spares us. I want us to have grandchildren and I want to spoil them rotten. I want us to have a normal life, perhaps travel, perhaps stay at home. But I want you out!"

"Out of what, darling?"

"Joe, I've been at your side for over a quarter of a century. You're of Italian stock. I'm aware of your business associates. I'm aware of your role in the business side of things. Do you imagine it's likely I've been at your side for all this time and not overheard the occasional telephone conversation, seen the occasional letter? I was an investigative journalist before we met, and a damn good one at that. I'm no fool. But I loved you and I decided that I'd just live with it. I know you're not a violent man. You're a decent, honourable man. But you associate with men who are criminals. Men who gave you the money to build this hotel. That's why I'll never visit the place. Because it's built on the proceeds of crime." She gathered herself. "Well, Susan and I deserve better. So I want you to retire. Now. Today. Immediately!"

Joe embraced Liz and held her tight. Both were weeping, Joe more gently in counterpoint to Liz's tearful sobs.

Jimmy St James cleared his throat. "Liz, I think it's appropriate if *I* respond to your concerns in this instance. Let me start with a reassurance. I've spoken with Joe on the way over from hospital and we've both agreed that the events of the last couple of days have presented us with an ideal opportunity for Joe to retire from all of his activities, including the hotel. Now, it seems only fair for me to confirm your worst fears about your husband's involvement in his business activities. Mine too, as a matter of fact."

He paused to accept a glass of whisky Joe had poured for him. Liz refused with a tearful shake of her head.

"As I imagine you were alluding to, I can confirm that Joe is a senior member of the Mafia and has been for many years. He has not shared that with you, and has not done so for a very good reason. But, before I explain further, I must ask that you retain this information in the same complete confidence as I have done for the last thirty odd years."

The word '*Mafia*' slammed into Liz's consciousness. Although Liz had known in her heart that this inevitably was where the conversation would lead, she felt sick at the thought of the man she loved participating in organised crime. Nevertheless, she had gone too far not to hear the whole story, as difficult as it was to hear the words spoken. She found herself agreeing to keep the information to herself.

"If what I am about to tell you leaks out, Joe would certainly be killed. I regret therefore that this must go with you to the grave. You cannot even tell Susan."

Liz found herself gripping Joe's arm so tightly, her knuckles were white. Jimmy continued.

"Your husband is a very brave man, Liz. In addition to being an active Senator and a senior member of the Mafia, he has, since his time with Bobby Kennedy, been working for the FBI."

Liz looked at Joe who nodded the truth of Jimmy's assertion. He took over the explanation himself.

"Honey, you know that when I was younger, I worked for Bobby Kennedy, who placed me in the office of Jimmy Hoffa, in order to pass him information on his links with organised crime. Essentially, that arrangement continued over the next four decades. I found myself trusted by both sides. I was rewarded with a political career due to Bobby's influence and my contacts with the Mafia saw me become their respectable face. They saw that it was more helpful to them because I was I'd become a Senator and that I looked after their commercial interests. I was never involved in the murky, murderous side of the families.

But everything I did was as a result of instructions I was receiving from my people at the FBI."

Liz looked at Jimmy who smiled. "Like I said Liz, Joe has been extraordinarily brave. Forty years working inside an element of organised crime, forty years an agent with the FBI, forty years of not knowing whether he would be found out, forty years of not being able to tell the woman he loves that he led a dangerous life, a double life." He lifted his whisky glass in a toast. "Joe Lattanzi is an extraordinary man."

Liz sat beside Joe, still holding his arm. "I'm sorry, I can't take all of this in right now. You're both telling me that Joe could have lost his life at any time because of his involvement in all of this and I would never have known?"

"That's pretty much why I didn't tell you darling. We've had a happy, relatively carefree life. I figured that the life you led would have been ruined if you spent your time fretting about my safety every night. Also, because by then I was a Senator, I couldn't just disappear overnight or tell the Mafia families that I wanted out. It doesn't work like that. They see me as an asset in which they've invested time and money. They still do. They trust me and see me as a straight shooter. Paradoxically perhaps, they place real value on my integrity."

Liz intervened anxiously, "What can we do?"

Joe and Jimmy shared a glance. Jimmy spoke. "Your husband is about to suffer a contrived nervous breakdown as a result of this latest escapade. The FBI will be asked to arrange for a psychiatric analysis of Joe from a trusted professional who will pronounce him only half the man he was and unlikely to recover his confidence. The report will show that he is still in full possession of all of his faculties - the families will want to be assured that he's not so damaged emotionally that he might break *omertà*, his vow of silence - and he'll retire to his ranch with his wife and lead a normal, if quieter life."

Liz looked at Joe apprehensively. "Will this work?"

"I think so, Honey."

"Will the FBI let you go?"

"I'm the friend of American Presidents, honey. I've still got a bit of pull there. They won't mess me around."

"But Jimmy, this doesn't explain your own involvement. What's going to happen to you? Does Helen know about all of this?"

"In a sense she does, Liz, but it's different for me. I'm afraid I'm still involved in a trap not unlike Joe's. However, I'm a lawyer. It's easier for me. I just happened to become involved in looking after the legal concerns of people associated with organised crime. I didn't realise what I was getting involved with at the time, but I suppose that they are entitled to protection under the law just like everyone else. To be honest, I'm not in the same peril that Joe was. I'm just a regular lawyer running a legal practice. I'll be okay. And remember, I'm *Joe's* lawyer too so I don't have any problems with the authorities because of all of this."

The three of them talked for a while more, Liz and Joe holding hands like adolescents while a range of emotions swept over them - including, in the case of Liz, anger. She returned from time to time to a 'how could you' routine but was mollified by Joe and Jimmy, who were eventually able to reassure her that her desire to spend a contented retirement with her husband and daughter was about to be realised.

After a while Susan put her head round the door. "If you adults don't join us kids very shortly, this meal is going to be ruined."

Joe beckoned her to come in and sit down. "Darling, how would you feel if I retired from active life?"

Susan recognised the seriousness in her father's voice and attributed it to the events of the previous two days. "Dad, whatever you do is all right by me. Will you still be a rancher, or do you just mean stepping back from the hotel?"

"Just the hotel, darling. I'll still look after the ranch. I enjoy that."

"Then you go right ahead. It'll be better for your health." She thought for a moment. "What about Liam? Will he still keep his job overseeing the hotel development?"

"Well, Liam and I discussed some things by telephone last night. We're working on some ideas but he wants to tell you himself."

Liz had recovered her composure. "I'm starving. Let's eat."

**

The meal, although this was unintended, was cathartic.

All, but especially Liz and Jimmy, were introduced to the horrors of the kidnap, the attack on the cabin, the blaze, the shootings and the explosion from the perspective of the respective story teller.

Liam was off-hand, Joe was serious and Susan, from time to time was tearful as she recounted her version of events.

All three had been spoken to by police officers the day before, after leaving Joe in the hospital and had been protected from an army of journalist by a combination of Nick Guthrie arranging for the police interviews to be undertaken in the hospital - their departure from the underground car park surprising the waiting press contingent - and Joe's ranch hands maintaining a watch on all entrances to the ranch.

The telephone had been disconnected and Jimmy had issued a press release indicating that all were back home and under sedation. He confirmed the broad essentials of the story and indicated that all three would be speaking further with the police and would co-operate fully in their enquiries once they had recovered from their trauma.

Bilko had been detained in hospital due to the seriousness of his injury but was expected to be discharged within a couple of days. Jimmy St James had called Lieutenant Regan and had arranged that both he and Bilko would visit the Lattanzis and Liam on the ranch over the weekend to begin the series of interviews that would end with court appearances for them all in order to bring matters to a conclusion.

St James had been told by Regan that it would be co-operative of Mr Lattanzi *et al* if the role of Special Agent Montana was left to the FBI to sort out but that he should inform his clients that he and Bilko would discuss the matter with them before evidence was brought before the District Attorney. St James agreed, recognising the coded assurances of Regan that a testimony would be agreed before other officers took a formal statement. *For whatever reason, someone wants to wrap this up extremely tightly*, he thought.

After the evening meal, Jimmy declared himself tired and said he'd better drive back to his house just outside Vegas. Joe was still taking medication and couldn't enjoy the wine which Liz, Susan and Liam had sipped throughout the evening. He was still fatigued from his recent exploits and the effects of the medication and said his good-byes to his old friend.

He limped awkwardly to Jimmy's car using his crutches. "Jimmy, I want to thank you for your wise counsel on this. I'm glad I'm getting out. You're my oldest and dearest friend and you've been a source of great strength to me in all of this. We've still got a bit of work to do to get through any court appearance - after all, I did shoot and wound a man…"

"A man the police and the FBI don't appear to want to figure in all of this. Whether he was acting outwith his jurisdiction or whether they don't want their interest in *Posse Commitatus* drawn to the attention of a wider public, we'll possibly find out in time but at the moment, it looks like they want to secure our assistance in putting all of this to bed quietly."

"That was my reading of the situation but I'll still need your help in convincing the families that I'm fine but that my value to them is at an end."

"That won't be a problem, Joe. Not if the Bureau can fix you up with an appropriate assessment from a psychiatrist."

Joe nodded. "Drive safely. I'll speak with you tomorrow."

"Night, Joe."

Liz followed Joe out to the driveway as he watched the tail lights of his friend's car disappear down the road and away from the ranch. "Let's you and I get some shut eye. I just want to hold you close until sun up."

"Okay, honey, help this old man inside."

**

Susan had cleared the table and prepared it for next morning's breakfast while Liam had retreated to the lounge at Susan's request in order to light the fire. She came through to find him reading his book on the American Airline industry.

"God, Liam, you're one of the most laid back men I've ever met. After all we've been through, you can joke your way through supper, then sit down and stick your nose in a book as if this kind of thing happens to you every day."

"Oh, I was excited enough at the time all right."

"I guess you were, at that." Susan sat at the side of the fire. "Liam, would you put that book down while I'm talking to you?"

Liam closed the book and placed it on the coffee table. "I'm sorry, Susan. I forget my manners sometimes."

"Look, I just wanted to thank you for everything you've done to protect my father and me. You were a real hero. The way you fought these terrible men was … well, it was just marvellous."

"You remember it differently from me, Susan. All I recollect is people making my nose bleed."

"Will you join me in enjoying one of my father's classic brandies?"

"I'd love to. Frankly, I'd have to think long and hard before I'd ever refuse a request from you. I will always carry the image of you standing above that guy who was about to punch my lights out, hitting him with a log like you were a real street fighter."

Susan smiled, now quite proud of her intervention. "Yeah, well he should have known better to have mess with Susan Lattanzi." She flexed the muscle in her right arm in the fashion of a body-builder, surprising Liam as she did so as he realised that her life on the farm had provided her with an impressively muscular frame which was disguised by her slim figure.

"My God, let me see that again," said Liam as he reached forward and felt the firmness of her arm muscle. "Dear heavens, you're twice as strong as me. You'd beat me to a pulp any time you wanted to."

Susan felt ambivalent about his compliment. She'd rather he appreciated other aspects of her femininity she told herself. *He still sees me as his little sister.* "Let me get you that brandy."

Liam moved uncomfortably from his chair and seated himself at the fire, staring into its flickerings.

"I thought it was just my nose which attracted the attentions of my adversaries, but I'm aching all over. I'm just not used to people throwing me around."

"I'm sore myself," said Susan as she handed Liam his brandy glass.

Liam decided on another toast. "To Liam Brannigan and Susan Lattanzi, the meanest *hombres* west of the Pecos."

Susan clinked Liam's brandy glass. "To Susan and Liam."

"They're quite a team", volunteered Liam.

"They sure are … yes sir," said Susan, her gaze falling to the fire as a look of sadness descended on her delicate features. After a silence, she cleared her throat, plucking up courage to ask the question which had been on her mind since her father had announced his retirement.

"Liam, now that my father's retired and won't be involved in the hotel development, what's going to happen to you? He said you'd both discussed it, and that you wanted to tell me yourself what you're going to do." She looked back into the flames. "You're going back to Ireland, aren't you?"

Liam took a sizeable draught of his brandy. "Well, I did ask Joe if I could raise this matter with you myself."

Susan felt the hurt rising within her. "And when are you going?"

"Well, that depends upon a couple of things. I'm leaving the hotel business along with Joe. I was there only because of him and due to my friendship with him. But, to tell you the truth, I've been thinking of leaving the business for a while now. I just couldn't bring myself to do it."

"Why not?"

"Just figuring out whether I had the courage to do something on my own."

"You want to set up on your own back in Ireland?"

Liam laughed. "No, I'm not that entrepreneurial." He finished the rest of his brandy in one gulp.

"Liam, that's a classic brandy. It's meant to be sipped and appreciated. What's the matter with you? Is all this talk of Ireland affecting your drinking behaviour?"

"No, it's not that. It's not that at all."

He took a deep breath. "Right, I'm going to say this once and then that's it."

Another breath. "It's true I'm thinking of going back to Ireland and it's true I've been thinking of leaving Joe's employ. But the reason I've been thinking about these things - especially over the last few days - has all been to do with my feelings for one Susan Lattanzi. I'm playing for high stakes here, Susan, because you really *are* my best friend and I'm not prepared to put that friendship at risk.

*God, we're covering some familiar territory here*, thought Susan.

"But put it at risk, I have to. Because … well, I think …. well I know …. look, I'm sorry if I'm embarrassing you, Susan, but I think I'm in love with you. And I know that me just saying these words changes everything. You can't put the toothpaste back in the tube. But it's out now and I'm sorry if this messes everything up between us but …."

Susan had been listening to him blurt out his ramblings with initial confusion but then, as appreciation of his feelings began to sink in, she threw her arms around him.

Holding him close, eyes tight shut she spoke to him, her voice wavering. "Liam, I've waited for a long time to hear you say these words. I thought I was going to lose you when you were fighting these men and everyone was shooting. I thought I was going to lose you when you said you were going to Ireland …." She realised that he had indeed confirmed his intention to go to Ireland.

She pulled back. "You did say that you were going back to Ireland?"

Liam laughed, as much from the relief of Susan's reaction to his confession of love as to her misunderstanding of his Irish trip. "What I actually said was that 'that depended on a couple of things'. I promised my parents that I'd go back over for a visit when the dust settled on this court case and I was wondering if you'd like to go over with me … only for a couple of weeks."

Susan was now completely happy. Joyous at the unexpected turn of events and inclined again to tease this man who had befriended her, had protected her and had now professed his love for her. "If I remember correctly, you thought I had a lovely singing voice and that I'd go down well in some of your Dublin pubs."

"You would charm them and you would charm my mother and father."

"Just as you've charmed mine, Liam. They both think you're marvellous." She giggled. "In fact my mother has made it her business to bring us together as a couple."

"I know," said Liam.

"And how on earth do you know that, might I ask?"

"Your father told me last night when I decided to resign so I wasn't impeded by being in love with the boss's daughter."

"What? You discussed this with my father before you discussed it with me?"

"I did."

Susan thought it through and decided it didn't warrant her wrath. She smiled. "How chivalrous. How old fashioned."

"Hey, let's not get ahead of ourselves here. I didn't ask for your hand or anything. I just said I'd become very fond of you but that I couldn't share my feelings with you while I was the hired hand."

"Did you tell him you loved me?"

"No. I kept that part for you."

Susan stared into his eyes. "We've never even kissed."

"Don't think it's not been on my mind."

"Hmm. Well, I think you should know a couple of things about how I feel about this. Number one, just in case you were wondering, I love you too, Liam Brannigan …. *very* much … although I was about to give up on you because you always treated me like your little sister."

Liam started to respond but Susan silenced him by placing her finger on his lips. "Number two, I would love to go to Ireland with you and meet your parents. I really would." A thought occurred. "You didn't ask my father permission for that as well?"

"As a matter of fact, I did."

Susan had doubts about this trend. "Hmm. I think from here on in, all decisions about you and me will be made by you and me. Are we agreed on that?"

"Sounds fair enough to me. As long as that's okay with your mother and father," he teased.

Susan smiled. "And there's a third thing. Number three."

"And what might that be?"

"I've been brought up well. I'm a good little girl and I wouldn't dream of going off to Dublin with a man I've never even kissed. Now did you get father's permission for that too?"

Liam laughed happily. "No, I thought I'd ask you first. But if you refuse, I might just throw myself off a cliff."

Susan looked deep into his eyes as the humour faded slowly from his face. "Liam Brannigan, if you don't kiss me right now …." Their heads moved closer together.

"Just what'll you do?"

"Then *I'll* just have to kiss you." Their heads moved closer still until they could feel each other's breathing.

"This'll mean we're not friends anymore," said Liam.

"I never much liked you anyway."

They kissed for the first time.

# Epilogue

"Where the Moun … tains of Mourne … sweep down … to the sea."

Susan bowed and took the enthusiastic applause from a busy bar room full of Dubliners as she finished the Irish song she'd insisted that Liam teach her before leaving Las Vegas. She returned the microphone to her lips, enjoying the reaction and playing up her American origins.

"Well, thank y'all kindly," and bowing several times before returning to join Liam, who was still whooping his appreciation at their table.

"Ah, you're a natural. I told you they'd love you."

Susan kissed him and sat down. The two guitarists broke into another driving rhythm. They were joined by a beard with a fiddle, who had the crowd stomping and shouting encouragement, as the Irish reel gave way to 'The Atholl Highlanders', a Scottish jig which accelerated the perilous pace of the set. Fingers flew across fretboards and applause broke out spontaneously midway through the performance at the rousing virtuosity of the musicians.

"Liam, I just love Dublin. What an atmosphere! And you say all the bars are like this?"

"Perhaps not every single one, but we all enjoy the music and the *craic*. I can tell you as an economist that the Irish spend more of their disposable income on what the European Commission call 'leisure and entertainment' - and the rest of us call drinking Guinness and putting the world to rights through the ancient art of conversation - than any other country in Europe."

"Well, I approve anyway. I'm having a great time." She cupped her hands round his ear and shouted into them, protecting her words from the cacophony of the raucous music, "I love you, Liam Brannigan," and leaned back to see his reaction - which was pained, as his eardrums almost burst with the decibel count focused so directly at the side of his head.

Laughing, Susan repeated her action, "I don't think I've ever been so happy."

Liam mimed his happiness at her sentiments, pretended to rub the pain from his ear, and headed towards the bar for another pint of Guinness for himself and a coke for Susan, who had struggled with her first pint of Irish ale before surrendering and declaring it 'an acquired taste'.

Liam returned, pushing his way through the throng, both drinks in hand. He sat down and took a long draught.

"Ah, it's nectar, y'know. You can't get this stuff in the States - at least not like this."

He looked at his watch and shouted at Susan. "He's late."

The words had just left his lips when Paul Kinsella edged through the crowd, waving a welcome. Liam rose and both men embraced. Liam shouted an introduction to Susan then suggested that they all move through to the snug bar which was situated along a hallway in another part of the bar where a conversation might be had in a less frenetic atmosphere.

"Well, I must say, Liam wasn't exaggerating when he spoke on the telephone of your great beauty."

Susan laughed. "I'll have to come to terms with the Irish. I can see that now. You're all a bunch of shameless flatterers."

"Aye but it's true enough, though. You're a lovely lookin' woman. Nothin' at all like the horrible oul' trouts he used to hang around with when he lived in Dublin," smiled Kinsella, lapsing into the Dublin vernacular.

"Oh, I can see you and I should have a long chat. He's been very coy about his love life before he met me."

"Little wonder. It was non-existent. All he had time for was his studies."

"Ah, now you're changing your story, Paul."

Liam returned to the table with Kinsella's Guinness.

"I've been getting a potted history of your romances before you met the love of your life," chided Susan.

"What, from that reprobate?" laughed Liam. "Sure, half the lies he tells aren't true and he just makes the rest up."

They all laughed.

Susan continued the theme. "Well, Paul and I are going to have a long chat about you anyway. I'm determined to find out all about your murky past."

"You might be able to have that long chat rather sooner than you think," said Kinsella offering a serious note to the conversation.

"And why might that be?" asked Liam, curious at Kinsella's change of tone.

"You mentioned on the phone what you and Susan here have gone through and how she knows everything that you and I have done?"

Liam nodded. "We have no secrets. We can talk openly."

"Well, the link I put your way resulted - however indirectly - in the FBI raiding the compound your man Wallis had up in the mountains. They found all sorts of stuff relating to the Militia and *Posse Commitatus* and doubtless they'll use that information locally one way or another."

"Yeah, we know all that. They're going to indict a whole lot of American citizens on different charges. Some of them are men of the cloth. Christ, they're as bad as the Irish."

"What I only just found out from one of my sources is that they also found information on arms shipments to the IRA. Late this afternoon, the *Garda* picked up half a dozen men and are questioning them as we speak here tonight. Now, most probably they'll see the arrests as a direct result of the raid on Wallis' camp but one of the fellahs they've arrested is a guy called Eamon O'Farrell and certain circumstances might pertain where he'll want to finger me as having provided the link. Probably not, but it's not a chance I want to take. I'd end up on a slab. Nothing's surer!"

"So what the hell are you goin' to do," asked Liam.

"It's a done deal. I leave tomorrow on a bit of a holiday. My workmates will be told I've resigned and I'll make sure that they get a postcard from Paris where I'll be writing the book I've always said I had in me."

"And in reality?"

"Well, I *will* go to Paris, but only for a couple of weeks. Then, well, I'll be heading off to the US of A."

Susan and Liam looked at one another. "Really?"

"Although technically I'm freelance, I'm fixed up with the Washington desk for the *Irish Times* although I'll have to submit my pieces under another by-line."

"Things are so bad you'll have to leave your own country?" asked Susan incredulously.

"Well, I'll not be the first Irishman to seek fame and fortune in America."

"Still and all, you must be pretty down about all of this," suggested Liam.

"Not really. I don't suppose I'll need to stay away forever. I've already got lots of friends over in the States and I've no real family ties here in Dublin. Three brothers and two sisters, all grown up and married. But my mother and father are both dead and I find myself hangin' around with oul' trouts the like of which I've been accusin' you of seein' before you went over to the States. To tell you the truth, I'm quite lookin' forward to it. Once I'd discussed it with our editor, Jack Prentice, I had quite a spring in my step."

**

The night wore on, punctuated by more drink, laughter, storytelling and plans for the future. A television in the corner had been on mute all night with little heed being paid to its entertainment value. Liam's attention was taken by a news item which confused him. With no volume to guide him, the pictures of a building destroyed fairly obviously by a massive bomb had him intrigued. He was used to seeing bomb damage up in Belfast but couldn't place the building. He nudged Kinsella.

"Jesus Christ, would you look at the state of that building," said Kinsella. "It's blown the whole front of the place to smithereens."

Susan looked at the pictures "My God, I hope no one was in there. There's no way anyone could survive that blast." They continued to watch the pictures in the absence of any commentary.

Susan stiffened and grasped Liam's arm.

"Liam! Look! That policeman on the screen. He's *American.*"

**

In an office in downtown Oklahoma City, a group of FBI agents gathered around a television screen. Behind them, other of their colleagues spoke urgently into telephones as all tried to make sense of the explosion which had blasted the entire façade from the front of the Alfred P Muragh Federal Building throwing shards of glass for hundreds of yards in all directions.

Injured people wandered around dazed and bloodsoaked as the emergency services carried dead bodies from the pile of rubble. Terrified mothers looked for their children, dropped off earlier that morning. Television commentators speculated on a gas explosion or even Iraqi terrorism.

**

At the rear of an office in Washington DC, Special Agent Steve Montana, now just plain John Miller, watched the news item, his arm in a sling. He poured himself a cup of water and raised it to his lips in a silent toast. Protected by senior people in the Bureau, he had been quickly removed from Nevada, and relocated under a new persona to tend the right-wing interests of the John Birch Society, the best financed, best organised conspiricists in America.

He sat and placed his booted feet on the desk opposite, permitting himself a smile as he quoted to himself his favourite passage of the American Bill of Rights. '*A well regulated Militia, being necessary to the security of a free state, the right of the people to keep and bear arms **shall** not be infringed.*'

*Just like I told that sonovabitch Bilko. Us Militia boys are everywhere!*

Lightning Source UK Ltd.
Milton Keynes UK
10 December 2010

164200UK00002B/15/P